The Urbana Free Library

To renew: call 217-367-4057
or go to *"urbanafreelibrary.org"*
and select "Renew/Request Items"

BOARDED WINDOWS

4-12

		DATE DUE	

H-12

BOARDED WINDOWS

A NOVEL

DYLAN HICKS

COFFEE HOUSE PRESS
MINNEAPOLIS
2012

COFFEE HOUSE PRESS books are available to the trade through our primary distributor, Consortium Book Sales & Distribution, cbsd.com or (800) 283-3572. For personal orders, catalogs, or other information, write to: info@coffeehousepress.org.

Coffee House Press is a nonprofit literary publishing house. Support from private foundations, corporate giving programs, government programs, and generous individuals helps make the publication of our books possible. We gratefully acknowledge their support in detail in the back of this book. To you and our many readers around the world, we send our thanks for your continuing support.

Good books are brewing at coffeehousepress.org.

LIBRARY OF CONGRESS CIP INFORMATION

Hicks, Dylan.
Boarded windows / Dylan Hicks.
p. cm.
ISBN 978-1-56689-297-1 (alk. paper)
I. Title.
PS3608.I2785B63 2012
813'.6—DC23
2011029253
PRINTED IN THE UNITED STATES
1 3 5 7 9 8 6 4 2
FIRST EDITION | FIRST PRINTING

ACKNOWLEDGMENTS

Thanks to Samantha Gillison, Nor Hall, J. C. Hallman, and Brad Zellar for their generous advice and assistance. Thanks to Chris, Anitra, Jessica, Tricia, Linda, Andrea, and all at Coffee House. My parents have always been wonderful and supportive: in alphabetical order, they are Don and Elaine Hicks, Robert and Terry Roos, and Margaret Stewart. Jackson Hicks's talent, wit, and kindness is a constant inspiration to me. Above all I want to thank Nina Hale, who's even more impossibly great than John Coltrane's solo on our apt wedding song, "My One and Only Love."

CREDITS

Lyrics from "Let the Wind Carry Me" by Joni Mitchell reproduced by permission. All rights reserved. Used by permission of Alfred Publishing Co., Inc.

For Nina

BLUE

THE LAST TIME I SAW WADE SALEM WAS THE MORNING of December 21, 1991, through the window of a green-and-white taxi. I stood on the sidewalk's lumpy mattress of snow and watched him toss a backpack to the other side of the seat, and pull off his pomponed Washington Redskins cap with a nod toward urgency. The taxi was overheated, it's safe to imagine. I had recently turned twenty-one. I had even more recently lent Wade the backpack, in the way one lends out a quarter or a piece of gum. In the trunk was my former guitar, a midpriced acoustic on which three or four nights earlier Wade had played "Gentle on My Mind" and "The Poor Orphan Child."

Something—my sticky-zippered backpack, or, more likely, the Redskins cap—must have slid off the backseat's slippery vinyl, because just as the taxi was about to pull out into the lane, its wheels creaking the snow, Wade leaned over (to pick up the cap, I'm speculating), erasing himself from the rear passenger-side window, like I and millions of others had slide-erased stale sketches from our magnetic drawing toys, such as the one Wade long ago brought home to me, unwrapped, as an ingratiating gift. His head reemerged as the taxi made its first turn toward the airport. For a moment I lingered on the sidewalk, across the busy westward one-way from a pretentiously named Nixon-era apartment building, its mansard roof covering most of its face like the *Fat Albert* character's nonpomponed cap. The bare trees and dirty boulevard snow were aptly gloomy, but the sky was blue, seemed too blue for the nostril-stinging cold. I felt tired and brittle, wished my feelings of good riddance weren't so mixed with longing.

man WiTH a PiPe

HE HAD CALLED ME IN EARLY OCTOBER. HE SAID HE'D heard through one of my erstwhile Enswell "playmates" that I was living with a woman, "an *older* woman," he added, belaboring the jokey condescension. He asked a few questions about Wanda (only five years older than I). He asked about my mother. He said he was moving to Berlin, after a final tour of the States. He said something about Hank Snow and the incantatory power of American town and city names, and that he'd be in Minneapolis soon. It was probably six days later, around midnight, when he called. Wanda was already in bed. "I'm at a pay phone on Lake Street," he said. "Looks like I'm sharing the corner with some working girls." At most he was ten minutes away, but an hour passed before he buzzed. He smiled broadly when he saw me coming down the stairs; the immoderate width of his mouth made it hard for him to smile narrowly. We pumped hands in the vestibule, somewhat awkwardly, either for emotional reasons or because, having left my keys upstairs, I at the last second remembered to stop the fast-closing door with my left foot (resting demi-pointe, it might have looked to a fanciful observer), and as a result was slightly off balance. "I'm still taller," he said. He was holding a yellowed pillowcase, presumably containing clothes and toiletries.

His American hatchback, also yellow and about a decade old, was filled, to an extent that would have frustrated visibility and fuel economy, with about a dozen square cardboard boxes filled with LPS. Loose LPS had been stuffed like Styrofoam sea horses in the car's few unfilled spaces. Quite a few discs had slid out of their jackets—Wade always threw away the inner sleeves (the bunchy plastic ones he threw away with particular contempt)—and I mentally cringed at how roughly he stacked and fingered the unclothed vinyl, and how some of the discs had picked up flakes of peanut skin and other car-floor garbage. "These are just my country records," he said. "I sold everything else—everything, barring the car and the contents of its glove box, and the road atlas and the clothes off my back, as well as the clothes off my feet, legs, groin, and head, and a sleeping bag that I intend to keep rolled up and stashed behind your couch indefinitely." I nodded. "And the few items in this pillowcase," he said, swinging the half-empty pillowcase till it wrapped one and a half times around his index finger.

Having forgotten to prop open the door, we had to buzz Wanda several times to let us in. She was a heavy sleeper like me. (These days I have trouble sleeping and suffer from nocturnal polyuria.) I staggered two or three ineffectual buzzes, then Wade stepped in to accelerate things. "She's probably incorporating the sound into her dreams," he said, buzzing with the resoluteness, I thought at the time (now I dislike the analogy), of a lab rat attempting to self-administer a drug, the supply of which has been depleted or removed. "Right now she's dreaming of a reversing forklift," he said. I caught a whiff of the sweat-abused sheepskin lining of my calfskin slippers, my mother's last gift to me, it turned out, or last antemortem gift, since I did, only a few months later, begin to inherit some of her things. Wanda finally came down, squinted irritably through a quick introduction, and trudged back up to bed. "She's exactly my height," Wade said, palming the top of his head, extending his arm as if Wanda were still there to vindicate his estimate, then retracting his arm to scratch his head, whose hair, excepting one handsome gray cataract, was still shiny and black, as black as an Ad Reinhardt canvas in an attic at night, as black as the vision of the painted red door, the black of the blackest stereo component, the black that, like the song by Los Bravos, *is* black, with the same shoulder terminus I remembered, the same way of falling over his cheeks yet leaving most of his forehead rampart exposed, the same slicing part down the middle, like Geronimo, or Neil Young circa *After the Gold Rush*, James Taylor circa *Sweet Baby James* and *Two-Lane Blacktop*. (Although I see now from a photograph that Taylor's part was softer than Wade's.) "Exactly" went too far, but later I confirmed that Wanda's and Wade's driver's licenses each read "6-2." Of course, such numbers are self-reported, and my sense is that DMV agents challenge only the most outlandish misrepresentations.

"We've got a little storage locker in the basement," I said, pointing to the record boxes. "About this time last year, I was *living* in a storage locker," Wade said. "Just me and my sleeping bag, my books, my records, a few minor works of regional art—solitary refinement, you might say, a condition the NoDak aesthete grows accustomed to. Has the basement ever flooded?"

I didn't know that history, so we humped the heavy boxes up to the one-bedroom apartment. Once inside he pulled a boot-jack from his pillowcase and took off his orange-brown cowboy boots, then his fringed suede coat and flannel shirt. Underneath those layers he wore a faded blue bandanna and a black T-shirt that read, "Here comes one good-looking Indian!" a feather serving as the capital *I* in the word *Indian*. And he was, no question, exceptionally good-looking. I'd heard my mother say some bitter things about him. "A dirtbag," for instance, and more colorfully, "the scum lurking under the ridge of a penis acorn." But usually at the same time she'd recall his looks. "God, he was good-looking," she'd say. He was macrocephalic, as movie stars are said to be. His jaw was almost squared, with a mild cleft. He had glassy, orangy skin, an aquiline nose, brown eyes under heavy lids. If one were to draw a circle between his arching eyebrows, one would have the simplest frontal rendering of a midsized bird in flight. I motioned to a seat on the couch, but he sat gingerly on one of the box towers, drinking tap water out of a filmy tumbler while I found him some couch-clothes, a pillow, and a scratchy, football-themed comforter mottled in ways redolent of male adolescence. (He didn't bring his sleeping bag in the house till a few days later, and never used it.) I offered him the polenta Wanda had brought home a few nights earlier, and he ate from the glossy to-go box without complete decorum. He took out a lighter and an ornate metal pipe from his jeans. "There's only one hit left in here, but I'll pack more if you want," he said. Uncharacteristically, I declined. He'd driven that day from Columbus, he said. "You must've left early," I said. "I left late," he said, "late last night. I have to stop all the time to piss, so I like to give myself a nice time-cushion. I almost hit a fawn outside Tomah. You're not supposed to swerve, but I did, and it worked." When he got up for more water, I read the back of his T-shirt ("There goes one good-looking Indian!"), and noted the saggy seat of his dull dark jeans, epigones of the faded and close-fitting yet not teasingly feminine Erizeins he had worn when I was a kid.

That's more than I remember from that night. It was nearly twenty years ago. What was it Wade said? It was something like: "I've done a shitload of skinny-dipping in the River Lethe, taken in many mouthfuls." He liked to blend the demotic and the fancy, liked to be imagined naked. In any case, I've done some embroidering, intentionally and unwittingly, and will continue to flesh things out with invented details and almost wholly reconstructed dialogue. My story is in part drawn from other stories, from the colored and conflicting stories that Wade and my mother told me, so in spots this book will be embroidered embroidery, in service, I hope, to some fundamental emotional truth, even if at times I fear that such foundations elude me. I've been said to be cold, passive, and evasive; a nonprofessional once spittingly diagnosed me with borderline adult autism, and while I trust she overstated the case, it does often seem as if I'm experiencing things at one remove, that my feelings, like an elusive sneeze, vex and tingle but don't really come. The problem has worsened over the years; I haven't cried in a decade; I don't hear music in the same flooding way I used to. For a long time I blamed this growing coolness on everything that happened and all that I learned in late '91, defined myself through those events and their numbing, sometimes twisting effects. I'm not sure yet whether writing this book will combat or continue this pattern, but I suspect it will only further blur and tangle my legitimate, fabricated, and passed-down memories, and I suppose that's what I want. "Why are you people so tirelessly/tiresomely [the exact adverb escapes me] obsessed with the limitations of memory?" someone once asked me. I didn't pursue whom she meant by "you people," didn't come up with an incisive rebuttal. It was she who was really on the defensive. I had challenged one of her stories, a rather too psychologically pat story, or a story imputing dubious and convenient motives to some ex-boyfriend or relative, a story from her deep, amnestic childhood, a story for which she seemed an unlikely primary source, a story derived from photo-album captions ("into dolls"), photo-album commentaries ("you loved that doll"), from movies or books, an epistemologically untenable (I argued) story of some type, patched together in some way, I can't be more specific, in part because I can't remember the story, only that I couldn't accept it. Had it been cooked differently or with less certainty, I might have hidden my skepticism. "It's my story!" she said, more than once, but that was precisely what I was trying to question.

embourgeoisement looms

I WAS DUE AT WORK BY NINE THE MORNING AFTER Wade's arrival, but if I was following my normal schedule for days on which I worked the nine-to-six shift, I got out of bed about twenty minutes after eight. I wasn't so much lazy as efficient: my showering and tooth-brushing were nearly symbolic; I hadn't yet taken up coffee; and I wasn't delayed by vestiary decisions, since I only had one pair of work pants (cavalry twills in Lake Michigan blue; at the time I thought they were called "Calvary twills"), one pair of work shoes (postiche-cordovan loafers aged to a clownish red at the toes and heels), and four or five billowy button-downs, white or pastel and always dirt-checkered on the inside cuffs. Most days I made it to the corner—often with wet, sometimes freezing hair and an ersatz bagel in my hand or mouth, some crumbs dangling below my lower lip—in time to catch the bus that got me to work ten to fifteen minutes late. I worked in downtown Minneapolis at an unhip record store, a shabby, not terribly profitable branch of a locally based national chain, now shuttered. For the purposes of this book, I've been tempted to give myself a different early nineties job, something comparable to the record-store job in terms of status and remuneration, yet more fertile, original, and attractive. For example, I have an acquaintance, roughly fifteen years my senior, who makes hand-carved Judaica and Nativity scenes (his latitude and large collection of Coltrane bootlegs are just two of the things I admire about him), and there's no reason I couldn't have served, during the early nineties, as his assistant or paid apprentice. I'm picturing it now: the wood and so forth, the tools, the bench or what have you, the dusty tape deck playing Hedy West. Considering the work, it'd be natural for master and apprentice to talk of theology, philosophy, history, politics. An antimemoir of ideas might result, the carver playing Plato to Wade's Diogenes. But no, it wouldn't work. One must write the tedium one knows, on top of which the carver has never been in a position to hire help. My title at the record store was full-time keyholder.

That first morning of Wade's stay, I had time to eat my bagel at the unsteady Formica table in our small dining room, which was also a library for some of my records, and an office, in that it lodged a sewing table on which Wanda and I kept a collegiate dictionary, its spine held together with packing tape, and a word processor, whose alien-green letters shimmered around their edges as I typed my mostly plagiarized and unpublished record reviews. From this axislike dining room one could potentially see into all four of the apartment's other rooms, though on that morning I could see only a buttery sliver of the sun-lit bathroom and none of the bedroom, its door closed to give Wanda privacy from our potentially lupine guest. In the living room, Wade had thrown off my comforter and stripped down to his briefs, socks, and bandanna. The socks were the same shade of white but of unequal length. A thick patch of hair protected his sternum. His left leg hung over our spongy, thrift-store sofa, between whose back and cushions his right foot was burrowed;

one of his hands rested atop his head (itself resting on the sofa's arm, my pillow pushed to the floor) as if he were securing a hat (cowboy? beret? cockscomb?) from the wind. An apparently uncomfortable pose, of the sort Lucien Freud favors for his portraits of sleepers and recliners, though I wouldn't have made that association then. Wade was even thinner than I remembered him—his spidery legs were especially arresting—but it wasn't a druggy thinness. When I put on my coat, he roused, looked at me confusedly, smiled slightly, and asked a few groggy questions about my job. For instance: "What kind of keys do you hold as full-time keyholder?"

"The one for the front door," I said. "And a few others." I'd in fact been given more keys, duties, and privileges than the FTK was officially entitled to.

"That's a start," he said. "Later you'll need the keys to the kingdom and the keys to the highway, maybe those of D and B minor." He cleared his throat and spit some phlegm into his loosely tied bandanna. "I'm gonna be a deejay in Berlin," he said.

"Berlin Berlin or Berlin, North Dakota?"

"Berlin Berlin. That's what the records are for. I need to ship them over, over the world-sea. I'll need some information about your post offices."

"Okay," I said.

"They're bats for c&w over there, man," he said, now sounding more awake. "Cowboys and Indians, swinging doors, sawdust floors. They can't get enough."

"They'll have to self-destruct," I said.

"Come again?"

"'Disco Inferno.'"

"Oh yeah," Wade said, "Tavares."

Disco Purgatorio

OR SOME OF 1977 AND MOST OF '78, I CALLED WADE my stepfather. He didn't have a legal claim to the title; he was just shacking up with my mother, and wasn't even doing that in earnest. He had a basement apartment below our two-bedroom, and while he spent much of his time upstairs, and the advantages of rent-sharing would have been felt by all, he never officially moved in with us. I suppose he would have had trouble fitting his store of records and books into our place, and in fact he kept all but his essential toiletries in his basement apartment, even kept a few items in his fridge and would often walk downstairs to get a beer, a TV dinner, or a cucumber, which to my mother's amusement he ate uncut and suggestively, not bothered by the bitter, waxy skin. I turned seven during that period. I spent a lot of time listening to music and playing Odin or Pete Rozelle to teams of plastic, green-pedestaled football figurines that ran, stumbled, and waltzed on a vibrating metal field, their numbers stuck crookedly to their jersey backs by my undexterous young fingers. Every month or so my mother would let me pick out a forty-five from the Top Forty endcap of what was then Enswell's leading discount store. I chose Melissa Manchester, Barry Manilow, Mike Sands, the Trammps ("I couldn't get enough, so I had to self-destruct" still one of my favorite lyrical sequences), yet defied certain predictions by turning out prevailingly heterosexual.

Occasionally one of my friends would come over after school. Wade only worked his straight job twice a week, and one of those shifts was the Saturday graveyard, so he spent most afternoons in our living room—reading, dozing, watching TV, taking up most of the couch in a pose somewhere between that of an odalisque model and a park-bench hobo, or a sculpture of a park-bench hobo. He had a particularly artistic way of filling a couch, as I've perhaps by now overstressed. Sometimes he'd ask if my friend and I wanted a snack. He didn't care if the snack was big and junky and likely to spoil our appetites for dinner. Other times, not only times when he was dozing, he wouldn't even say hello.

After my friend and I were in my room, or out in the parking lot of the neighboring Lutheran church, a good spot for bike tricks, I'd say, "That's my stepdad." I don't know if I came up with the euphemism on my own or if I was following my mother's protective lead. On one hand, conceivably a hand of four fingers, Enswell was a live-and-let-live place with much lawlessness and iconoclasm in its past, a city whose knife-edged tent-town babyhood was led by unmarried railroaders and the scuffling demimonde they lured, whose adolescence found room for hopheads and rumrunners, blind pigs and cathouses. I'm told that for decades a red-light district thrived just a few blocks from the home Wade, my mother, and I shared, the women in spring and summer often sitting, like Rahab with Joshua's spies, on their rented roofs, awaiting customers, but also just talking or comfortably not talking, sometimes calling out to other groups of two or three women on nearby rooftops, and maybe,

I once imagined, finding some of the restorative grace described in Goffin and King's "Up on the Roof," so elegantly performed by the protean Drifters, lead singer Rudy Lewis battling the production's dinky, quasi-Latin rhythm but not surrendering in full to a melancholy that, unchecked, would have destroyed the song. It's after all not supposed to be a roof from which you might jump, but a roof that keeps you from jumping, by being a serious but not lugubrious place, a place where mindless cheeriness is as unwelcome as mad cruelty, a roof, then, that discourages jumping and falling, through gravity. So while that dinky, quasi-Latin rhythm is in fact terrible, without it Lewis might not have struck the right ambivalence, and the record might have failed, might not have become the sort that enlightens thousands on thousands of radio listeners, that unites the scattered lonely, that seems to sanctify the radios themselves, as "Up on the Roof" may have done, even in North Dakota (where the rats don't really race and the sidewalk ballet seldom reaches a crescendo) in the fall of 1962, the same fall in which the Jaycees and other blight-fighting civic leaders got the red-light district slated for the bulldozer and wrecking ball.

On the other hand, Enswell was a conservative North Dakota city where, even by the late 1970s, unmarried cohabiting couples may have been sinners in some townspeople's eyes, such as those belonging to my friends or, more likely, their parents, who, if given the choice, would have preferred to picture their kids being casually watched over by a stepfather instead of some mere boyfriend, long-haired and nearly jobless.

Since I was already lying about Wade's relation to me, I don't know why I didn't just say, "That's my dad," the assumption my friend likely would have made had I, most wisely of all, passed over the matter in silence. More than once the stepfather fib invited unwelcome questions about my so-called real dad, whose identity was unknown to me. There weren't so many friends to fib to, at least, nor too few. Then as now I was neither popular nor unpopular. My unusual handsomeness—really, alas, it's a kind of electric cuteness—didn't fully reveal itself till I was in my teens, and by then I'd taken on a tentative antisociality. Now I'm very lonely, an impermanent condition, I hope, not squarely resulting from unpopularity. "It's a hell of a lot easier to be free of things than to be free of people," Wade once told me, "but you've got to be capable of that too."

He left us on Saturday, November 11, 1978, his ears no doubt still ringing from the previous night's Bolling Greene show at the Enswell Municipal Auditorium. It was somewhere between seven thirty and eight o'clock when he left. I have a fumelike memory of watching him leave, of watching my mother upbraid the fat country singer in the havelock and bandolier, the men standing on our lawn, she standing on our stoop, I peering through the mail slot. Later, however, my mother insisted that I was hard asleep when the silver tour bus pulled noisily away, its scornful exhaust tones, augmented by a hard-to-attribute auroral whoop, still reverberating several minutes later through the dirty white sky. And that makes sense, since I was coming off a late night and was known to sleep soundly through noises louder than shouts and whoops, louder even than Detroit Diesel 6v-71s. Once during a thunderstorm, Wade carried me from my bedroom down to his apartment and put me in the caved-in middle of his hideaway bed, where I dreamed and drooled between my mother and him, reportedly staying as still as the dead throughout my relocation, staying nearly that still when the thunder got louder and then louder still, though I do remember waking up long enough to feel Wade and my mother holding heavy hands on my chest. In the morning I disbelieved there'd been a storm at all, till an exclamatorily headlined *Enswell Century* was laid next to my plastic, remotely porcelaneous cereal bowl, a Piggly Wiggly premium as I recall, decorated with irises, blueberries, and chubby-legged girls, their bonnets leaking blonde ringlets, the same bowl I used this morning for my sugar cereal. I inherited some of my mother's things, as was said, such as the cereal bowl and several other things, though pride, impetuousness, or asceticism led me to refuse anything of much monetary value.

miles of aisles

I WAS DISTRACTED AT WORK ON THAT FIRST FULL DAY of Wade's stay in Minneapolis, and my till came up ten dollars short. A few years later, the store (notwithstanding the just-noted shortfall) was granted an expensive and predictably vulgar remodel, but during the period I'm now describing, its fixtures were as battered and wobbly as some of its drunker customers, several sections of carpet were held down with duct tape, the slatwall was badly divoted, and the typeface used for what HQ insisted on calling "signage" featured a no longer fashionable variety of shadow. We—I did see myself as part of the store's *we*, not just one of its employees, though I subjectified only with our underdog location, on a long-struggling block of the city's busiest street, and tried not to introject the corporation's rhetoric and policies—we barely survived selling hip-hop and R&B cassettes (sometimes CDs), plus double-A batteries, oversized headphones, softly pornographic posters, and trashy portable tape players that at least expired, against cliché, before our thirty-day warranty, leading to seemingly infinite return-exchange loops. A few professional-types came in during the lunch hour and at Christmas, but most of our regulars were young or poor or both: teenagers killing time on weekends or during the store's relatively rushy weekday hours after school before dinner; families splurging on the first of the month; clerical workers; hotel workers; out-of-work workers; tramps (very few trammps); community collegians; lumpenproletarians; lazzaroni; strippers from the club down the street (usually buying hard-rock tapes, sometimes R&B tapes, hip hop being forbidden at the club so as not to alienate the predominant clientele of older, mostly white alcoholics). I loved helping the strippers; I tried to be calm and solicitous.

I used to say that the majority of our customers were black, but maybe that wasn't true; maybe only forty-eight percent of our customers were black. Whatever the demographics, the chain's faceless buyers and their digital hegemons often didn't understand or couldn't predict our customers' tastes and demands, which I believed to be less manipulable, more willed, though collectively willed, than those expressed at most of the chain's mall locations. Back then I still held the American teenager to be the greatest invention of the twentieth century (the thermos, Wade countered), had a particularly patronizing and romantic view of black youth culture, and was a dogmatic opponent of the suburbs, where I now live, alone and unprosperously. I granted that our customers' tastes were largely sculpted and given meaning by showbiz schemers and their media collaborators, just as mine were, despite my dubious claims to bohemianism, but I was heartened to see or imagine that these schemers and collaborators were often working at low levels out of home offices, their wallets fat with unconvincing business cards, their faces fuzzy on the J-cards of dusty consignment cassettes.

Frequently, headquarters would send us scores of some expected blockbuster, some big-budget follow-up or ballyhooed debut (remember Randi Randall?) that as it turned out few or none of our customers wanted, and in the same shipment send just one or two of something (AMG, Tim Dog, Marcus M., Ed O.G. & Da Bulldogs, M.C. Breed, Bytches with Problems, LX2, Geto Boys, Lacē, Compton's Most Wanted) piercingly coveted by every third person through the door. Corporate buying I'm sure is a tricky gig; I'm not here to sling old arrows at the faceless. But sometimes it was hard to turn folks away, especially the teenagers who'd had a particular tape in mind on their long bus ride downtown, who'd have to ride home in the dark with no new tape (the store across the street had a smaller selection of R&B and hip hop), or a substitute tape, and whose headphoned bedtime might as a result be inferior, untranscendent. (Although the substitute tape is sometimes the one you really need.) Occasionally, however, we were able to step in with our own buy from a one-stop distributor, and a day later we'd razor open a drop shipment of, say, an especially communicable, bubbling-under cassingle, sometimes of a song getting little or no radio or video play, a song being promoted in school hallways, on phone lines, on boom boxes at awkward parties, through the pores of cheap headphones blasting from the back benches, or the vertiginous aisle-facing benches, of happier city buses. If we timed our buy correctly, we could sell a hundred copies of such a cassingle in a week—an abnormally large volume for our store. Cassingles sold for $2.12 including tax, and the margin was minuscule, especially after paying one-stop wholesale, but I (didn't care about the company's margin, and) thought of these lucky or prophetic buys as simultaneous triumphs of populism and benevolent capitalism. Always I'd buy a copy of the biggest cassingles for myself, and would write, on the cassingle's cardboard pouch, the week of its sales acme at our store. I still have three long cardboard boxes filled with those cassingles; they should make, I exaggerate, an interesting time capsule for whichever bureaucrat sorts through my surviving things.

Fear of obsequiousness keeps me from calling the store's "employee discount program" generous ("The program is that they get a discount on their employees," joked one backroom Bakunin), but to me it didn't seem mustache-twistingly stingy. I probably returned ten percent of my wages to the company (a kind of tithe), every few days buying a CD, tape, or one of the few LPs we still stocked or could order. Our in-store selection was lousy in most genres—the jazz section was particularly tasteless and ahistoric—but we could special-order most things in print domestically. That was boom time for CD reissues and anthologies, and I bought a lot of those, including 1991's Bolling Greene anthology, *Greener Pastures* (Rhino 70598). Start there if you're curious about Bolling's work, even if I'd dock a star for a few painful omissions, especially "West Texas Winds" (an absence rebelliously noted, at least, in Cub Koda's liner notes), and 1983's "High Heels, Tight Jeans, and Single Overhead Camshafts," a cunningly self-parodying rockabilly single, cowritten by Wade Salem, that failed to meet even its modest sales expectations, despite being ably produced by Tony Kinman of then-ascendant cowpunks Rank and File. I was one of the few who did buy the single, with my paper-route money in my first Minneapolis fall. The cover featured a black-and-pastel photo of Bolling standing next to a men's-room door, still wearing his havelock, armadillo T-shirt, and bandolier, fatter than ever, though thanks to his prominent chest and comparatively thin legs he always seemed more bisontine than hippopotamian, more gallant than galumphing. "What a stupid song," my mother said when I played her the A-side.

We did employ some deadbeats at the store, it's true. And I did spend some of each day leaning on counters and fixtures, chatting with colleagues, sometimes with customers. But unmistakable loafing accounted for a small fraction of my work-day. I suspect I robbed my employer's time considerably less than did the average American worker. Then as now I showed little ambition, but not because I was merely lazy. I realize that already in these pages I've twice denied laziness; the reader is free to interpret my repeated denials in the conventional way. I nonetheless want to stress that the full-time keyholder position wasn't a slack job, or at least I didn't treat it as if it were: stand-ing for nine hours (minus a thirty-minute unpaid break); argu-ing the store's return policy, stricter and more mistrusting at our location than it was at most of the chain's suburban stores; stocking and restocking; tagging and postering; alphabetizing and categorizing; finding remote new homes for our white secu-rity bandages; correcting the mistakes of the sloppier part-timers; hounding shoplifters; ignoring generally correct accusations of retail racism, sometimes most fervently articu-lated by boys and men in parkas that looked like relief sculp-tures of portable CD players; chasing the more hapless, alarm-sounding shoplifters through the alley, blurring past the blue dumpsters so often bulging with and expectorating trash from the movie theater (now closed), the costume shop (also closed), the magazine shop (closed), the strip club (still going), giving chase sometimes all the way into the flagship of Minneapolis's leading department store (closed—I'll stop this now; it's hardly worth noting that businesses close), chasing because the chase was proverbially thrilling and because to return to the store with re- and slush-covered merchandise in hand was to return a hero, a comic hero, and indeed some of the less indoctrinated part-timers, which is to say all of them, would laugh, smile, or shake their heads at those of us who were willing to risk, in the interest of a few nine-dollar cassettes ($9.62 with tax), being stabbed with a Swiss Army corkscrew behind a strip-club dumpster (I'm fabricating; nothing so violent or ignominious ever went down, though one time a crying prepubescent essayed a pathos-rich uppercut in the general direction of my chin before dropping the goods in a puddle and disappearing around the corner)—all this conflict and tedium and tedious conflict amounted to something more taut than slack, and sometimes, for instance while riding the bus home to Wanda and suddenly Wade, I lamented my decision to be so quickly kicked out of our enormous, bacon-eyed state university.

SHADOWS AND LIGHT

THAT FIRST EVENING (AND SECOND NIGHT) OF WADE'S stay with Wanda and me, when I climbed with tired legs and eyes up to our third-floor apartment, I heard Pat Metheny's *Bright Size Life* playing through our door at a volume perhaps beyond the bounds of neighborliness, though Metheny's music, with the possible exception of *Zero Tolerance for Silence*, which hadn't been released yet, is neither in itself nor socioculturally the sort to goad fretful calls to the police. The music, at any rate, was loud enough to cover the sound of my opening and closing the door.

The apartment was cozier than it had ever been since Wanda and I began our tenancy about a year earlier. We didn't trouble ourselves much with décor and atmospherics, so this isn't saying much, but we did trouble a little, so it is saying something. One late-spring Saturday shortly after we moved in, for instance, we took a walk and wandered into an estate sale at a long-neglected Queen Anne–style house, where we bought a pastel rag rug and two unsigned oil paintings (a daub of an Ayrshire cow, a seascape not unlike one of Courbet's elegant toss-offs). For the walk home, we hoisted the heavy rolled-up rug over our shoulders and each tucked a painting under a free arm. Before long we had to rest, using the rug as a log bench. I rubbed and rotated my neck; soon Wanda took over rubbing, and we smiled at each other because the neck's soreness was cunnilingual. Cottonwood inflorescence and a pleasant breeze were making the city a snow globe (I collect them), and I believe I made Wanda laugh by catching some of the fluff on my tongue. At another point along the walk home, both of us, almost at the same time, noticed a smell coming from the rug, a subtle but nagging urinous smell, entirely resistant, the coming weeks proved, to various nonprofessional cleaning products and techniques. The urine, Wanda insisted from the moment we first smelled it to the moment she hefted the rug into a dumpster, was human. Feline, I suspected. She propped the paintings against the same dumpster, because she could no longer enjoy them aloofly or ironically, she said, having envisioned the deceased's solitary, incontinent final years of endless television, the blue light gleaming through the window at indifferent neighbors. (Last night I walked by a house whose living room was TV-lit in flashes of all the primary colors, and maybe some nonprimary ones too. Do the new TVs offer more heterogeneous window light to passersby, or has blue's dominance been overstated?) Also during our first months in the apartment, Wanda and I (I really) often lit candles from a package I'd bought one payday at a grocery store. After this supply ran out, though, we normally dwelt in bright overhead light, either because it was easier to flick one switch—or, sometimes, push one (the living-room overhead was operated by two resistant buttons, not a toggle switch)—than to spend several seconds fishing under our askew lampshades, or (we dwelt that way) for other reasons, such as Wanda's preference for sex in the sharpest, least flattering light available.

But as you may have deduced from the above use of the word *cozy,* the living room's overhead light was off when I walked into the apartment that first evening of Wade's stay. He had bought a package of red dinner candles, had jammed four or five of them into our tritely bohemian wine-bottle holders, caked with piebald wax, had jammed another four or five into unfamiliar wine bottles probably scavenged from recycling tubs. The bottles were ingeniously diffused throughout the living and dining rooms: on speakers and tables, on the TV and the floor, on Wade's record boxes and our small bookshelf; the light balance was perfect, I thought. Our two living-room lamps (one a twin-goosenecked floor lamp with megaphonic shades, the other intending to look like Hank Williams) were on, but Wade had swapped their abrasive light bulbs for softer versions ("glow pears," he called them). Incense was burning. The whole room was yellow with red accents, cavelike and warm, warm figuratively—literally it was hot: the apartment's radiators overtaxed themselves in fall and winter; October through March we walked around in T-shirts and unbuttoned pajama tops, shed much nocturnal blood through our noses.

Wanda: "Part of it's just run-of-the-mill ironizing, but really I'm working with entitlement, appropriation, displacement, trying to interrogate who owns these jokes." She was sitting at the Formica table explaining her work to Wade, who was preparing a mostly premade pizza in our tunnel-like kitchen. They greeted me and she carried on. She nearly had to shout over the music, but she had a strong, performer's voice. For money, she answered phones for a catalog run by the public radio station, taking orders for jocular sweatshirts and

Garrison Keillor cassettes, but mainly she was a cover comic, collage comedian, or conceptual stand-up. She performed under the name Shucks Miller and built routines out of old jokes by Sid Caesar, Cap Dolen, Herbie Dodd, Henny Youngman, Harry Kobinz, Robert Klein, Gabe Kaplan, Richard Pryor, Morris Wohl, Lenny Bruce, Blowfly, Barry Greer, Rodney Dangerfield, Futz Kruger, Alan King, Nat Davis, David Brenner, Jimmie Nichols, Woody Allen, Mort Sahl, Russell Jones, David Steinberg, Dick Gregory, Don Rickles, Bob Hope, and others, plus anonymous jokes from out-of-print anthologies, jokes from allergenic back-issues of *Playboy, Passages,* and *Reader's Digest,* jokes from the squarest daily comic strips (Mort Walker, Harry Scott, Dik Browne, Bil Keane, Ted McKinley, Cathy Guisewite), these last especially awkward to cover since Wanda would have to describe the drawings as well as recite the bubbles of thought and speech: "So this youngish yet frumpy woman is standing glum-faced in a dressing room, all manner of bathing suits tossed higgledy-piggledy around her . . ." It was stock postmodern shtick, unserious, many would argue, but Wanda was serious about it, tried to use the method as a path to something larger. She spent a lot of time in the library, sometimes eleven or twelve consecutive hours, listening to old records under big beige headphones, poring over joke books, filling her notebook. When she got home, her ears were often still sweaty, her fingertips still dusty, and I'd kiss or lick them to reward her labor. She had several cardboard fruit boxes filled with notebooks, themselves filled with jokes she'd considered promising enough to write down, but almost all of these jokes she ultimately rejected. The second stage of keepers she wrote out on cards taken from a board game, fairly large cards (5½ x

3¾ inches), the kind that can only be read through a tinted viewer, though of course Wanda's felt-tip writing could be read without the viewer. When planning a set, she would obsessively arrange and rearrange the cards in arcs and other potentially engrossing shapes on our scratched hardwood living-room floor, making it tricky to walk around without disturbing her provisional outline. "How much longer about do you think these will be on the floor?" I'd say. And she'd say, "Someday I'll have an atelier for this shit, but for now we'll just have to embrace the obstacle-course thing." She used words like *atelier* aggressively, I thought at the time, to stress that she was smarter or at least better-read than I was, but now I think she took more pleasure from the words themselves than from the humbling effect they may have had on me.

I went to turn down the music a notchette, and took a seat across from Wanda at the table, on which there was a fat, impressively rolled joint sprinkled with brown sugar. The table no longer wobbled; someone, surely Wade, had made a shim out of a shard of cracker box. "My till came up ten dollars short," I said.

"Can I borrow ten bucks?" Wade said while rubbing butter on the pizza crust's rim with a satirical flourish. Then to Wanda: "So you do this act in comedy clubs?"

"Sometimes. I'd like to do that exclusively, but they don't invite me back. Mostly I work in small theaters, cabarets, some queer stuff."

"One of her shows turned into a real cause célèbre awhile back," I said. Probably I didn't come up with the worldliest pronunciation of *célèbre*.

"Yeah," Wanda said. "I did one of the Jewish sets in a Shylock costume, with a butcher's knife and a giant papier-mâché beak. Some people got upset and I had to be part of this panel discussion. Of course all the jokes were by Jewish comics. No one bitches when I do the misogynist stuff." (The panelist who called Wanda's Jewish set "falsely provocative" was right, I think, though this panelist hadn't actually seen Wanda's set; when Wanda looks back on her early work, she must feel some remorse or humiliation, as I do about my less public mistakes.)

"Also her great-grandmother might have been Jewish," I said, tonguing the edgy mouth of my night's first can of beer. There were already six or seven empties on the kitchen counter, most squeezed into approximate hourglasses.

"You ever work in blackface?" Wade asked.

"Not yet," Wanda said.

"You guys don't remember Grace Slick on *Sullivan*," Wade said.

"*Smothers Brothers*," I corrected.

"You do anything by—who's the guy? With the big red hat."

"Licitra?" I said.

"Yeah." Wade put the pizza in the oven.

"No," Wanda said. "Too obvious and not funny."

"She wants people to laugh *with* the jokes, not at them," I said.

"I'm not sure I'd put it that way," Wanda said. "If everyone laughs it doesn't work, but if you get islands of laughter, especially male islands, or oblivious female islands, then I get the room tension I'm after."

"That's all I meant," I said.

"Sometimes I'll catch a dyke flash some frat dude a cold stare," Wanda said. "That's the sort of thing I want, not to see the dude shamed—'cause they're both right and both wrong. But just to enact something."

"Enact now," Wade said.

"I'm trying to revivify these jokes. Like with digital sampling, how the source material a lot of times is reborn through fragmentation, deracination."

"Right, yeah, that sounds good," Wade said, leaning against the stove. "I mean, I don't know anything about computers, but I used to be what you might call a reproduction purist. I'd read Benjamin's 'Das Kunstwerk im Zeitalter seiner technischen Reproduzierbarkeit' and Berger's *Ways of Seeing*"—this title he pronounced with a funny German accent: *Vays ohf Zeeink*—"and my response to the ultimately liberating 'withering of the aura' and all that shit was not just to accept but to prefer and demand everything at one remove, at least one: so the record, I thought, was better than the band; the Memorex better than the record; the Marcantonio engraving better than the Raphael original; the painting inspired by the engraving better than the painting inspired by the original; the coffee-tabled color plate better than the framed canvas; the grainy black-and-white detail better than the color plate; the photocopy of the grainy black-and-white detail, stuck to the fridge with a service-station magnet, better than the black-and-white detail; the belch better than the hot dog; the photo-booth polyptych better than the kiss; the memory better than the affair; the shadow, in other words, more compelling than the figure."

"Yeah," someone said.

"'Cause shadows add layers of mystery," Wade went on, "nimbi of abstraction, suggestions of perfection, and in so doing climb like dark horses closer to the fab Forms of the intellectual ether."

I said something inarticulate, closed my eyes, softly pulled the hairs on my Adam's apple. I liked listening to Wade's voice, fast and mellow like Charlie Parker darting through a ballad—"Bird of Paradise," say, which is really "All the Things You Are" or all the things you are. He could talk and talk, and it wasn't windbagging, I thought, it was bullshit artistry, at once seductive and irritating, often most convincing when I didn't quite know what he was saying. "An intelligent man would often be much at a loss without the company of fools," La Rochefoucauld wrote. Certainly Wade spent time with intellectual equals, but I think he was happier away from them. No mistake: Wanda wasn't a fool, far from it, but she was only twenty-five (or twenty-six—it's sad that I can't remember her birthday) and didn't debate or refute Wade as often as she could have even then. As for me, I might have been a fool, though possibly in this book I'll exaggerate my younger self's foolishness, and my current self's, either out of modesty or because readers find foolishness endearing, and because now is the era of the man-boy fool, or because I aspire to become a wise, truth-telling fool, for which plain foolishness might be good preparation.

"Of course the 'figures' of my little examples," Wade said, "if transferred to Platonic metaphysics and psychology, are themselves copies of, or copies of copies of, the universal Form." (To me) "Did you get to Plato before you dropped out?"

"A little."

"I only dredge him up because it's hard to talk about copies without him. It's fitting that *xerography*, whence the trademark and metonym *Xerox* comes, derives from the Greek."

"I thought it came from Bud Xerox," Wanda said.

"So maybe you remember," Wade said, "that art, as Plato had it, is two steps from Absolute Being, the Form, the Idea, the definite and fixed grades of the will's objectification, just like Bobby Bland was two steps from the blues."

I stood up but gestured that I was still listening.

"So for One"— Wade made a capital *O* with his arms— "there's Absolute Beauty; then there's temporal, palpable beauty, such as a beautiful woman, exempli gratia Wanda—rolling her eyes as I speak—a beautiful woman who copies or partakes somehow of Absolute Beauty; and lower down the line let's say there's a painting the woman modeled for. Then there's the reproduction of that painting in a much-manhandled edition of *Erotic Art through the Ages,* the prize of my coffee-table porno-art books before I sold all my stuff."

"How much did you get for all that stuff?" I asked from the other room.

"It's impolite to ask about money. So about this updated Platonic ladder let's agree that one can take Plato seriously without taking him literally, and that the antithesis of his intolerable aesthetics, that art of true sublimity not only improves life but improves *on* life, won't do either, at least not as an abiding faith."

"Where the fuck are my Bobby Bland records?" I said.

"I moved him to R&B," Wade said. "It's bad taxonomy to put him in blues."

"What? You can't be moving my—"

"Aristotle, better of course on art than Plato—" Wade said.

"But worse *at* it," Wanda said.

"That's true, that's true," Wade said, "to judge from the extant record. Complicating things further."

Wanda smiled.

"Aristotle says in his *Poetics* that Polygnotus's paintings and Homer's poems 'are better than we are.' You could read that as just a simple acknowledgment of artistic idealization, but he also suggests that such an improvement is possible even in dancing and flute playing—"

"Except that's not possible," Wanda said. "Flutes are horrendous."

"You just haven't heard the right flutes," Wade said.

"James Newton's good," I said, back at the table. "Dolphy."

"Don't underrate Herbie Mann," Wade said.

"What I'm saying is I hate flutes. I don't care whose fucking flute it is."

"Do you like steel guitars?" Wade said.

Wanda hesitated for maybe twenty seconds. "Yes," she said.

"Okay, so by the time Aristotle says we can be better than we really are by playing steel guitars, we're well on the way to art as religion, art as transcendence, art over or against Earth and all its stuff, though also art that uncovers that stuff's truth and esse, as when Hegel says that a portrait by Titian or Dürer, or any portrait finely attuned to the sitter's spiritual vitality, is more like the individual than the actual individual himself."

"Except Hegel wouldn't have seen any of the actual individuals Titian or Dürer painted portraits of," Wanda said, "unless they were painting Methuselah."

"Well, that's a simpleminded complaint," Wade said. Wanda defended herself without excitement but Wade cut her off: "Anyway, I've become something of an art-as-religion apostate. It just doesn't seem to sustain me anymore."

"Can we smoke this spliff?" I said. Wanda gave me an amused look at the word *spliff.*

"That's what it's there for," Wade said.

"Right on."

"This record used to be a real make-out favorite for his mother and me," Wade said, looking at Wanda while wave-pointing in my direction. "Something about Jaco's Fender, those rubbery bass glissandi, like a tongue in your ear."

"But kind of flatulent, too," Wanda croaked midinhale, then imitated the sound.

"Jaco turned his Fender into a fretless by himself, you know," Wade said, insulted it seemed, "with nothing but a toenail clipper and a half-empty tub of oleo."

"I was just kidding," Wanda said, "it's really nice." Her smile, as a rule and in that instance, wasn't especially warm, was cooler than she was. Her features were in general severe. The bridge of her nose was particularly knifelike. These descriptions aren't intended to be physiognomic, however. She could be harsh sometimes, sure, but in terms of kindness and warmth she bettered me and would have measured well against a higher standard.

"Yeah, but it's not wallpaper," Wade said. "You have to listen to it. It's not pretty, it's beautiful. Mysterious. The oldest known ancestor of the word *pretty* is a West Germanic word meaning 'trick,' but there's no trick to this stuff, no wool-pulling." He nodded my way: "I'm impressed that you have this CD. You need to do some weeding, though. You've got a lot of crap in there, impoverishing the collection."

"Some of them I get for free at the store," I said.

"Well, you can get matches for free, but that doesn't mean you should use them to burn your house down."

"Kind of an over-the-top analogy," Wanda said.

"I used to have a tape of this album," Wade said. He was cutting the pizza with a pair of scissors. "Listen to that bass." He hummed along with a few bars, conducting a bit with the scissors—or, not so much conducting as describing a finchlike flight pattern.

"A genius," I said.

"I sold to Jaco one time," he said.

"Really?"

"Just once, down in Atlanta. We walked together for a block or two. The whole time he held a catalpa leaf in front of his face to avoid recognition."

"Wow," I said.

"That was Jaco," Wade said. He brought the pizza to the table and sat between Wanda and me with his back to the kitchen. "Yeah, this album sounds exactly like the drive from Enswell to Grand Forks, but not at all like the drive from Grand Forks to Enswell. In fact clashes with the ride home. Dissonant where it doesn't want to be. I've tested this several times. I used to have a Rand McNally extensively marked up with that kind of research." He looked into Wanda's eyes. "His mother and I, we listened to a lot of this one, a lot of Joni, the jazz Joni, Jaco Joni, Jarrett, J. J. Johnson, Jimmy Giuffre, Jimmy Webb, Jimmy Reed, Jim Reeves, Johnny."

"Which Johnny?" I asked.

"All of 'em: Hartman, Hodges, Coltrane, Carson, Mathis, especially Mathis. We'd recite Baudelaire, Rimbaud, Bataille. We were D-Luxe Frenchies. Have you met his mother?"

"No," Wanda said. "I've talked to her on the phone."

"Seen any pictures?"

"Yes," she said with put-on affection.

"Lord," Wade said, now drawing a figure in the air. "Legs like inverted traffic cones. She was a Lachaise sculpture. And a real voluptuary. I trust she still is."

"Okay," I said, trying to move things in another direction.

"A beautiful woman!" Wade said. "Not pretty at all. I've thought about calling her before I leave for Berlin, but . . . to what end? She probably wouldn't want to hear from me anyway." He looked at me.

"Yeah, I don't know," I said. The pizza sauce was oversweet and the cheese kept sliding from its base like a slapstick toupee.

"The early Joni—not the early Joni, but the second phase, star-made Joni, *Ladies of the Canyon* through *Court and Spark*—that period doesn't work for me as bedroom music. The lyrics are too distracting, like having your lover's roommate in the corner talking on the phone, about you. That's a male perspective, I know," he said, glancing at Wanda, who may have found the glance patronizing, may have found the word *lover* oily or square, though the more up-to-date substitute words tend to be cute, imprecise, or overslangy.

"I don't like vocal music at all during sex," Wanda said, "unless it's in a foreign language—"

"A foreign tongue?" Wade said.

"Yes, a foreign tongue," Wanda said. "Or in English but indecipherable. I think I'd like to live where hardly anyone spoke English. People say that's the best way to learn a foreign language, but I'd want to stay ignorant, maybe choose somewhere with a language I had no interest in learning, with a different alphabet so I couldn't figure anything out. Maybe then everything would be dreamlike and romantic. You could imagine people were reciting poetry and plotting revolutions when really they were just gossiping or asking for change."

"They'd probably ask for change in English, if they were asking you," I said.

"Maybe," Wanda said.

"But you're right," Wade said, "words are complicated in that context, the bedroom context."

"I don't like anything rhythmically straightforward, either," Wanda said, "in that 'context.' I dated a woman for a while who could only fuck to John Philip Sousa."

Three sharp laughs shot staccato out of Wade's wide mouth.

"Almost all the music we listen to is rhythmically straightforward," I said. "I mean, not the free jazz or some of the syncopated stuff, but—"

"Well I'm not speaking in like technical terms," Wanda said. "I'm just saying I want the music to be more flowing than driving, not because I want the sex to be dainty, I just don't want anyone to be overly influenced by the beat, you know. That's happened a few times, where I found myself getting fucked to the beat—one-two-three-four, one-two-three-four . . .'"

This aroused and accused me, and I considered two things: that with Wade sleeping in the next room, Wanda and I would be deterred from having sex, and that the length of his stay was unsettled.

"Sousa *is* strange," Wade said.

"Yeah, who was that?" I said.

"He was an American composer of marches and—"

"Yeah, yeah, I mean who wanted to fuck to his music?"

"No one you know," Wanda said.

"It sounds kind of made up," I said.

"Well, it's not," she said. In the dim light, her inexorable acne was significantly obscured and her hair looked blacker than it was, though not as black as Wade's. Her hair was in fact brown, but brown on the border of black, with a few prominent tufts curled into loose spirals. She was wearing a one-pocket crew-neck T-shirt from a discount-store three-pack, or rather a former crew-neck, since she'd ripped the collar into a jagged scoop neck while we sat next to the coin-operated amusements on the store's sidewalk. I couldn't understand the urgency. "Why not wait till we get home?" I said, and I remember the look of mournful surprise on a little girl's face when Wanda started biting and tearing the three-pack's top shirt, how ashamed I was when the girl's possibly poor and affronted mother pulled her daughter away toward the mechanical doors. I liked how those T-shirts came out, though. Once on one of our early dates I blurted, "I'm not looking down your shirt." "There's not much to see," she said, and it's true that one noticed more clavicle than breast; I even came to eroticize her clavicles, would sometimes lick or nibble them from left to right as if I were eating corn on the cob in summer (when sweat would rest on her clavicle's upper ridge and I'd relish the salty taste).

Wade cleared his throat. "In some ways—to get back to what I was saying—in some ways those Joni albums, from a certain masculine perspective, are ideal make-out music, since they're so resolutely, even if remorsefully, against domesticity." Neither Wanda nor I took up this thread. After some silence (the CD had ended a few minutes earlier), Wade closed his eyes and in a tarnished baritone began to sing from Mitchell's "Let the Wind Carry Me," a great work of art with which I have a deep and increasingly lachrymatory connection: *Sometimes I get that feeling and I want to settle and raise a child up with some-body.*" (I love that folksy *up.*) He stopped, to my relief; he was making me uncomfortable. But he was only counting the beats in his head: "*I get that strong longing and I want to settle and raise a child up with somebody.*" He had a tender, expressive voice, as fine as ice on eyelashes, and he was really stretching and bluesing some of the notes and phrases, though not the same ones Mitchell stretches on the record. I hadn't remembered him being much of a singer, but he was outstanding, and there was something superbly unfashionable about the sweet yet burry tone of his voice—singing voices are as much expressions of fashion and history as they are of self, and Wade's seemed locked in 1974. His singing face was nearly as expressive as his voice, though not in an actorly way, or it was expressive in an actorly way so accomplished that the artifice seemed to slide away. Wanda shifted (lustfully?) in her seat. Few of us are immune to the tall-dark-and-handsome type. Wade, his "Here comes one good-looking Indian!" T-shirt notwithstanding, was a Lebanese American. His grandfather's first name had been Saleem, self-Anglicized into the surname Salem. Quite a few Syrian-Lebanese people, mostly Maronites, came to North Dakota around the turn of the century, settling in towns and small cities such as Williston, Rugby, Hunch, Ross, and Goldenrod, where Wade grew up, working at his parents' grocery store, serving as the Bruins go-to wide receiver from '64 through '66, inheriting his grandfather's Little Blue Book on Schopenhauer, which for a while Wade carried "talismanically," he told me once, in the crumby pocket of his letter jacket. He went on with the song: "*But it passes like the summer, I'm a wild seed again. Let the wind carry me.*" He opened his eyes, Wanda complimented his singing, I murmured a second. "Anyway," Wade said, "it's not a perspective I'm bound to, a so-called male one, that is, or isn't. 'Everyone is the other, and no one is himself.' I still believe that."

"'I is another,'" Wanda said softly.

"Exactly," Wade said. He closed his eyes again but didn't sing this time. "I have to have music. I have to have music." He opened his eyes. "I'm not above pulling out midcoitus to flip over the record, and have been criticized for doing so. After I'm settled in Berlin, I'm gonna buy a really good sound system. Everyone knows the Germans are great audiophiles. Phonaesthesia is fantastically common there. Hundreds of car accidents happen each year on account of folks swerving and braking to avoid collisions with music."

"How'd you meet up with Jaco?" I asked.

"Oh, that's kind of a sad story." He turned back to Wanda: "The music has to be perfect; the wrong music destroys. I can't perform with rivals on the stereo, either: Marvin Gaye, Robert Plant, Larry Wood, Barry White, Teddy Pendergrass, the later Rod Stewart, any of those Casanovas and Lotharios. The real outsized ladies' men of mood music are destroyers, absolute destroyers. I've gathered some empirical evidence as to their pernicious influence on potency. My needle rusts, to quote a line, paraphrastically, from 'Phonograph Blues.' That's one of the reasons I like Mathis. *Open Fire/Two Guitars.* You know that one?" He looked at me.

I didn't.

"Another instance of beautiful-not-pretty. What he does to those notes—all the bending and massaging, the holding, the vibrating, the dilating—every phrase a gloss on the terrible pleasure of longing. Maybe during side one you recite a couple of Dickinson poems or a bit of Kierkegaard on Regine." He hooked a few strands of hair out of his mouth with one of his Lisztian fingers. "A story about *Open Fire:* One night I'm at Oran's. This was the bar I haunted in Enswell." (The exposition was for Wanda; I remembered Oran's.) "A buddy of mine owned the bar—he'd inherited it from Oran himself—and another buddy, Karl Tobreste, played drums there on weekends: on Fridays with me and a couple other guys in the Seed Sacks; on Saturdays in Hailstorm. And then later on Karl and I were the rhythm section in Bolling Greene's little touring band." Wanda nodded. "So one night I'm at Oran's, sitting in my regular corner booth in the band room, and I look up from my book just as this beyond-belief fox is bending over to pick up a matchbook or something. Long blond hair, tight jeans, the kind of ass that begs to be spanked hard with a paddle. Oran's had a Ping-Pong table in the basement. Well, she turned around and it was like something out of Ovid, Tiresias and the snakes or what have you, 'cause she instantly turned into Gary Rush, this stereo salesman I knew."

We all laughed. "That's also like this one *Benny Hill* sketch," I said.

"Gary Rush," Wade said, shaking his head, this gesture perhaps actorly. "I'd bought an expensive pair of headphones from him one time, studio quality, with an amazing bass half-loudness point and a ten-foot cord. I could cover a good chunk of my apartment with no tugging or unplugging. I miss those headphones." He shook his head. "Stolen." He looked at me. "Did you take them?"

"What?" I said.

"Did you take my studio-quality headphones?"

"No."

"Well, you took that sawbuck from your register today, and my headphones went missing during the time you had access to my apartment."

"I didn't take your headphones or the ten bucks," I said.

Pause.

"Okay," Wade said. "It's just: they were outstanding head-phones. The stereo separation, it seemed really extreme, and the stuff in the center of the mix did strange things, seemed to come out of my eye sockets." He brought his hands to his face and danced his fingers like crepitating fireworks away from his eyes.

I asked if Wade planned to eat the crusts he'd arranged in a campfire-like mound on the side of his plate. The customary tentative negotiations over the last pieces had been skipped; Wade ate like a child, sloppily and with no sense of equity. It was okay for me to eat the crusts, he motioned, and continued his story: "So every once in a while I sold Gary Rush grass. He looked like Gregg Allman, but much shorter. Karl used to call him the Midget Rider. After 'Midnight Rider.'"

"Right," I said.

"So I called Gary over to my booth, and we talked for a while, went out to my car to smoke a couple joints. The grass wasn't as potent back then, you know, so smoking a joint by yourself was roughly equivalent to the three of us sharing this one now. Anyway, we eventually wound up at my apartment."

"This is the apartment below ours?" I said.

"Yeah, but your mom and I weren't together yet."

"Oh."

"Things started to move down a pretty obvious road, and I put on *Open Fire/Two Guitars*."

"Is that like 'open fire' with a gun?" Wanda said.

"What? Oh, yeah, I never thought of that. So a few songs in—we're shedding some layers at this point—and he gestures to the stereo and says"—Wade switched to a low, burned-out voice—"'Look brother, can we nix this faggot shit?'" We all laughed again.

"He's dead now, Gary is," Wade said. "Been a long time gone." Wanda and I tried to respond with a shift toward sobriety.

"Nothing to do with me," he said.

For argument's sake, I much later looked into the cause (heart disease) of Gary Rush's death. Wade I think was an essentially moral man—by no stretch heedless of right and wrong, at least, if not always upright and trustworthy—but there was a slight sinisterity to him that made it momentarily conceivable that he *had* killed Gary Rush, and for no good reason. (For snoring, say.) Although I'm hard put to evince this sinisterity; the illustration I recur to is more subjective than I'd like: It was about two in the morning after our little pizza party. Underfed at dinner, I got up for a snack and saw Wade silhouetted in front of my stereo. He didn't notice me, didn't or pretended not to notice the refrigerator light. He was wearing headphones and a long scarf (Wanda's—I didn't like the idea of him getting used to her scent), his spidery right leg propped on one of my particle-board record shelves in the subjugating way guitarists sometimes prop their legs on stage monitors, and in my memory he looks fantastically rubbery and seriocomic, like one of Kafka's drawings, or even vaguely and more to the point like the shadowy, sticklike figure in

Félicien Rops's *Satan Sowing Seeds*. Wade wasn't satanic, I should stress, but his just-mentioned air of sinisterity, though slight, was thick enough to emit bursts of Mephistophelean elegance and allure.

He wasn't a violent man, though, or no more than most. The next morning, he and I had breakfast of a kind at the convenience store where he would spend many of his Minneapolis mornings—drinking coffee, eating doughnuts, and playing chess with down-and-outers at the store's one table, a high round table granted two uncomfortable stools—and it was there that I heard what I took to be his only partly facetious claim to ab ovo pacifism. He was born, he told me, at 11:59 p.m. on October 17, 1947. That birthday, for men born between '44 and '50, was drawn 228th in the December '69 draft lottery; October 18 was drawn fifth. By the time of that first lottery, Wade, earlier awarded a student deferment, had dropped out of college, so had he been born just a minute later, or had the nurse for whatever reason recorded his birth-time as midnight instead of 11:59, Wade almost certainly would have been drafted and might have served. "So you see . . ." he concluded. He'd fired a gun only once, he also told me, while pheasant hunting one cold fall morning with his dyspeptic father, and hadn't hit anyone with his fists since the third grade. He couldn't remember what the fight was over, but clearly remembered its last few minutes, how straddling and punching the boy repeatedly in the chest was one of the times in which pleasure and sadness were as hard to distinguish as minnows in a large school. Some of Wade's sexual proclivities involved violence as well, I came to learn. So when I say he wasn't a violent man, I mean that he wasn't routinely, menacingly violent, not prone to freakish, unprovoked, or disproportionate acts of violence of the type one might expect from a criminal.

He'd spent some of the midseventies in Grand Forks, where he first added cocaine to his inventory of marijuana, psychedelics, and pills. Grand Forks, he said, was North Dakota's "top toot town." He left that city because he missed Enswell, he said, but also because a pair of rival dealers may have been threatening him. He'd gotten an unpostmarked manila envelope containing a pamphlet called *Home Remidees* [sic] *for Gunshot Wounds*. He left three days later, though for several years he carried on a modest grass trade in Grand Forks. He kept the pamphlet, he said, and eventually gave it to my mother, who he thought would enjoy diagramming some of its barbarous sentences. The pamphlet, I suspected, was Wade's invention. Only reluctantly would he talk about drugs or dealing—"it's not interesting"—and when he did it was often tongue-in-cheek, though I think he was sincere when he said it wasn't interesting.

At some point when Wade was more or less living with my mother and me, she told me he sometimes sold marijuana to friends, in the way, she said, that one might sell an extra concert ticket to a friend. I'm not sure why she offered this misleading explanation and its even more disingenuous analogy, since I'd suspected nothing and didn't quite understand what marijuana was. Perhaps she was preparing me for rumors. She smoked a fair amount of pot herself, and though she didn't proselytize on its behalf, she was never furtive or apologetic about it. (She did sometimes complain of grogginess in an explanatory way related to apology.) After Wade left us to go on the road with Bolling, first as a batman or Doctor Robert, then as a bassist, I learned from my mother that he'd in fact been dealing more coke than pot, and that the short trips he took, putatively to visit family or play an out-of-town gig, were really visits to his supplier in Los Angeles. To throw off the authorities, my mother said, he'd fly to Los Angeles out of a different city's airport each time—Bismarck, then Sioux Falls, then Duluth. The more she revealed, the more glamorous Wade became and the more I distrusted my mother.

But surely not all of those trips were to L.A. Some must have been Wade's semiregular sales trips to Grand Forks, often soundtracked by *Bright Size Life*, though not, eventually, on the return trip, for which the album was or is somehow ill-suited. A few years ago, I tried to verify that hypothesis, playing Metheny's album repeatedly from Grand Forks to Enswell, Enswell to Grand Forks, Grand Forks to Enswell, Enswell to Grand Forks. It was a peaceful, trancelike weekend. I thought of Jaco and the catalpa leaf, thought of Wade, thought of Wanda, thought of a giant, blanketing catalpa leaf with raindrops on the outside, fur on the inside. But I couldn't grasp what Wade was getting at; the album sounded great in both directions. My ears aren't his ears, though, and the scenery had changed over the decades, and no doubt for other reasons the experiment can't be meaningfully reproduced.

THE END OF ART

B
Y THE TIME I WAS A TEENAGER, MY MOTHER, WHO
as I'll later explain was my adoptive mother, had
forgotten much of the French she'd learned in school,
though she hadn't entirely forsaken the language. Once I saw
her reading *Les fleurs du mal* in the original, a French-English
dictionary and a cup of her surprisingly feeble coffee at hand.
Probably she continued to work slowly through other French
literature too, I don't know. I didn't pay close attention to everything she was reading. I know she often read Montaigne's
essays, but these she read in Donald Frame's translation. I have
her old edition of Frame's Montaigne; I like to note which passages she check-marked (e.g.: "A feeble struggle, that of art
against nature"), though the book, bought secondhand, is
inscribed by a previous owner, so really I don't know if I'm pausing over her check-marks or Frank Wiechman's. Sometimes she
came close to finishing French crossword puzzles out of a
water-puffed paperback, or diagrammed French sentences,
though these, I calculate, made up less than two percent of the
countless sentences she diagrammed in her relatively short life.
After we moved to Minneapolis, she sometimes went to French
movies, or, after we got a VCR, rented them—there was a period
of about six weeks in the fall of 1988 when she watched fifty or

sixty French movies, working through the local video store's small selection, then tapping the central library. Before watching one, she'd put two slightly overlapping strips of masking tape on the bottom of the screen, to prevent subtitular cheating, insulting a directorial vision already injured by square-screen reformatting. Sometimes she asked me to watch the movies with her, especially if it was something she hoped would speak to my inchoate bohemianism. "Come on," she'd say, patting the couch, offering to translate for me ("in more idiomatic English than the subtitles"). Usually I declined. In later years I would watch some of those movies on my own with considerable sadness and some boredom.

During those weeks of fairly intense French video watching in the fall of '88 (possibly the spring of '89), my mother didn't bother to peel the masking tape off the screen after finishing a movie, since she'd likely watch another one soon enough. I didn't bother to remove the tape either. But whereas the tape annoyed me when it covered parts of the few French movies I did agree to watch with my mother (*Shoot the Piano Player*, *Pierrot le fou*), the partial concealment seemed to improve my own programs. I suppose the tape lent obscurity and mystery to hopelessly clear, unmysterious stuff, mostly sitcoms and game shows watched slouchingly after school. That said, I did peel off the tape one afternoon to get a full view of a pornographic movie I'd managed to rent, and though I remember nothing specific about the movie and can't cite its title for cheap laughs, I do remember how nervously careful I was afterwards to stick the strips of tape back in their precise former positions, how the task seemed doubly stressful and humiliating because my penis was bothered in my jeans from having been washed in the bathroom sink under water not given enough time to warm, bringing to mind a chilly swim in Devil's Lake when I'd gotten scared a few too many yards from shore and had to be rescued by a boy just one grade ahead of me in school. The tape had left gummy traces, as well as a faint outline from having shielded the screen from several weeks of dust, so I was eventually able to restore the strips almost perfectly, though an end of the upper strip started to curl away from the screen like the front of a toboggan and wouldn't restick. My pains were pointless from the start and proved even more so: removing the tape wouldn't have been incriminating; I might reasonably have done so to watch *Jeopardy!*; moreover I forgot to take the video out of the player and was thus discovered more directly. My mother left the video on my pillow but never mentioned it. Tactfully, I suppose, or maybe by then she considered her parental work mostly done, didn't have the energy to deliver a futile lecture or suffer my mumbling shame. She'd adopted me under odd circumstances, without great forethought, and I've sometimes wondered if she didn't come to regret the decision, not that her behavior ever betrayed regret beyond the mild and occasional variety presumably common to many parents.

She had started as a French major at Northern Illinois University, but later switched to English with a French minor. She was a gifted grammarian, though not pedantic, not snobby about everyone else's solecisms. Many friends and relatives suggested she become a schoolteacher; perhaps no one suggested she become a professor. But she was never interested in teaching at any level, or so she told me when I was twelve or thirteen. Just the thought of standing up all day playing a role or rôle exhausted and even sickened her, she said, and besides, she'd met only one sufferable child (she patted my shoulder). It was bad enough to play a role in an office or shop, she said, but there at least you weren't performing all the time, unless everything was a performance, and she wouldn't accept that. She liked movies, certain movies, and a few plays, but held actors in low regard. Not artists, she said, especially those who claimed to be. Nothing ruins Shakespeare quite like its performance, was another thing she said. But, she added, almost all artists, not just actors, were half-talents and tagalongs. Art, once a fruit of prosperity, was in her view now a symptom of it, and she despised the airy promotion of "creativity" that so marked seventies pedagogy. The half-talent's failure will hurt her as much as the genius's, she said, and the half-talent's success will hurt the rest of us. On top of which, all the major art forms were in irreversible decline. When I took up the guitar, callusing a few fingertips for my life as a supernumerary of the artistic proletariat, she looked at me dryly and said, "Just what the world needs, another guitarist," though it was her old guitar, a beat-up Kay, and later that night she picked it up to play "Will You Still Love Me Tomorrow?" and "The Poor Orphan Child," her pitch-challenged voice cracking throughout the former's final chorus.

In her sophomore year ('67–'68), when she was still a French major, she spent a term studying at the Catholic University of Paris. She had a choice to spend either fall or spring term there. Because she liked spring in DeKalb, she chose fall in Paris, thus missing the heady student-and-worker triumph of May '68. (She also missed that summer's Chicago DNC, during which she was at a Wyoming dude ranch serving as nanny to a French professor's three insufferable children.) She had a good time anyway, not at the dude ranch but in

Paris, even fell in love with a quiet, dark-haired intellectual whose name I don't remember. Two or three times she told me about him and her term abroad, but mostly through murky impressions and stray details: a rented car that may or may not have been a convertible, her Tuileries-dusted shoes, the unanticipated cold, a party on a bridge, a joint dropped in the Seine. Let's call the intellectual Étienne, though he wasn't a Frenchman; he was another American exchange student, Steve it might have been. He wore oxford shirts from Brooks Brothers, always with one of the babyish collar buttons undone, and wrote poetry, bad poetry, my mother said, had learned all the wrong things from John Ashbery and early Tristan Tzara, she didn't add, but my invention is probably close to the mark since she disdained amateur modernism more than amateur trash. On Étienne and my mother's last night together—they never talked about continuing their affair in the States, where they were separated by several thousand miles as well as Étienne's undiscussed homosexuality—he gave her a cheap but attractive necklace and a recent book by Gérard Zwang called *Le sexe de la femme*. She never described the book to me, or if she did I've forgotten what she said, but I remember the slow, ironically bombastic way she pronounced the title: *Le sexe . . . de la femme*, with the word *sexe* hissed and drawn out like the sizzle of certain tracks in the seconds after a train has passed, then suddenly muted like a hand grabbing a cymbal, after which she included an aroused growl where I've placed the ellipsis dots, and finally a quick, coup de grâce–like *de la femme*. It's hard to convey the humor of this on the page, but I remember us laughing over it more than once. She had a fizzy, gluggy laugh like soda pouring from a two-liter bottle.

Her copy of the reportedly beautiful and limited original edition of Zwang's book might have fallen into my hands in early '92, had she not lost it to theft two decades earlier. Were one of the originals to turn up, I could never afford it. I am unexpectedly poor. But from an internet retailer I've just ordered an imported, late-nineties reissue. Only a paperback, but who knows. It was Wade who taught me to revere the paperback. The mass-market paperback, he said, did more for art and ideas than the popularization of higher education. All his heroes were autodidacts. In any case, this paperback reissue's arrival, supposedly within two weeks, is, under uncompetitive conditions, the thing I'm most looking forward to.

mingus

THERE WAS A BOTTLE OF REGIONAL ROOT BEER ON THE cloth passenger seat of Wade's car, along with an emery board and a copy of the *Saginaw News*. When I moved the newspaper, I glimpsed a brown stain (root beer, I inferred) shaped like a fat comma. The shotgun floor was covered with Styrofoam coffee cups, peanut shells, hardened banana peels, two tennis-ball cylinders, two unsleeved forty-fives, and a dozen or so candy-bar wrappers. I cleared a level surface for my feet while Wade talked about Berlin, about the obsessively regular morning walks he'd take down Unter den Linden, the museum gift shops he'd visit, how each time before going on air he'd kiss the rank pop guard in front of the studio's enriching Neumann microphone.

It was a sunny Tuesday or Wednesday not quite a week after Wade's arrival. I had the day off. We were driving down to Owatonna, where he wanted to scope out Louis Sullivan and George Elmslie's famous National Farmers' Bank. He visored his eyes with his hand and asked me to look in the glove compartment for a pair of sunglasses. During the search I noticed a rusty fork, a retracted instant camera, a matchbox girded by a green rubber band, an unused early pregnancy test, and a map of Indiana tucked inside a field guide to Eastern birds. "They must not be in there" he said irritably while patting the floor, steering with his knees till the car passed briefly over the shoulder's teeth-buzzing cautionary furrows. "Oh, here they are," I said, and handed him the tortoiseshell aviators, very large though not too large for his face. I couldn't tell if they were seven-dollar sunglasses or hundred-dollar sunglasses. He was wearing his slightly dirty suede coat and his pomponed Washington Redskins cap, folded above his ears in some cleverly unridiculous way, and when he put on the glasses, I saw for the first time during his visit that he was still something of the style bricoleur I remembered from my childhood.

I picked up the three tapes in his dashboard cubby: Harlan Montgomery's *K.O.*, in one of the thick, unhinged black plastic cases with adhered cover art; a homemade c-90 in a scratched, cracked, and cloudy case, Gary Stewart on the A-side, Earl Thomas Conley on the B; and Bolling Greene's *The Infractor*, from the short-lived era of cardboard cassette cases and emblematic of that packaging's sentimental deterioration: the fraying on the edges, the fanning out on the sides, the cola stain on Bolling's jowly face. Wade said he needed a break from his tapes, so we listened to the radio, first to the better of the Twin Cities' two country stations, then to the station for defeated hippies, chronologically confused nostalgics, lawyers in love, et al. On this latter station we heard 10cc's "Dreadlock Holiday," one of Wade's favorite reggae tunes, he said. The chorus ("I don't like reggae—I love it!") reminded him of something Werther says about Ossian. At some point during Wade's visit, I learned to use the phrase "You have me at a disadvantage" when a reference drew from my cavern of ignorance, but I must have picked that up later. Now I call on the phrase all the time. Apparently it's unclear to a lot of people, and though my aim isn't to obfuscate, it is much rather to affect a refined, confident modesty, it's not as if I haven't noticed that when my interlocutor fails to grasp the phrase, the scales of power are right away balanced if not tipped in my favor. Occasionally I say "You have me at a disadvantage" when someone references something of which I only wish I were ignorant.

The drive from Minneapolis to Owatonna takes about an hour and fifteen minutes, though it probably took us longer since Wade drove unexpectedly under the speed limit. Shortly after we cleared Minneapolis's southern suburbs, he pointed out something about an airplane passing over us, something semi-technical that I didn't understand, and from there he segued into a story, both titillating and dull, about how he'd once managed to get a blowjob in his booth at Airport Road Enswell Parking. For a few years he was ARE Parking's utility attendant, working two shifts a week, Tuesday afternoons and Sunday mornings (comin' down). The gig was something of a cover for Wade, who made most of his money dealing, but I suspect the meager supplemental income came in handy. My impression is that he never made much money as a dealer, and wasn't terribly ambitious or competitive regarding his share of the market. My observations of his work, however, were fragmentary. I've long imagined that he made some transactions at the ARE Parking lot, if only because it was a frequently underpopulated place where passing money through car windows was sanctioned. But dealing there was probably more trouble than it was worth. Mostly he operated out of Oran's Bar, arranging house calls or rendezvous from his regular booth.

I got to join him in that booth one late afternoon in the spring of '78. I'd come in looking for him because I couldn't find my skateboard. I was really worked up about having misplaced, lost, or been burgled of this thin, yellow skateboard, which I'd only had for a few months. I walked tentatively into the bar like the start of a half-remembered joke. I was wearing, to paraphrase Gogol, whatever God or JCPenney sends to a provincial town (now the choices in Enswell are wider, though no better): slightly diluvial jeans, it might have been, and a screen-printed tank top on which a beer-guzzling rat raced a speedboat (caption: "River Rat"). Millie the tenured barmatron was patrolling the place with a bottle of off-brand glass cleaner and a loosely balled newspaper while Oran's son Marty built tumbler ziggurats on the long, rectangular bar. Everyone—Millie, Marty, the seven or eight pensioners and early-shifters around the bar—stared at me, and I pointed to the adjacent room, the band room where the Seed Sacks and Hailstorm played on weekends. "My stepdad's in there," I said. Marty, an old friend and probable client of Wade's, knew I wasn't Wade's stepson. He gestured in some smirking way that welcomed me with reservations. From North Dakota's finest jukebox, I want to say, Tommy Duncan moaned, "My brain is cloudy, my soul is upside down," but maybe I've just put that in there along with the high-waters and the off-brand glass cleaner because it seems right, because Tommy Duncan is moaning now in my low-ceilinged, carpeted apartment. Wade was reading alone in the band room. He didn't know where my skateboard was. As I turned to leave, he touched my arm and gave me some money for a soda, said I could hang out with him awhile. "Thanks!" The cola foam danced like ocean spray on my hand as I walked carefully back to Wade's booth with one of Marty's hot, just-washed tumblers, and I remember how impressed I was with the slice of lime, how good it felt to squeeze it into the cola. By that point Wade's friend Karl Tobreste was onstage setting up his drums, a cheap kit from Sears but he made it sound like a Ludwig. Wade closed his book. I asked if he ever wanted to be a kid again, like my age, but with his adult brain. He said no, because he would just become a disappointing prodigy. Then he made some convoluted objection to the question, said it relied on a strict Cartesian mind-body dualism that could no longer be supported, argued that right-thinking monism renders all such switcheroos meaningless or undesirable. I don't actually remember what his objection was, just that it was over my head, and that I sensed it was spoken for Karl's amusement. Wade was a great one for that, talking indirectly to others within earshot while pretending to talk to me. It's not unique behavior. I sucked on my soda-sopped ice, then sucked on the lime, until a tall, high-foreheaded man in a khaki shirt approached Wade's booth, and I was gently told to go home.

The story of Wade's parking-lot conquest had given me an erection that I hoped wasn't obvious through my twills. As I shifted in my seat, he started another story, and continued with stories or fragments of stories till we got to the bank. Although I broke in from time to time and some back and forth resulted, at one point I imagined that he might have told his stories even if I hadn't been in the car. It occurs to me now that Wade might have made his monistic objections (or whatever objections they were) to my time-bending fantasy not for Karl's amusement but for his own. Sometimes during his stay in Minneapolis he'd talk without looking at Wanda or me, or without looking at our faces. He'd turn his head from side to side or toward the floor, as if he resented our being in the way of his voice, as if he didn't really want an audience. But of course he did, and at other times, I recall, he stared at us too intently.

On the drive he told me that his older sister was a decent pianist, that he used to help her push the untunable Salem spinet out from the wall so he could lean against the soundboard and listen to her play show tunes at incongruous tempos: a dirgeful "Surrey with the Fringe on Top," a sprightly "Ol' Man River." He told me about the time he was hit, while jayrunning so as not to arrive even later for a dishwashing shift, by a Dodge Dart "the color of a jaundiced pear," and how useful it is to know "severe collisional pain." The restaurant's manager, who had strange, winged hair like Schopenhauer's or Bozo's, Wade said, called the hospital to find out when the accident occurred, then fired Wade for tardiness. He told me about a Grand Forks doctor, a sometime customer, who for a few years offered back-alley vasectomies to the promiscuous and uninsured, either as an act of Malthusian charity or because he was a sadist, Wade wasn't sure. A Yellow truck passed us going north, and he said he'd often thought about getting a trucker's license. "Isn't it disorienting to see these huge orange trucks rolling down the highway with the word *yellow* painted on them?" he said. "Ceci n'est pas un camion orange." He told me again about Jaco and the catalpa leaf. Since we were sharing encounters with jazz bassists, I told him my (light-on-action) story about shaking Ron Carter's hand, and he answered that one of his ex-girlfriends had gotten a splinter from Charlie Mingus's bass lodged in her ear. Mingus, Wade said, telling his ex-girlfriend's story, had been plagued at a Chicago nightclub by a pair of incessant chatterers near the stage, loud chatterers and glass-clinkers who wouldn't shut up even after repeated calls for attentiveness from the bandleader, who finally picked up his double-bass by the neck and brought it down like a hammer on the middle of the chatterers' table, not more than a ruler's length from the table occupied by Wade's girlfriend. "Mingus himself tweezed out the splinter with a pair of dessert chopsticks while Dannie Richmond took a long solo," Wade said. "Then Mingus brought his totaled bass backstage, grabbed another one—a wasted old thing with just three strings—and finished the gig, playing better than before."

"Man," I said.

"Her implication being that something magical happened to the ear as a result of the splinter. But I have my doubts. This gal, she lacked discernment; her ears were too soon made glad."

"Maybe before the splinter they were—"

"Even sooner gladdened? It's possible. I don't even like to think about some of the crap she made us listen to. Mingus and Van Morrison were the only worthwhile musicians she liked, and probably their music sounded especially strange and unprecedented to her 'cause she listened to no other jazz or blues or soul, not even fusion or blues-rock or blue-eyed soul, unless it came on the radio or I put it on at home."

"You lived together?"

"For a while."

"What was her name?"

"How's that?"

"Her name," I said.

It seemed like he couldn't remember or was reluctant to report it.

"Rae," he said after another moment.

"Ray?"

"Rae, R-a-e. Rae Morgenson."

"My mom was a big Van Morrison fan. Both my moms were."

"Yeah, well, everyone was," Wade said.

"Not everyone," I said.

"I would rather you not question the universality of the white hippie experience."

I laughed. Then, "Do you consider yourself white?"

"I consider myself blue."

It was a cool day, but the car's heater worked surprisingly well (and still does). I shimmied off my L.A. Kings starter jacket. "So what kind of crap did she listen to when she wasn't listening to Mingus or Van?" I asked.

"I just told you I don't like to think about that."

"Yeah, but—"

"I don't know. Commercial stuff, phony head music: the Other Knee, the Cryan' Shames, Iron Butterfly, Wind Shadows, Vanilla Fudge, the Eggs of Misconception, the Ghosts of Electricity. A lot of questionable shit. She'd dated the drummer from the Other Knee. Frog, he called himself. I think he was the one who gave her the Mingus album. She liked Mingus's music purely, you know. She didn't like it 'cause it was cool or sophisticated, 'cause it might intrigue someone who called on the phone and heard it blasting in the background, she having turned it up before answering. She just liked it."

"What did Ellington say? 'If it sounds good, it is good.'"

"But I couldn't figure out *why* Mingus sounded good to her, because as I say most of what she liked was garbage. I tried to listen to her music with new ears, you know, thinking maybe she was hearing things I couldn't hear, me being too much the yeasayer of prevailing critical opinion. Didn't work, though. I've always been mystified by people like that, the sporadically, randomly tasteful. My problem isn't indiscrimination, it's that I have such a painful sense of where my discrimination gives out. Hank Adams said he knew his inferiority in taste just like he would've known it in smell, had he been hard of smelling."

I grunted.

"A lot of times I've felt too smart for my life, but too dumb for another one. You'll probably find that too."

I didn't like the sound of that, and we drove without talking for a few minutes. Then he told me about some of his other girlfriends. He said he'd had a "soap-bubble affair" with Mollie Katzen, the beautiful author of *The Moosewood Cookbook* and *The Enchanted Broccoli Forest*, and that he'd spent one night with Bolling Greene's ex-wife, the singer and one-hit-wonder Penny Sakes ('77's *For Heaven's* . . . holds up pretty well). Also he'd loved a woman whose great-great-grandmother may have been the model for Courbet's *The Origin of the World*. "I'm a bit of a starfucker," he said. He'd also gone out with an artist who believed in "booksong," the idea that one could develop a "mystic's ear" for which book to read next. He'd dated a court reporter who was into bondage and discipline and some sado-masochism, he said, and from her he'd picked up a mild taste for that sort of thing. He'd grown equally comfortable as top or bottom. One of his favorite things was to be punched in the eye while coming, he said, but the court reporter didn't always get the timing right—apt, he said, since she was also a not fully competent percussionist in a folk-rock band. Desire, Wade told me, wants nothing more than to destroy itself, as the Trammps had more or less maintained. He said he'd had a lot of girlfriends and had loved them all, but none as much as my mother. "She was a real connoisseur of coffee on book leaf," he said, as if that were her defining trait. "Probably still is. She loved to stare at the stains and wonder over the words they'd landed on. She was deliberately careless with her cup. Your mother appreciates things, you know: black birds on white skies, raindrops on sidewalk gingko leaves. She would never explicitly point those things out, but . . . she'd draw your attention."

"I don't remember any gingko trees in Enswell."

"But I saw some raindrops like that the other day and thought of her. So this is it," he said, parking. I leaned against the car while he studied the bank for two or three minutes. "Can you grab me the sx-70?" he said.

"What?"

"The sx-70, please."

"What?"

"The Polaroid in the glove box."

He took a photo of the bank, and did a few dozen squat-thrusts. "Okay, let's split," he said.

"You don't want to go inside?"

"Not really."

"You want to stop for lunch at all?" I said.

"Let's just grab sandwiches at a gas station."

"A lot of those sandwiches are slimy."

"This place isn't happenin' for me right now, okay?"

About twenty miles out of town, we stopped at a gas station where I bought sandwiches in triangular containers while Wade altered his Polaroid photo with the rusty fork I'd seen in the glove compartment. The sandwiches were slimy. The rest of the way home we took turns naming professional or notable collegiate football players. To make the game more challenging, we had to circle through the alphabet, forward and backwards, him saying "Grady Alderman," me saying "Fred Biletnikoff," him saying "Jimmy Conzelman," me saying "Tony Dorsett," him saying "Bill Earley," and so on. We were allowed to skip *X*. The first person (me) who couldn't come up with a name lost. I challenged some of Wade's names—a few seemed patently fictional—but each time he unhesitatingly offered corroboration: always a position and a team, often a jersey number or a metaphorical description of the player's style and form, maybe a bit of human-interest trivia, the marital history of some ancient Canton Bulldog or Rock Island Independent, the stray border collie that really taught him how to run. I held a few of the suspect names in mind, and, sure enough, they turned up in a football encyclopedia. It was hard to know when Wade was telling the truth, and I think one of his tricks was to make some truths sound like lies, so that if you discovered enough of his seeming lies to be after all true, you might start to think that everything he said was true.

THE ORIGIN OF THE WORLD (1)

I MENTIONED ABOVE THAT THE WOMAN I'VE BEEN calling my mother, Marleen Deskin, wasn't my biological mother. This fact was never kept from me. Martha Dickson was my biological mother. Between my mothers' names there's obviously much similarity—alliteration, assonance, consonance, and so on—and perhaps this similarity (unfortunate in the present context, and I apologize) readied or at least encouraged my mothers' short but important friendship, since all sorts of superficial similarities can at least briefly make a friendship seem inevitable.

At some point in my antememorial days my mother Marleen must have sat me down for a bowdlerized version of the following story, beginning, it may have been, with a tenderizing plate of runner-up brand cream-sandwich cookies and a gentle yet distinctly portentous prelude. I don't remember these cookies or this prelude, but neither do I remember a time when I didn't know something of my spectral biological mother. I do remember two times on which she, Marleen, told a more or less complete version of the story: (1) on a road trip to the Grand Canyon during my twelfth summer, and (2) in the kitchen while she made a taco salad during my sixteenth spring. Fragmental-anecdotal parts of the story came or were drawn out on several other occasions. Certain fragments came out with relative frequency, such as the part about Martha's homemade embroidered blouses, how ineptly they were sewn, or the part about her copy of Van Morrison's *Astral Weeks*, how and where it skipped. (No doubt Marleen repeatedly recalled this skip as a reflective joke, and would be pleased to know I finally got it.) As I grew up, the story and its fragments got darker, more specific, less euphemistic, and maybe Marleen altered, added, or subtracted some of the particulars along the way, just as I've done with the benefit of scattered research.

Marleen Deskin first met Martha Dickson on February 7, 1969, when they, along with two other Northern Illinois University students and one alumnus, got in a beaten brown Buick and drove from an imperfectly cooperative five-bedroom Victorian in DeKalb to a sit-in at the University of Chicago's administration building. The sit-in had started after the University announced it wouldn't rehire Marlene Dixon (again, I apologize for the similarity of all these names), a young, fairly popular assistant sociology professor and Marxist-feminist-activist whose three-year appointment would end the coming September. Dixon's work, argued the sociology department's tenured faculty, failed to meet the intellectual standards required for reappointment. The demonstrators attributed the dismissal to sexism and revanchism, said the administration overvalued research and publication, undervalued teaching; they demanded an equal student voice in the hiring and firing of professors. In the first days of the sit-in, about four hundred students occupied the administration building, whose everyday occupants were temporarily relocated. As the sit-in went on, student leadership changed and more demands were added, many of them unrelated to issues of hiring and firing or to Dixon, who visited her supporters a few times but generally kept out of the way. The administration's response was hard and cool: they didn't meet with the rebels, they didn't call the police; they handed out suspensions, they waited for spirits to sink.

Since mid-January of that year (so for about three weeks), Marleen had been dating an NIU graduate named Barry Morton, a former SDS member and a friend of one of the U of C sit-in's organizers. Barry was a Marxian, self-described, though others (at least one other) described him as a moneyed liberal who'd learned to use New Left rhetoric with moderate facility but incomplete conviction. Barry wasn't all talk, though, and in fact he preferred spear-carrying to, say, speaking at demos, writing for underground newspapers, or drawing attention by other means. (Barry and I are now friends on Facebook.) He had delivered sandwiches and some other provisions to the sit-in on its third day, when the administration building was still bustling, triumphant kids talking all night, laughing, swaying, poster-making. "Welcome to the Winter Palace," read one of the posters, and Barry was among those outside cheering when it was first unfurled, descending like a tingle down a spine, from a second-story window. He'd only planned to stay for a short while, but the mood was so exhilarating, he hung around for ten hours, had to call Marleen to postpone an informal date. Each day, however, the numbers dwindled and spirits indeed sank, so Barry recruited Marleen, Martha, and the two others to offer further support to the flagging protest. Marleen, who would graduate that spring, only had an early morning French class on Fridays and didn't have to miss any school to make the trip. Martha, an unserious junior, played hooky.

The car was huge and cold. The men sat in front, Barry in the middle. The driver, whose name my mother had long forgotten by the time she told me the story, wore an unseasonable porkpie hat and smelled in some inexplicably bad way like pancakes. The other young man, his name also forgotten (Barry remembers: John), was possibly hoping to usurp Barry as the co-op's de facto leader. He was the one who'd accused Barry of being only rhetorically radical. He rarely challenged Barry directly, however, even when given semiformal opportunities. A few miles from the house, Barry, turning around to look at the women, said, "If any reporters try to talk to you, don't give them your name."

"What about a fake name?" Martha said from the back.

"A fake name's okay, but nothing clever, no anagrams," Barry said.

"So not *too* fakey?" Martha said with what my mother Marleen called her "Saharan sarcasm."

"Probably there won't be any reporters left," Barry said. He was wearing a Donegal tweed overcoat, its frayed collar partly covered by the hooklike ends of his blond hair. He had agreed to pay a disproportionate share of the co-op's expenses for seven more months; then new arrangements would have to be made. He had a straight job as a copywriter and rumored inherited wealth, including some obviously hypocritical investments.

"We're not going to give them our names," Marleen said.

"Sociology's a rinky-dink field, anyway," the driver said.

"This isn't just about Dixon," Barry said.

"I just don't think it's a serious field," the driver said.

"Well, you're the expert," Marleen said, and Martha stanched a laugh.

"Regardless," Barry said, "it's in our interest to have anti-Establishment thinkers in sociology departments, if only to act as foils to those who dreamed up Muzak."

The co-op housed six to eight people, depending on whom you asked, and was supposed to and sometimes did run on Marxist principles, to which its residents, in the normal way of things, were divergently committed. Martha was an ideological jumble, here radical, there conservative. Her short residency at the co-op might be called situational communism (not situationist, though there was some of that too, probably coincidental). Marleen had already been invited to join the co-op, but, somewhat cautious by nature, chose to stay in her dormitory. She too had a temporizing interest in Marxism, though she didn't pretend to more than a passing familiarity with its texts. Two women lived in the co-op, or so Marleen had heard from Barry, but before the drive to Chicago, she'd met neither one. The other woman, Martha explained to Marleen in the backseat, had moved out a few months earlier. "She's coming back," Barry said. "She's just taking care of some family shit." Martha turned to Marleen and shook her head with ironic affirmation. John snored, the driver turned on the radio.

For all I know the tension between Barry and Martha was romantic in origin, but if so, Marleen never learned about these origins, and it's just as possible that they simply disliked each other, or liked goading each other. "Unlike certain people in this bucket," Martha slipped in when she and Marleen's conversation returned to politics, "I actually come from the prolefuckingtariat." Profane tmesis, Marleen led me to believe, was one of Martha's trendy tics: *fanfuckingtastic, bullfuckingshit,* on and on like that. Barry moved his long legs from one apparently uncomfortable position to another. Martha's grandfather, his granddaughter added, joined the Socialist Party during its North Dakota heyday in the teens and never lost faith. "So all this stuff is old hat for me," she said, tapping the driver's porkpie. "What kind of work did your grandfather do?" Barry asked. "He was just a poor farmer," Martha said, "trying to set up farmer-owned grain elevators and whatnot." "Then he was a peasant, not a proletarian," Barry said. Martha held her middle finger behind Barry's head for several seconds. As she saw it, she said after collecting herself to some degree, there was no real revolutionary potential in the U.S., not for the foreseeable future, not in the way Marx imagined it, and certainly not from the proletariat. But widespread, ever-growing spiritual-erotic hunger, hunger for the stuff American capitalism trivialized, coarsened, and suppressed, that kind of hunger could lead to a bigger cultural transformation than *anyone* had imagined. She was showing off with her speech, but also her voice was shaking. The future's great works of art, she said, wouldn't look like art at all, would be mistaken for noneveryday life.

Martha took a pastrami sandwich out of her coat pocket, brushed it off, ripped it in half, cutting the meat with her fingernails, and offered the bigger half to Marleen. The unpainted nails on Martha's right fingers were long, but her left fingernails were short, because she played the gimbri. They also shared an apple, which picked up linty red spots from a cut on Martha's lower lip, the spots mirroring the red slubs on Barry's coat. They talked about poetry and a friend they had in common. Marleen, urged by Martha to speak a bit of French, quoted a few lines of Baudelaire's *L'idéal*, impressing Martha. "He's so repugnant, but I love him," Martha said, and a moment later, "That's something

I want to do, learn a foreign language." Barry turned his head partway toward the backseat: "I've heard college is a good place for that," he said. The driver laughed, Martha shrugged. Emboldened, Barry added that it was dumb to define the proletariat on nineteenth-century lines, as if we weren't living under a vastly transformed capitalism. A very much still possible revolution, he said, would be led mostly by enlightened members of the middle and intellectual classes, and he tossed in a few more points while Martha imitated a puppeteer with her right hand. "Barry's a perfectly enlightened member of the intellectual class," Martha stage-whispered when he'd finished, "until it's time to scrub the brown streaks off the toilet bowl. That seems to be where I come in."

When they got to the administration building, there were no more signs hanging from the windows and at most twenty students inside. Barry's friend, a grad student and a member of the New University Conference, was sitting on a slatted wooden bench at the end of a dim hallway, playing an unamplified bass guitar. Barry brought his two bags of groceries to the food station and introduced Marleen, Martha, and the others to the grad student, who, after some small talk and updates, offered to take the group on a partial tour of the campus-abutting Woodlawn neighborhood, some of whose poor, mostly black residents were about to be displaced by a U of C construction project. Momentum never built for this walk. A short while later a new group of students rotated in, and Barry's friend went home to take a nap.

Martha and Marleen sat against a wall, talking and smoking. It felt good to be away from the others. Martha was originally from Wheeler, North Dakota, she told Marleen, a town of six hundred people where she'd lost her virginity in a giant mound of hard red spring wheat. Later the family moved to Enswell, where Martha had been Enswell High's third prettiest cheerleader. Martha wasn't really half Marleen's size, but it seemed to the bigger party as if two Marthas could squeeze into one hollow Marleen. Soon Barry brought the group back together, suggested they all go out to a pizzeria he knew of and then catch the Sonny Stitt Trio at the Plugged Nickel. Porkpie had already assented this plan. "What kind of music is that?" Martha said.

"Jazz," Barry said.

Martha snatched the folded newspaper from under Barry's arm and scanned the concert listings. "Why don't we see Vanilla Fudge?" she said.

Barry shook his head no.

"I sorta know the drummer in one of the warm-up bands," Martha said.

"That's not what we're doing," Barry said.

"Don't be such a snob," Martha said.

"Taste and snobbism aren't synonymous," Barry said.

"We could see Baby Huey," Martha said.

"Yeah, let's see Baby Huey," John said.

"Let's see Sonny Stitt," Barry said.

"Baby Huey!"

"Sonny Stitt!"

"I just don't really feel like jazz," Martha said.

"I'm treating," Barry said.

Marleen rubbed Martha's arm and said, "You *sort* of feel like jazz."

At the Plugged Nickel, the four students and one alumnus pushed two tables together, but before long the conversation split up again along gender lines. The club was loud and warm. One of Martha's boots formed a puddle in which a fringed end of Marleen's scarf soaked all night. Martha had brown hair and a dimply smile and was wearing a clearly homemade embroidered blouse, one of her earliest attempts—the flowers wilted, one sleeve too tight, the other too loose. To Marleen she seemed a blend of restless confidence and twitchy vulnerability, completely assured and completely uncertain, and somehow these combined energies made Marleen feel at ease in ways she knew with no one else in DeKalb.

Between sets, Barry pulled his chair next to Martha's and said, "That toilet gibe—if you have a problem—I'm not saying the housework has been equitably divided—but if you have a problem, it'd be better to bring it up at a self-critique session."

"Why don't you?" Martha said. "I'm talking to my new friend."

On Monday, Martha moved into Marleen's dorm room, over the drizzly mumbles of Marleen's preceding roommate. "Why do you still live in this baby dormitory?" Martha asked Marleen, who shrugged toward inertia. Martha showered in the middle of the night and kept her hallway appearances brief (the floor supervisor never hassled her); she used her yellow Samsonite as a dresser, kept it under the single bed she and Marleen shared. Their relationship was more sororal than sexual, Marleen told me: mostly Martha was a cuddler; she'd nestle her head under Marleen's chin, and her hair would tickle and irritate Marleen's face. In the dorm room's cramped quarters Martha's charms began to wane. One night Marleen, statuesque and a restless sleeper, unwittingly pushed Martha off the bed, waking everyone up. Martha recovered and was soon chuckling over the accident, trying to steer the chuckling toward a discussion of chance and the unconscious. For about a week, Marleen had been discouraging the pair's carouselling small-hours conversations, mostly out of pretended courtesy for the now third-wheel roommate, who to all appearances seemed to be a contented eavesdropper. On the night of Martha's fall from the bed, Marleen let the talking go on for ten minutes or so and then said, "I'm sorry, but I'm really tired. I've got this paper to write. I can't sleep through more classes. Most of this stuff can't be resolved anyway, even by people who know what they're talking about." Martha, though sharp with comebacks, just turned away from Marleen. "I didn't mean that as a put-down," Marleen said. "I meant both of us, all of us." Marleen was sorry but didn't say so.

Some afternoon about a month after Martha had moved in, the largely forgotten Barry came by to say that Martha's brother had called the co-op. "Frankly, it sounded mortal," he told Marleen, and that night Martha learned that her parents had died a full three weeks earlier in a car crash. Marleen held Martha most of the night, stroked her hair, handed her toilet paper since there were no tissues. The other roommate watched them silently and creepily. The next morning Marleen and Martha walked together to the bus station, taking turns carrying the heavy Samsonite, into which Martha had earlier snuck Marleen's copy of Gérard Zwang's *Le sexe de la femme*.

Marleen didn't hear from Martha for over two years, didn't expect to hear from her ever again, didn't, after a while, think of her often. Then one weekend day in July of '71, Martha put a call in to Richard and Esther Deskin of Palatine, Illinois. Yes, he was Marleen's dad, Dick told Martha, and in fact she was back home for the time being and was already coming to the phone.

"I'm in bad shape," Martha said over the phone. "I'm in super fucking bad shape." She sounded drunk or high, slurry and tearful. She said she'd tried to start a small clothing line but it hadn't worked, and now she was broke and incredibly sad. She said she had a beautiful, three-month-old boy whose eyes played the music of the spheres, but that she couldn't take care of him. "I need you to help me, Marleen," she said. "I know I haven't kept in touch, but last night it struck me like lightning that you were the one, the one who could help me. It came to me as a voice, a totally external voice, your voice. It didn't sound like your voice, but it was, it was your voice." Martha started sobbing, and was still holding the phone sobbing when Marleen arrived two days later at a little rented house in Enswell, North Dakota. This time of course Martha was on the phone with someone else, but it seemed to Marleen as if the drive, which she'd alertly enjoyed, hadn't happened, as if she'd made it from Palatine to Enswell like a voice through phone wires.

Martha really was in bad shape, foul-smelling, Cubistic, often incomprehensible, constantly smoking PCP-enhanced grass or dropping acid, crying and talking to illusions, lying on the floor, sweating a lot, hearing the wrong things on Van Morrison's *Astral Weeks,* which she played over and over, often forgetting to place the needle after the skip near the start of the first band. Sometimes Marleen would come into the living room to find Martha lying on the floor listening to Morrison sing, "in the ditch, in the ditch, in the ditch, in the ditch, in the ditch, in the ditch," until Marleen, holding the baby like a football, walked over, turned down the volume, and with her left hand advanced the needle slightly, even though she was sick of the album and didn't think it was helping. Only recently did I realize that Morrison in truth sings "*and* the ditch."

One afternoon Marleen and the baby came home from Piggly Wiggly, and Martha, who hadn't left the house since Marleen's arrival two weeks earlier, was gone. She'd left most of her things, but Marleen knew she wouldn't be back. "I was sad for Martha," my mother told me, "but I was happy for me, because I really, really wanted to keep you." A year or so after Martha left, Marleen legally adopted me, and a few years after that Martha died of an accidental overdose somewhere in California.

aSTraL niGHTS

ON THE EIGHTEENTH OF OCTOBER 1991, I WAITED with expanding hunger and impatience for Wade and Wanda to pick me up from work. From there we were going to the Great Perusal, a St. Paul bookstore where an obscure poet named D. Michael Tauber was reading. I'm sure of the above date because this morning I found a calendar listing for Tauber's reading in the archive room of the Twin Cities' surviving alt-weekly. Wade's forty-fourth birthday, then, would have been the previous day; I'd given him a Nicholson Baker book that he received with some skepticism, in turn received with some defensiveness, though I hadn't read the book yet either. Anyway, I waited forty-five minutes or thereabouts for Wade and Wanda to pick me up, pacing on the sidewalk while my coworkers occcasionally looked on in entertained sympathy. This lateness doomed our plan to go out for dinner before the reading. When Wade's car finally approached, I had a few seconds to watch them through the windows before they stopped at the curb. He was talking enthusiastically, slapping the steering wheel for emphasis; Wanda was laughing, one of her clownishly large-soled shoes tapping the dashboard in time, I think, with her laughter. When I got in the backseat I almost sat on a rusty car jack, and they apologized without remorse for their tardiness and explained the flat they'd caught on Lyndale and Franklin. There was a short but possibly telling pause when I asked which tire had deflated, and then Wanda handed me a somewhat mollifying bag of barbecue ribs. Bolling Greene's underappreciated *Greenehouse* was playing on the tape deck.

While I ate, Wade and Wanda returned to the conversation I'd glimpsed through the windows, about the democratization of connoisseurship or the pornography of yoga, biological determinism or the extent of Browning's influence on Joyce, animal liberation or whether Heidegger, writing on Van Gogh's peasant shoes, had described something profound and far-reaching about art's power to unconceal truth (Wade's view, as I've reconstructed and distilled it), or whether the exhausting Nazi had misread the shoes and used his misreading to reframe a silly agrarian romanticism that undercut his larger and rather commonsensical point (Wanda's view). These at least were things they talked about during Wade's time as our lodger (Wade always dominating the discussions), though to be honest I don't recall what they talked about in the car that evening, only that I felt a bit childlike and superfluous in the backseat.

In front of the bookstore, Wade, in one easygoing attempt, parallel parked into a space that would have deterred some motorcyclists. A passerby applauded; the passerby, I gathered, was crazy, but the applause wasn't. Wade was so facile that night, so at one with everything; he was a raindrop on a sidewalk gingko leaf. I couldn't sort out my admiration from my envy from my jealousy. Wanda went inside the bookstore to get seats ("which I'm sure are in high demand," Wade said sarcastically, though it was his idea to come to the reading), but I stayed outside for a few minutes with Wade, who was doing squat-thrusts on the sidewalk while studying the store's window display. He was wearing close-fitting, boot-cut Erizeins, faded to stratus-cloud white-gray. There were a few stores with selective inventories of used jeans near our apartment. I watched him for a few seconds, then turned to look at his hatchback. "Your spare is the size of a regular tire, huh?" I said.

"That's right," he said.

"I thought the Leveret came with a doughnut." An affinity for the doughnut wheel might have led me to some expertise on its history, but I was bluffing, trying ineptly to catch Wade in some lie.

"Nope."

I turned again to face his back. "Are those jeans new?"

"Do they look new?" he said, turning around while still in a squat. The jeans were particularly bleached at a quarter-sized spot to the right of the zipper's end point, I noticed.

"I just haven't seen them before," I said.

"These are my reserves. You like them?"

"Yeah," I said. "But the other night you said you only had the clothes off your back and all that."

"And a few other items, such as those in my pillowcase, where I've been holding these jeans. I never said the clothes off my back et cetera made up the whole of my wardrobe, just that they were notable among my monkishly few possessions. Sixty-two," he said, finishing his exercises.

The reading had already started when Wade and I joined Wanda in the back row of folding chairs, two or three empty rows between us and the next clot of attendees. When we sat down, Tauber paused briefly to acknowledge us with an appreciative smile. He had Redford-like hair and a trim, cheek-proud beard.

He couldn't have been much more than forty, though according to Wade he'd been publishing since the late sixties. His reading tone: self-satisfied; my attention: sporadic. After the reading, the three of us browsed separately for half an hour. In the music section I found a used copy of 1979's *The Rolling Stone Record Guide*, and with a *Greenehouse* melody circling my mind turned to Frank Thiesan's summary of Bolling's work up to that point:

BOLLING GREENE

★★ Days of Dayton, Nights of Columbus / Beachwood 45789

★★ Hosses / Epic KE-35287

★★★ Greenehouse / Epic KE-34738

★★ The Infractor / Epic KE-34039

★★★★ The Old Chisholm Trail Revisited, or Come-a Tie-Dye Hippie / Two Deuces 2014

Hippie cowpoke quasi-intellectual without Kris Kristofferson's academic credentials but with a better singing voice (faint praise, that). The deleted Fab Four homage *Dung Beatle* has amusing cover art and a clever take on "Being for the Benefit of Mr. Kite!" that might justify picking up a used copy, if priced to move. After that slender triumph, Greene found himself still much smaller than Jesus and quit Austin for Nashville, where he had some success as a songwriter, penning "Boarded Windows" for Porter Wagoner and "Helen of Troy, Alabama" for Freddy Weller. Greene's versions of those and other wry, often plaintive country-rock gems can be found on *Chisholm Trail*, recorded back home in Austin with a sympathetic five-piece, including Michael Murphy on second guitar and high, throaty harmonies, a nice complement to Greene's black-coffee baritone. That album's gorgeous "West Texas Winds" finds Greene singing with the sort of unpretending emotion all too scarce on his later outings.

With *The Infractor,* Greene was positioned as an original scofflaw, a role that seems to suit the portly singer about as well as the snug leather vest and bandolier he models on the cover. "Sorrow Has a Basement" is a drowsy blues with a few twists, and the title track tempers the macho posturing with melancholy, but Greene mostly sleepwalks through the ramblin' gamblin' paces. Austin pal Hubie Cutler lends some guitar and background vocals to *Greenehouse,* featuring the spirited "Renegade Ticker" and the dusty-road ballad "Penny of My Thoughts," a paean to Greene's then wife, singer Penny Sakes (the marriage barely outlasted the song's huffing climb up the lower reaches of the country chart). The slapdash, guest-star-larded follow-up, *Hosses,* was a product of collective unconscionableness. Greene switched labels for *Days of Dayton, Nights of Columbus,* an imperfect union of unfunny novelties and laughable epics that seems to point the way back to obscurity. —F. T.

I closed the book with miffed force, then roamed without purpose till I came across Wade standing shut-eyed and motionless in one of the store's back corners. I watched him from two bookcases away for a long five or six minutes, during which I caught not one faint motion from him, though he seemed ever on the brink of movement, on the particular brink of raising his arms slowly in a spiritual gesture, perhaps Buddhistic, perhaps evangelical. His arms stayed at his sides, though. The unbroken calmness on his face was intense, if that's not too cheaply paradoxical, and his smooth facial skin looked even more vitreous than usual. I saw that another customer, a young woman probably from the neighborhood's tony private college, was watching Wade too. She gave me a collusive smirk. I made a subtly discouraging face and returned my full attention to Wade, who wasn't, I decided, on the brink of movement after all, that on the contrary he'd hold his living-sculpture pose till Wanda, I, or one of the bookstore's staffers spurred him. As if to refute this new prediction on cue, he opened his eyes like a magician's curtain, alerted the rest of his face, and without transition walked briskly and purposively to the fictional L's (I followed him unnoticed from several steps back), where he picked out a paperback (Antony Lamont's *Fretwork,* it turned out) in the easy way one retrieves one's bright plaid coat from a sparse rack. Next he talked the cashier into letting him exchange Baker's book for the Lamont, though I'd bought Baker's book elsewhere and hadn't altogether peeled off the foreign sticker. He also bought *Asymptote* by D. Michael Tauber, who was browsing not far from the counter and soon in conversation with Wade. A few moments later I was spotted, called over, and introduced. "I was just telling D.," Wade said, "—is that right? D.?" For some reason Wade was messing with the poet.

"My friends tend to call me Dan," Tauber said.

"I was just telling Dan how I've been following his work for a long time now. All the way back to the *Crossbar* days, in fact."

"*Crossbar*? Wow, that does go back," Tauber said.

"Dan was a serious bicyclist back then," Wade said to me.

"Probably more serious about biking than poetry," Tauber said. "Now I could probably stand more biking." He patted his stomach.

"An old friend of mine had a copy of *Crossbar* and passed it on to me," Wade said. "I don't know, it just really got under my skin."

"Thank you," Tauber said tentatively. "It was juvenilia, but I guess something shone through."

Wade held out Tauber's new book, said, "Well listen, maybe you could sign this for my young friend here."

Back in the car, Wade reached across Wanda to retrieve his ornate metal pipe, already packed, from the glove compartment. "What was all that about?" I said. "*Won't you sign this for my young friend?*" Wade wiggled a transparent green lighter out of his tight jeans. "I just think it's a book you might want to have," he said, offering Wanda the first hit, their fingers touching for a second longer than needed when he handed her the pipe. I read the poet's bland inscription ("Hope you enjoy. —Dan Tauber, winter, 1991"), put the book down. Since we were parked in front of the bookstore, I wondered aloud if we shouldn't move to a more discreet spot. Wade started the engine but didn't move the car, while I singed my bangs on a tall flame. Wade and Wanda rolled down their windows to diffuse the smell of burning hair, and I objected to this indiscretion too, since we'd soon be letting out smoke. "Relax!" Wade commanded, and I adjusted the lighter and took an exceptionally burning and potent hit, its effects nearly instantaneous. "You gotta cough to get off," Wade said, taking the pipe from me and smiling. In ten minutes or so we were all pretty high, still sitting in the humming car, by then more redolent of the rich weed than of my hair. Wade turned up Bolling's "Hot Flash" at the last bar of its second chorus, just as Pig Robbins's circular clavinet solo trips through the door like some famous farceur you've never heard of. Wade sighed.

Later we were all in the living room, passing around a pint of gourmet ice cream, when Wade got a call. I handed him the phone and he and the caller started talking about Dylan bootlegs. A minute later Wade hung up, said he had to make a quick house call. "Can you also drop me off at Wilson?" Wanda asked. It was a bit late to go to the library, I thought. "What if you get shot in this guy's apartment," I said to Wade, "and then the guy comes out to shoot Wanda in case she saw something?"

"I'll leave the keys in the car. She can just peel off when the gunman comes out."

I looked at Wanda: "Why not just go tomorrow when you'll have more time?" And less pleadingly: "Then we could all hang out here tonight."

They left. I sat awhile on the couch, scratching my head. My scratching was freeing a lot of dandruff and hair, and that interested me, so I picked up one of Wanda's spiral notebooks and started scratching over the notebook. The notebook had a black cover, on which my dandruff looked like stars, stars joined by strands of my brown hair, which I took for comets, though they didn't really look like that. As I went on scratching, the notebook got denser and denser with stars, and for a while I thought I'd be able to cover the black entirely. That proved difficult, however, so after fifteen minutes or so I used a subscription card to push the stars and hair-comets into a pile in the notebook's center, and brushed them behind the sofa.

On the way to bed I tripped over and picked up a book Wanda had been struggling to finish. The night before, she'd thrown the book on the floor in frustration. When I asked her why she didn't just move on to another book, she said something about the pleasures of intermittent brilliance, and told me that for a while as a girl she'd gone to the driving range every afternoon because, though she hated the game, she loved those rare times when it flew off the tee without sending any vibrations through her arms, when it seemed to shoot out of her. So I knew she'd carry on with the book, a recent work of critical theory whose author and title I've forgotten; Wanda preferred laborious, recondite, sometimes nonsensical books touched here and there by real intellectual fire to reader-hungry books of everyday smartness. I wasn't intellectual enough for her, I worried, or my intellectualism was the sort requiring a humbling prefix.

I lay down, opened the book at random to one of the middle chapters, and may have lucked onto one of its brilliant passages, though I can't recollect anything about it, and before long I started to drift, stalling for a half hour on two pages, one partially illustrated, getting no pleasure from the words but some from the type, first from the subtly decorative curve of the *j*'s, then from how the type blurred, doubled, and levitated when I forefingered round my half-shut eyes.

A few hours later, Wanda tiptoed into the bedroom, gently released the book from my fingers (their tips still oily from over-scratching my scalp), and helped me worm out of my twills. Or so she told me the next morning, when I didn't remember any of her ministrations, and in fact had a hazy memory of setting the book on her bedstand and taking the pants off myself, and of later hearing soft voices from the living room in deep night.

court and spark

WANDA AND I MET IN THE SPRING OF 1990, AFTER one of her rare gigs at a conventional comedy club. We had a friend in common who'd taken me to the club over my protests. I hated most stand-up comedians but admired Wanda's set that night. Every so often it was amusingly uncomfortable, occasionally it was amusingly tedious, but never, a few moments excepted, was it funny or embarrassing, and I suppose it was that difficult negative combination that I admired. She went over poorly; when I tittered in those exceptional moments of funniness or embarrassment, my titters were heard. Afterwards, however, she didn't seem to need consolation from the four or five of us standing around her in front of the stage. She was laughing, sipping rather than guzzling a bottle of green-bottled beer, touching some of our shoulders, still performing but not in an overpowering or giddily fragile way suggestive of deep insecurity or predictive of a crashing sadness to visit her room later than night. (I just learned that *boudoir*, a woman's small, private room, literally and patronizingly means "a sulking place.") Granted, I don't know what she did or how she felt later that night. (There were times, however, when I felt she was . . . not by any means annoyingly happy, but perhaps insufficiently sad. During a fight much later I told her she was "not soulful," which I meant to be somehow softer than "soulless," though it was still a cruel, false thing to say. More or less the same thing has been said of me, so this might have been projectional criticism.) That night at the club she was wearing a fedora and a man's suit, a baggy, broad-shouldered two-piece from the fifties that delayed my discovery of just how thin she was. (As a girl she'd been likened to Olive Oyl.) She did a funny impression of a local sportscaster for our little group of hangers-on, but she also listened carefully to me and the others, carefully enough at least to ask a few savvy follow-up questions—nothing too bland, nothing too intrusive, nothing too clever. She didn't seem bored when the talk moved away from her or her performance and its dimwitted, mismatched audience. Her equanimity was impressive. When I wrote above that she'd gone over poorly, I was too tentative, just as I was when I called her "thin" instead of "skinny." The crowd had hated her. About halfway through the set, a man up front had reached into one of the patch pockets of his long-in-the-tooth charcoal overcoat and thrown a pebble at Wanda, had continued to throw a pebble every half minute or so, stage-whispering "You suck," stressing the word *you*, with each aggressively dainty throw. A command, then, more than a judgment. Viewed from the back, the pebbler looked old—stooped and with coarse gray hair— but when he turned and I got a better look at his face, I saw that he was only in his forties or early fifties. No one reprimanded him. Clearly the silent majority opposed Wanda even more than this pebbler, and it was as if they'd telepathically agreed that their silence, coupled with the prematurely gray man's strange harassment, would be more punishing than conventional heckling, spitting, or belligerent coughing. My friend and

I joined in the silence, save for my occasional titters. Later I regretted my passivity, though I doubt it was ever resented. Wanda, I came to think, wasn't desperate to be loved, as most performers and artists are, nor did she thrive on a crowd's animosity, as some performers and artists do, though she did, I think, genuinely fear a crowd's indifference, a fear so many performers and artists assume, mimicking each other, while all the same giving performances and making art or art-related stuff to which indifference is the only reasonable response.

A few weeks after that performance, in what must have been mid- or late May, Wanda and I ran into each other at a party. The party was in one of the second-story units of an old brick fourplex, but the whole building seemed to be participating. We first saw each other near midnight, on the front steps. She was walking in, I was walking out, as in the Bruce Springsteen song, except that I wasn't planning to leave for good; I was just going out for a soda and a candy bar or one of those depressing convenience-store hot dogs. There were probably twenty people standing in front of the fourplex, on its porch and small lawn. Cigarette tips were darting around like fireflies. Wanda was with a friend, a woman, but not a lover, I found out later. When Wanda said hello, I walked slowly backwards away from her and said, "I'm going to get a pop and a candy bar or a hot dog or something." The relevance of my announcement was unclear, and she answered with a silence I took to be curious. "You wanna come?" I said. "I just got here," she said. "But j'you wanna come?" For punctuation of some sort, I casually picked up and Chinooked two maple samaras and made peripheral note of their perfect descent.

On the warm and breezy walk to the store Wanda and I slipped easily into talking, first about candy bars, then about music, comedy, North Dakota, the hosts of the party (schmucks, Wanda said). I wasn't walking with absolute straightness, and a few times our shoulders brushed. Later that night she said I was "astonishingly good-looking, like Wittgenstein, except it's not him you look like." (Immodest of me, having already established my handsomeness, to report this compliment. I'll contritely add that I'm not aging well.) "Who's that?" I said. Now I pretend to more erudition than I really have, but in those days I aimed for downy-cheeked humility. I was bookshy, but not actively anti-intellectual. Wanda explained who Wittgenstein was, and, nodding at my homespun model, admitted to not understanding much of his work. The elliptical expansions on and refutations of Frege's and Russell's logic gave her toothache, she said, albeit in another woman's mouth, and the mystical stuff she'd already half-learned from pop songs and the Bible, though she hated to say such a dopey thing. "But about which we can't talk, we must shut our tater traps," she said in a goofily sultry Southern accent, and we kissed without tongues, then with. I'd never kissed anyone with such besieged skin, and she had a touch of b.o., something I have a double standard on in terms of gender. But it was easy enough to look past those errors of nature and grooming; she had an enticing, before-picture kind of beauty, and I fell in love with her quickly.

People sometimes say that the pain of a breakup should last about half as long as the relationship. By that measure I should have gotten over Wanda around Thanksgiving of '92, even sooner if the end of our relationship coincided more with Wade's arrival than with his departure. But twenty years on I still picture her face all the time, still want to fall asleep with her reading next to me, still picture the troubling last time I saw her naked, still listen to her favorite music with pangs of longing, still feel her breath on my face, still hope with a restless stomach to run into her, and will sometimes, with no other incentive, go to a play or concert that raises hopes for another such encounter, though the encounters are frequently wordless. Of course it's hard for me to untangle my feelings for Wanda from everything that happened during our last months together, and doubtless my current loneliness has made my old loves seem deeper than they really were. I'm sorry to be such a lugubrious Narcissus. I woke up sad today and got anxious and colicky after a cup of coffee, began to obsess over a seemingly cutting email I got a few days ago from a not-close friend. It doesn't take much coffee to make me anxious these days; I'm about to give it up. My increasing abstemiousness might be a symptom of my neurosis, however, so for a while I'll probably continue to drink a cup in the late afternoon, which seems to focus me with less pronounced psychological and intestinal side effects.

in THE DiTCH, in THE DiTCH, in THE DiTCH, in THE DiTCH, in THE DiTCH

TODAY I WALKED FROM MY SUBURBAN STUDIO APART-
ment to a member's-only warehouse where I bought an
enormous jar of pickles. There's no real walking or biking
route from my apartment to the warehouse, and I'm currently
without a car as well as a job—I should clarify: my car just needs
a new intake manifold, and though I'm not steadily employed,
I've been doing some second- and third-rung modeling, catalog
work as a paternal type when I'm lucky, and some more embarrassing shoots—so for most of the way I walked on the inter-
state's shoulder, with the burger wrappers, the tire molt, the
bottles of motor oil, the cans of soda, a Sudoku book, a pair of
women's underwear (someone has been raped, I thought), the
fallen animals: doe; fawn; raccoon; rabbit; a surprising, heart-
tugging number of large, disgustingly mangled turtles. A few
drivers slowed down for me, yelled solicitously out their windows; some honked and heckled, but most whizzed by, their
cars and trucks blowing hair (my own) into my face, billowing
my T-shirt, atypically tucked into my cut-offs to keep the wind-
lifted grit out of my underwear. Scores of grasshoppers hopped
at my sneakers and seemed to singe my calf hair.

I spent a long time in the warehouse. It was dark outside by the time I started for home. For safety, I walked most of the way in the ditch, and down there I especially wished I'd worn long pants and more supportive shoes. It was a walk that, afterwards, had to be described in English, American English. I don't quite know what that means. It's a variation on something my mother Marleen used to say, which as it turned out wasn't hers either. For a few years in Enswell she routinely took long walks. On some weekend days, she'd walk for three to four hours, probably covering nine to twelve miles; on some weeknights, she'd walk about half that distance. From time to time I joined her, but as a rule I stayed home, watched TV or played with my plastic football men. She liked to walk in long lines rather than big circles or squares. She'd walk to a set destination by the straightest route possible, stand in place for a few minutes, then turn around and walk home. Most of her destinations were specific, such as a bingo hall, but some were vague, like: a ways out of town. And sometimes, to get to these spots, she walked on the highway's shoulder. So my walk today was in part a tribute to her.

She walked for meditation, exercise, and, especially during my elementary-school years, almost all her transit. At some point toward the end of the '76–'77 winter, the transmission of her demographically predictable strength-through-joy subcompact gave out, and since money was tight just then, she decided not to have it fixed, to get by awhile on foot. When spring came and smiled on our carless existence, she sold the subcompact to a lay mechanic. Enswell wasn't and isn't a big city; one could negotiate a pedestrian life. It was a haul to get to the fairgrounds, say, but most things were within what an average healthy adult in no hurry would call walking distance: my school was only three blocks away; Tuttle Ag Pumps, where my mother worked, was a mile and a half away; and we lived right off Foster Avenue, the main drag, and were thus close enough to the essential stores (grocery, drug, hardware) and to several restaurants, Bey's Food Host by far my favorite. Still, it was often inconvenient, not having a car, especially during winter. Sometimes we had to cheat by calling a taxi or a friend. Some people took us to be poor, which we weren't quite.

When Wade more or less lived with us, my mother occasionally and grudgingly borrowed his car, a muscular dolphin-blue coupe with the abbreviation *SS* on its grille and elsewhere. Or he gave us rides, or we all rode together, if that's what we were doing, going somewhere together. I loved that car and its radio. Almost always I got to ride in front, between Wade and my mother. Wade wasn't really into engines or exhaust tones or remedies for axle tramp and so on—he'd gotten a good deal on the car from a luckless client and didn't keep it long—but he was a good, relaxed driver, and once between Enswell and the village of Frith, after the rolling hills, now sometimes scarred with ATV tracks, gave way to a long stretch of flat, he got the car up to 120 and stayed there for several miles while the Atlanta Rhythm Section made love to phantoms and Paul McCartney turned his back on inclement weather. My mother's whoops and gurgling laughter filled the car despite the blasting wind and radio, and as I remember it the laughter wasn't at all borrowed or obligatory, though probably there was something movieish about the drive. I suppose most automotive fun carries a cinematic taint.

We went without a car for six years. Then, within a month of our arrival in Minneapolis, my mother and I traveled by city bus (on which two unchaperoned boys my age shot me mocking stares) to a large suburban car lot. It was a hot morning in August. We each carried a small plaid suitcase from a set. As we walked through the lot to the showroom, I lagged ten paces or so behind my mother, as if with our matching suitcases I could feign independence. The showroom was vertiginously cooler than it was outside. My mother walked up to the first free salesman she saw and set her suitcase in front of him. He looked down at it. "I'm going to buy a cheap used car from you today," she said. "Cash on the barrelhead." The salesman scratched the back of his left knee with his right toe. "Then my son and I are leaving for the Grand Canyon. I want to make it to Kansas City today. If you can sell me a car in a half hour, we'll be there by dinner." This salesman was mellow. He didn't comment on my mother's speech or ask her to clarify "cheap," he just motioned for us to follow him, led us to a disregarded part of the lot behind the service garage, and showed us a dented but low-mileage American sedan going for three thousand dollars, painted a caramel not unlike my mother's hair that season. "The Grand Canyon is an incredible place," he said. My mother smiled. After that, she generally lost interest in long walks, or maybe her interest had already started to wane during our last year or so in Enswell, I'm not sure.

Anyway, when she got back from her walks, I would ask her how the walk had gone, and she'd say, "It would have to be described in French." Decades later, I realized that she'd been borrowing one of Malte Laurids Brigge's lines from Rilke's novel, which I suspect she first read on Wade's recommendation, since it was a novel he "loved." Wade was a lover; he claimed to love people or at least women liberally, but he didn't apply the word glibly to things. I don't recall him ever saying, as I do, "I love this song!" or "I love that shirt!" No misunderstanding: I don't think it's silly to love a song or a book, and in some cases one might forgivably love a shirt. But for some reason when Wade told me he loved Rilke's novel, a book then unknown to me along with its author, the words seemed wrong from his mouth, perhaps disappointing. "To be loved means to be consumed in flames," [Malte Rilke] writes in the novel. "To love is to give light with inexhaustible oil. To be loved is to pass away; to love is to endure." So by its own terms, it's selfish to love *The Notebooks of Malte Laurids Brigge;* it aligns one with the book burners, though a book burned privately and in the right spirit, a spirit in fierce yet pacific opposition to hate and fear, could be a sort of offering, and I can almost imagine how beautiful such a ceremony might be.

FOR THE ROSES

WANDA'S SUNDAY NIGHT GIG WAS AT A NEWISH comedy club in the warehouse district called Jest in Time. The club was unexpectedly light, woody, and contented, its small round tables, armless Windsor chairs, and newly refinished floors all softly dyed in close shades of beige or natural. Two of its walls were mirrors, but despite that clue it took me awhile to remember that the space had previously been a dance studio, the Belknap Center for Dance, where a friend of mine's much older half sister had taught and once in my presence done something unorthodox with a portable barre. Wade and I were happily not talking at a table near the knee-high stage, above whose cream backcloth was a vinyl banner, its squiggly lavender stripe the lesser of the room's two intrusions of bold color. I scanned the room, counted heads (sixteen nonstaff, some of them presumable members of the headlining improv troupe), and was momentarily tempted to move to one of the white beanbag chairs tossed pixieishly in the club's northeast corner, shaded by a large plant that I couldn't identify. A red leather coat—here was the other show of bold color—lay on one of the beanbag chairs. My Coke was Pepsi and came in a heavy tumbler, clinging to which was a cocktail napkin featuring, I saw after the napkin fell on my lap, the club's mascot, a

laughing alarm clock whose pipelike limbs seemed to be dancing to the Dire Straits album playing on the club's glassy sound
system. I stared at the damp napkin, torn around the mascot's
face, and started to feel sad about the club's impending failure.

The emcee introduced Wanda as Shucks Mueller instead of
Miller and ignored Wade's shouted correction. Wanda had
tucked most of her hair into a frayed straw boater and was wearing her light-green houndstooth sports coat, a wide-lapelled
size forty-six that held her trunk like a hot-dog bun round a
pencil. Her floral kipper tie was of the same vintage (early seventies) and taste (bad) as the coat, but her trousers—cream flannels once worn by her remarkably thin Rockefeller Republican
grandfather—were elegant, although short, even in this satirical
context, complicating the rest of the costume's easy-target vul-
garity. Her set was a slightly modified version of one I'd seen a
few times before, made up mostly of domestic jokes about
shrewish, foolish, or whorish wives. At the start of the performance, she or Shucks was uxorious, slouchy, beleaguered; by the
end s/he was bumptious, enervated, abusive. At one point, the
dildo strapped to her (let's stick with feminine pronouns) waist
must have slipped through the slit in her (my) boxers, and she
pitched the proverbial tent in her grandfather's flannels, which
were stained at the crotch with my semen, and which, along
with Wanda's white Corfam loafers and her pale skin, blent into
the backcloth so that she sometimes looked like the floating
torso of a minor-market weatherman.

Only the most perceptive audience members would have
noticed that stain, but it was the kind of detail Wanda cared
about. One night several months earlier, I'd come home from
work to find the flannels laid out on the living-room floor and

Wanda reading in her underwear on the couch. As a greeting she asked me to unzip my pants and hover over her grand-father's. She pointed to a piece of red sweater lint to the right of the zipper, my target. At first the idea seemed disrespectful to her sweet, still-living grandfather. "These are really nice pants," I said, kneeling to palm the soft fabric, reaching inside to finger the silk lining. But then Wanda got on her knees and elbows (her knees near the one-and-a-half-inch cuffs, her elbows on the thighs), unzipped me, and started sucking deeper and rougher than normal, which encouraged me to grab her hair and carry on with an aggressiveness that later engendered some guilt along with decades of masturbatory support. Eventually she pushed my thighs to slow me down, and with my cock still partly in her mouth said, "Tell me well in advance of when you're going to come." "It's gonna be hard for me to hit that exact spot," I said. She stopped sucking and said, "If you miss, we can try again later." That promise and her breath on my penis acorn elicited a drop of pre-come, and she slowly pumped my cock over the target (my knees hurt on the hardwood floor) till I came quite precisely where she wanted me to, shooting just one errant, briefly shaking glob on the floor, which she scooped up with a grapefruit spoon and rubbed into the trousers. The stain hardened to a faint caramel similar to the paint on my mother's old sedan.

Wade laughed heartily throughout Wanda's set, not at every joke but at quite a few, and sometimes punctuated his laughter with a startling clap. In imitation, and because of the weed (the smiling box officer had sniffed conspiratorially at the smell floating off our hair and skin), I laughed a lot too, more than I usually did at Wanda's act. Wanda's steadiness as a performer was nearly professional, but our laughter seemed to distract her. "Maybe we should cheese it," I whispered to Wade. He looked at me quizzically and continued as Wanda's volunteer claqueur, and I, against my will and without reinforcement from the rest of the crowd, continued to find his laughter infectious.

After the set, Wanda, carrying two rum and Pepsis and now in jeans and one of her hot-rodded t-shirts, joined us at the table. She graciously if coolly accepted Wade's compliments and my less effusive ones. The crowd had doubled by the time the improv troupe, Without a Paddle, went on. Their set was boring, inane, beneath satire. Here and there Wanda and I exchanged groaning glances, while Wade's head kept bobbing in and out of a churchy doze. My interest endured mostly by dint of the five-person troupe's one female member, a short, wide-hipped woman, about my age, whom I'd noticed jittering around the club before the show. Onstage, the Without a Paddle players sometimes wore wigs, lab coats, or grass skirts, but mostly they wore their own clothes—drab, state-university clothes except in the case of their token woman, who came out in the more bohemian outfit I'd seen her in earlier: white jeans; Doc Martins; and a mannish V-neck sweater, now topped with an unbuttoned red leather jacket, the one seen earlier on the white beanbag chair. One of the arrowhead ends of the jacket's belt was now tucked into a slanted pocket, but the other end dangled toward the floor. The jacket was just slightly darker than the red-red of stop signs and fire trucks, and accorded perfectly with the woman's sangria lipstick and short, almost en brosse dyed-black hair. In my memory, I suppose this jacket has become the "rose to match my red ideal," to traduce a line from a Baudelaire poem notably interpolated and given a honky-tonk mise en scène by Bolling Greene.

The beautiful woman in the red leather jacket wasn't an especially gifted improvisational actor, but she was better than her colleagues. (Irrespective of her superiority, I was more embarrassed for her than for the others.) One of the sketches was set at a driving range—I lightly slapped Wanda's arm—until the woman came onstage as an NBC producer and the scene became an audition for Johnny Carson's replacement. In another sketch, her character unsheathed a ridiculous, piercing laugh, a true cackle, that itself drew the biggest laugh of the night.

"Well, I didn't mind the ass on the gal," Wade said when the set ended. He wasn't shy about making lecherous remarks around Wanda, who I think endorsed his boycott of false gentility. "I'd like to be around her *with* a paddle," he added. "Is that a big thing for you, paddles?" Wanda said. They discussed that further while I played with my napkin. We would have left, but the club's manager was stalling to pay Wanda her twenty-five bucks. She was about to ask again when the woman from Without a Paddle approached our table. "Shucks?" she said, and started praising Wanda's set, first generically, then in more detail, repeating a few punch lines and making a flattering reference to a reasonably well-known performance artist. She'd grabbed a seat from another table while delivering this long compliment. There were two tomato seeds stuck to the left sleeve of her sweater, one seed stuck to each side of the elbow like fish eyes. Her name was Marianne. She'd seen Wanda perform before, had recommended her for the opening slot.

"When I first saw Marianne Faithfull's name, I thought it was pronounced like *marine*," I said. "Isn't that dumb?"

"My name's spelled with a *y*," Mary Ann said.

"Oh," I said.

"But not like the *Gilligan's Island* chick; it's one word like Marianne Faithfull's, but with a *y*."

"Wanda and I are big Marianne Faithfull fans," I said. "We listen to *Broken English* all the time."

"Well, we've listened to it a couple times," Wanda said.

"But we both like it," I said. "We each have a copy."

"They'll probably never make love to either copy," Wade said, "on account of it being for the most part rhythmically straightforward."

"To be honest, I've never heard Marianne Faithfull," Maryanne said. "She's just a name to me."

"Like Pete?" I said.

"Yeah, or Larry," Maryanne said. "I know she used to go with Mick Jagger." *Go with Mick Jagger*, I liked that. She was taking big sips of her clear cocktail, probably a gin and tonic. We all talked about Marianne Faithfull, and then our Maryanne, waving toward the stage, said, "I don't think I'll work with these guys anymore. It's"—she shook her head searching for a word—"asinine." It didn't seem like the word she wanted. "Every time we finish," she said, "I feel my dignity get carried off on a stretcher." I was about to contradict her. "Improv is tough," Wanda said, and she and Wanda talked about the form and its difficulties, Wade and I chiming in about jazz and bluegrass. "Yeah, that was my last Without a Paddle show," Maryanne said.

"Probably you could do better," Wanda said.

"Well, I thought you guys were pretty good," I said.

Maryanne shrugged and, mostly to Wanda, said, "I just wanted you to know that *I* know how stupid the stuff was tonight. These guys, their first ideas are always, I don't know . . ."

"Hard even to summon the energy for further critique," Wade said in too harsh a tone. At the ebb of his high, Wade got irritable. Wanda gave him a chastening look, then to Maryanne said, "But *you* were good, you almost saved them."

"That Carson bit was spot-on," I said.

"Thanks."

"Have you heard the Beach Boys song about Johnny Carson?" I said.

"No."

The waitress came around for an early last call, and I learned that Maryanne drank vodka tonics, not gin ands. She was an overnight baker, she told us, or had been at least; a few weeks earlier she'd been fired (coolly, and by telephone, she said), and was now living off her dwindling overdraft account. Soon she'd have to sell her motorcycle. She was taking one class, on the history of erotic art (among Wade's areas of expertise, he slickly conveyed), but her plans to enter a film program in St. Paul were on hold, and from there the three of us raced through our favorite movies, most of them unknown to Wade, a few of Maryanne's unknown to me. The waitress returned with the drinks and Maryanne nearly chugged the vodka tonic and got up to squeeze in an order for one more. Her voice got louder and stagier. She started talking about an idea she had for a movie, and about a large sculpture she was going to make out of cough drops. I began to think that too much of the group's conversation was being devoted to Maryanne's future achievements.

After Wanda collected her money, Maryanne suggested we all go to a late-night family restaurant not far from our apartment, but Wade said he needed to turn in for the night and I followed his lead. As we were all standing outside the club, Maryanne wondered aloud if a family restaurant that stayed open so late had been misclassified, or if it stopped being a family restaurant at a certain hour, such as nine p.m. As she pursued this fruitless riff, once cracking herself up (the jarring laugh that so charmed Without a Paddle's audience was closely patterned on Maryanne's normal laugh), I applauded myself for declining to join her and Wanda. Moments later, however, when they drove off on Maryanne's Japanese motorcycle, I regretted my decision, and felt guilty about my private dismissal of Maryanne's harmless joking and unselfconscious, one might say defiant, laugh.

On their way to the restaurant, Wanda and Maryanne hit a patch of gravel and dumped the motorcycle. No one was hurt beyond some skin abrasions, but the bike came out badly positioned for sale. My drive home with Wade was less eventful, mostly silent. "You think we should meet them after all?" I said as we were approaching home. "No, they want to be alone," he said. "That's why I said I was tired."

"Seemed like you really were tired."

"I am tired," he said. Then after a pause, "Wanda was good tonight. She's the real thing. The stuff she's doing now, it's not quite there, but she's on to something, just you wait." I took his words seriously, and several times during those last months of '91, even as I felt Wanda and I breaking up, I imagined myself as her lifelong aide-de-camp, doing mundane things for her that would make her art possible, leading the ovation when she merited one, leading it more commandingly when she didn't, getting teary when her name was called at some local awards ceremony. Though in truth I'm a tagalong not a votary, and I doubt I could ever play such a role, even for someone more talented than Wanda.

FROM NOW ON, THE POETRY IS IN THE STREETS

O N HALLOWEEN AFTERNOON IT STARTED TO SNOW heavily and continued through the night. I had to work the next morning, a Friday. Wade didn't stir on the sofa as I ate my cereal in the kitchen, or when I put on my rustly parka and pulled on my galoshes with some grunting difficulty. When I stepped outside, there were, as I recall, eighteen and a half inches of snow on the ground. All over the city, stems from the larger pumpkins barely emerged from the snow like snorkels round a touristy reef (I did a bit of traveling during my two-year affair [mid-'o1–late '03] with an ad-agency noncreative), but most of the pumpkins were submerged altogether, along with ashcans, oilcans, leaf piles, Tonka trucks, and some of the smaller grills and Coleman stoves.

Considering the size and prematurity of the storm, I was surprised when my bus arrived more or less on time, though after a while I realized that it wasn't my bus at all, but a much-delayed earlier bus, explaining why many of the passengers looked unfamiliar and more professional than those of us who didn't need to make it downtown till just past nine. The bus got stuck near Franklin Avenue, and about a dozen of its more spirited and sacrificing riders got out to push—against Metropolitan Transit Commission regs, repeated the gregarious driver. We managed to loose the wheels (one of them spewed grime on my pants), and I high-fived the thin glove of a fellow pusher wearing a stiff glen-plaid suit under his promotional letter jacket, the suit's wide trousers only grazing his pinchy wingtips. My ankle-boot galoshes weren't built for the task either, especially since the left galosh had a nickel-sized hole on its heel.

Timid or lazy stay-at-homes had given downtown a cheery holiday sparseness, and after I got off the bus I lingered awhile in the snow-global scene in front of the record store, even though my arrival at the store was recorded by two machines and I was often scolded for tardiness. Sometimes the wind would blow a cluster of flakes into curved feathers. When, a bit later, I got back from the bank in time to open the store, I was met by a somewhat mentally handicapped woman who came in every few weeks to ask after the same discontinued Bolling Greene cassette, *Hosses,* which had helped her through a hard time, she'd once explained. I unlocked the doors and she followed me into the store, stamping her boots on the welcome mat. "It's snow joke," she said, and we had our recurrent conversation about Bolling and the fickleness of the record industry, the decline of the cassette. After she left, no customers came in for several hours. I took a seat on the ledge of the store's plate-glass windows and watched the snow fall, listening to a Kentucky Headhunters tape at a higher volume than was usual for the store, until their music started to seem properly genial but improperly prosaic for the occasion, and I put on Joni Mitchell's latest, which I later brought home for Wade, not much taken with it. None of my coworkers made it in. I understood why Wade sought out nearly solitary straight jobs—filling up vending machines, watching over parking lots. At about four o'clock the district manager called to say that all the stores in his ambit were closing for the rest of the day.

After locking up, I went to the hipper record store across the street, where a party had sprung up. Maryanne was there, taking crouching hits off a one-hitter behind the imports rack, or so I thought for a moment, but it was just someone who looked vaguely like her. She and Wanda's friendship had developed quickly like a Polaroid, and now they saw or at least talked to each other every day: they took long afternoon constitutionals leading to the earliest happy hours; sat on opposite ends of our sofa, reading in silence save for explanations of hmms and chuckles; browsed the books from Maryanne's erotic-art class while I sat on the floor trying to fix a wah-wah pedal; chatted on the phone while watching TV; talked at the Formica table about dentists from their girlhoods (the dentist from Maryanne's childhood was kind but big-fingered and hairy-handed, the one from Wanda's gruff with his assistant, who did all the work).

I spent about an hour and a half at the party before calling home. Wade picked up. "It's really snowing," I said. By then the snowfall was getting closer to its ultimate twenty-eight inches (it looked like thirty). "What's this *it*?" he said. I told him I'd be home in about an hour, maybe longer since I planned to walk and it'd be slow trudging. Wanda's shift at the call center had been canceled too, he told me. "Listen," he said, "if there's a video shop still open, could you pick up some movies? Stuff from the past ten years." I asked if he could be more specific. "Good stuff from the past ten or eleven years," he said.

"But I need more direction."

"Try to get a dozen or so. Anything you get, I won't have seen. I have to catch up on film before my expatriation. No one reads anymore, even in Germany, is my understanding, so I'll need to hold my own on cinema if I want to be taken seriously."

"I thought you said the idea was not to be taken seriously," I said.

"People have to take you seriously before you can convince them not to."

"So should I be getting German movies?"

"It doesn't matter. Cosmopolitan."

"But art movies?" I said.

"Highbrow or low, just nothing in the middle."

The walk home was dark and windy, strange and slippery—no, first crepuscular, then dark, I now remember. When I think of that walk, I don't recall any of the discomfort I must have felt from the cold and the wind and the hole in my left galosh; I just remember a pacific dreaminess or nonmaniacal euphoria, the show-biz flakes in the streetlamp beams, how the Marxian snow leveled the parked cars (though you could still gauge their ages and values by their shapes), how the snowbanks were like the giant wave in Hokusai's endlessly reproduced woodblock print, though that's silly: they would have been nowhere near that size. The sidewalks were hard to navigate, so for most of the trip I walked in the tire ruts in the middle of the street, including the city's busiest street, like a lonesome protest marcher. Once in a while I had to step aside for a slow-moving car or truck, but no one got angry, even the honks were Samaritan little pips. Three or four times I helped someone push into an alley or out of a parking spot. Part of me wanted to walk the city all night pushing cars.

(I feel obliged to add here that people were hurt by the storm: there were meals lost to undelivered AFDC checks, fingers lost to snowblowers, shovel-clutching grandparents lost to driveways.)

The independent video store was still open and doing good business, so I spent an hour picking out a dozen movies from the eighties and incipient nineties. When I got home, Wanda was reading *Z* magazine and playing a Scrawl album too quietly for it to do its work. She was sitting in the sand-brown wing chair Wade had rescued from an alley and set among his record boxes in the living room. He was dozing on the couch, an open library copy of *The Ashley Book of Knots* resting like a cottage roof on his chest, his cream cowboy shirt (new, I think) mostly unsnapped. Without opening his eyes, he pantomimed knob-turning and made other gestures till I gathered he wanted me to turn up the stereo. "Certain volumes are an insult to music and to silence," he said hoarsely.

"I thought you were sleeping," Wanda said.

"Sorry, I was kind of sleeping," Wade said. They went back and forth like this some more while I went to the bathroom, where it took a lot of rusty hot water to warm my feet.

Wade had seen only three movies of the eighties, he was explaining when I returned to the living room, and two of those, screened as a double-feature at a pornographic house in Kansas City, "were not seen in their entirety." (He often used the passive voice when relating embarrassing anecdotes that clearly embarrassed him not at all.) He had, then, seen only one wide-release movie of the eighties, the coolly received *Gavel & Leisure*, about a vagrant (Bruno Kirby) who gets mistaken for a judge. I'd put the bag of videos in the upright fruit crate that held Wanda's TV, a red-white-and-blue bicentennial model she'd had in her bedroom as a girl. Wade reached into the bag and picked a video (*Sherman's March*) at random, put it in the player, and took a seat in the middle of the sofa. He didn't seem to mind sitting on the crack between the two cushions, or maybe he just wanted to be in direct line of the TV. It was a small TV (one inch of screen for each original colony) but precious, I suppose, in that it was one of those rare black and whites modded into color, its guts having been replaced at Wanda's request and considerable expense by a perplexed but masterly Russian repairman. It seemed like a silly project to me, but in the end the picture made its own case, the image sharp but not cutting, the colors warm and tingly, particularly attuned, I thought, to the oranges, reds, and yellows often seen through eyelids on swing sets.

After *Sherman's March*, we watched *Cautious of the Moon*, then *Stranger Than Paradise*. This last movie I'd first seen with my mother at Chicago's Fine Arts Theatre during a Christmas '84 stay with my aunt and uncle in one of the city's northwestern suburbs. It was sleeting on the night we went to see the movie, so the drive downtown took us even longer than expected, and once we got there we couldn't figure out where to park. "We should've taken the train," my mother said, a dig at me, since I'd pressed for driving. We did find a place to park, though not in the underground ramp that we later realized would have been much more convenient. We jogged gingerly on the slippery sidewalks that led to the theater, occasionally conquering a patch of ice by spreading our arms like a scarecrows. I especially remember the brown-gray wetness of the Michigan Avenue sidewalk in front of the theater's glass doors, and how my mother bent over and fluidly opened the right door as if she were ending a dance routine. All the actors were great, she said on the way home, hardly actors at all. Wade seemed moved when I shared this anecdote. "We played a show in Chicago around that Christmas," he said. "I might've been in town that same night, just a few miles from y'all." He reflected on that coincidental proximity, as if a chance meeting in a strange city would have made any difference, as if my mother and I had been missing all that time and he'd nearly found us. My mother and I had never been hard to find in Enswell or in Minneapolis. It's true that we moved into a different Enswell rental a year after Wade left, but Enswell is a small city and my mother was always in the phone book, which back then, I mention by the way, also listed the citizen's occupation and whether he or she was a homeowner, householder, or roomer. I was reminded of that while poking around the Enswell Public Library last year. My mother's entries read: "Deskin Marleen T [to economize space, no periods were used after middle initials] secretary Tuttle Ag Pumps," followed by the standard directory info. (When asked, my mother always called herself a "gal Friday.") In the 1971 phone book I found: "Salem Wade D cook Bey's . . ." He was missing from the directory for several years, then returned in '76: "Salem Wade D driver AAAA Vending . . ." And in '77: "Salem Wade E [sic] attendant ARE Parking . . ." He disappeared again until '87, but by then the phone book no longer listed occupations.

We finished *Stranger Than Paradise* around two a.m. Wanda had fallen asleep on Wade's shoulder and later drifted or was subtly lowered to his lap. When the movie ended, she stumbled off to bed. Wade and I moved to opposite ends of the couch, and were soon reclining on these opposite ends, his long legs resting on the back of the couch in his faded Erizeins, my not-as-long legs hanging in twill toward the floor. We stayed up to half-watch *San Pedro Cards & Gifts* (underrated), during which he started talking about Los Angeles, about the first time he'd gone there, in July of '77. Because it was so late and we were both tired, or because he was in a contemplative mood, he spoke at first with unwonted slowness, and in a deeper, softer tone than usual, a lulling tone, though I was tired and might have been lulled by Minnie Pearl's voice, besides which Wade's voice had a soothing, cello-like timbre even when he was more energized and the hours weren't so small. It was easy to grasp his appeal to a radio station's program director. His pace picked up and his voice got more voluble as he continued, but not alarmingly so, and I floated into a shallow sleep as he talked, though I believe I caught most of his reminiscence:

Wade had gone to Los Angeles to exchange five thousand not easily saved dollars for three ounces of not egregiously diluted cocaine, which he kept on the plane ride home to Enswell via Denver in his carry-on, in a baggie concealed, *entomed* as it were, in James Michener's *Centennial*, a Christmas gift from his mother. He had hollowed out Michener's book while watching TV in the Motel Hacienda. He'd brushed the book's shavings off the bed, but then envisioned the shavings as evidence and got on his hands and knees to pinch them off the musty olive carpet. The Motel Hacienda, it turned out, was not a nice place to stay. The soda machine's sold-out lights glowed orange for every brand except Diet Rite, whose column, he discovered, was also empty. The motelier coldly demanded payment up front and was missing a hand. In the parking lot, her uniformly tank-topped kids played at war, using steak knives wrapped in medical gauze and balloons filled with their own tears. It was the right thing to do, there being a drought under way. Nearby a man chained himself to his sprinkler, running full blast at midday in defiance of city orders, and drowned before the police could haul him away. A heat-crazed housemaid was caught trying to dip a soup ladle into a Hockney swimming pool; at hospital she got a gnomic telegram from the artist himself, followed by a visit from the ABC affiliate's top dispatcher of broadcast-closing human-interest stories. Someone in Santa Barbara flew a yellow box kite into a high-tension power line, setting off sparks that lit the dry brush and gathered into a wind-cheered fire that consumed two hundred homes, some of them said to be worth a half-million dollars. "Looks like God done switched sides in the class war," quipped a (white-sounding) community-radio deejay, who apologized insincerely during the next break. A pair of young, otherwise normal-seeming suburban men was off to jail for having hijacked a school bus. In his notebook Wade noted the confluence of yellow: yellow box kites; yellow buses; yellow balloons (some of them were yellow); yellow scoop-necked shirts on gallery owners; yellow notebooks; yellow pencils; yellow diving boards; pungent yellow paperback pages in West Hollywood bookstores; the yellow, nicotian teeth revealed by the motelier's provocative smile. Sometimes skin turns yellow when it's stretched over a person who's about to die. Of course, if you're looking for death or prophecy, it's not so hard to pick and choose images, perhaps especially in Los Angeles, where paradoxers of an apocalyptic Eden or Edenic apocalypse have the best shtick going. It'd be dishonest to omit how good Wade felt walking past a toy-strewn yard (one of the toys a yellow Tonka truck) where a man with wild salt-and-mustard hair was bent over playing Charlie Christian spirals with high feeling on a no-name guitar under the chicken sun. Wade's trip could have taken a day, in which case he could have made the Bolling Greene show at the North Dakota State Fair, a show his attractive upstairs neighbor, he'd overheard, would be attending with her vaguely poignant son. Instead he stretched his errand into a week of lonely tourism. Neither his disappointingly dull L.A. connection nor anyone else invited him to the bacchic party he'd imagined on the plane. Although for the most part Angelenos weren't as stylish as he'd anticipated, he often felt like a conspicuous provincial. He walked and drove and drove and walked. He often got lost on the highway and his shouts bounced around the protractor part of his rented steering wheel. He ate peanuts in front of Watts Towers, saw *Call Me Angel, Sir!* at an ironically named porn theater, waited in a depressing line at the Roxy to see priapic SoCal rockers Sideswipe, whose performance made him nostalgic for the line. He went to the UCLA campus, where he smiled enviously, contemptuously, and longingly at the students, sat tailor style before Lachaise's hermaphroditic *Standing Woman*, admiring her grapefruit breasts and watermelon hips, her impossibly thin waist, presidential head, shot-putter's arms, pianist's fingers not unlike Wade's own. If music is the breathing of statues, as Rilke had it, she was breathing *Das Rheingold* out of her mouth, "Muddy Water (A Mississippi Moan)" out of her nose. He went to the Los Angeles County Museum of Art, where he lingered at one of de Kooning's famous, infamous women—this one relatively gentle, partly pastel, but still strangely headed, moderately frightening. To a young, heavily lipsticked woman also looking at the drawing, he noted that in '53 Rauschenberg turned one of de Kooning's women into a kind of shade, by erasing the drawing and calling the palimpsest his own work. "*Erased de Kooning* it's called," Wade said, with an attempted sniff-laugh. The woman, in some kind of Continental accent, said, "Such gestures quickly grow tiresome," but which gesture did she mean: Rauschenberg's cheekily Oedipal response to the anxiety of influence, or Wade's pedantic come-on? He moved to another room. Modernism had been institutionalized long before Wade could get to it; so-called postmodernism was being institutionalized immediately. It was impossible to stand outside the mainstream in any meaningful way. Even a drug dealer stood outside only in technical and situational terms—the street dealer must stand outside, that being where streets are kept, but he's no genuine outlaw, only a nuisance or mirror or mirror nuisance, as the crime movies had so proudly discovered. Wade's criminal life led more plausibly to jail than to riches, but a straight, middle-class future was still an option, he thought, especially if he set his sights on the lower middle. Anything was possible. The upstairs neighbor seemed to have excellent taste in music.

FeSTiVaL

GETTING IN AS MANY MOVIES AS POSSIBLE OVER THAT blizzard weekend became a kind of game, for which we all invented and argued rules: As long as two people were in front of the TV, we agreed Saturday morning, the festival went on, lest things be stymied by someone's work shift or a run to get groceries or more movies. Intermissions were limited to five minutes. There was no rewinding for missed lines, no pausing for bathroom breaks—Wade had to pee with pitiable frequency, so efficiency particularly depended on this last rule. Sometimes during his stay with us, I heard him projecting horselike streams into, on, and around our toilet (in certain light, spots of dried urine gleamed on the white tile), but other times, especially when I was awake in bed, I heard him expelling what must have been mere tablespoons, only to return to the bathroom five minutes later with the same paltry offering, sometimes again and again like that till he or I fell asleep.

After *Tapani*, I think we watched *Wings of Desire*, then *The Eton Boy*, *Collaborators*, *Lisa in Slippers*, *Melvin and Howard*, *Liberty Farm*, *The Point of Boiling*, *Concrete Washout*, *Switcheroo*—in truth the order escapes me, but I'm pretty sure all those were in there somewhere. That afternoon ("It was evening all afternoon," Wallace Stevens wrote, "It was snowing / And it was going to snow"), Maryanne came over with a bag of day-old baked goods and some suggestions for the festival. She was dressed in an actual snowsuit, a tight old lavender thing that Wanda had to help her shake and twist out of. The bag of pastries, Maryanne explained, was a gift from one of her former colleagues. She was still out of work (her job-hunting seemed short of tireless). I ate a baby-face-sized cookie, ignored the film suggestions. I was less the cineaste than Maryanne but didn't want a shared curatorship, mostly because Wade had praised a few of my selections. Underneath the snowsuit, I see now from a photograph snapped that day, Maryanne wore ragg-wool socks; her white jeans; a cotton sweater with wide black and ochre stripes; and a probably secondhand silk scarf with olive, fingerprint-like markings on a cream background. Her arrival had upset the seating arrangements, and with no deliberate maneuvering I landed between her and Wanda, lightly touching Wanda's left shoulder and Maryanne's right hip. I was careful not to disrupt this equilibrium, and later suffered some neck and shoulder pain connected to prolonged stillness.

After sitting through two and a half movies, Maryanne confessed to antsiness and suggested we all go sledding. The rest of us were committed to the festival, though, or in Wanda's case had to leave soon for a short shift at the public-radio catalog. Besides, no one had a sled or could come up with a suitable makeshift. Maryanne proposed cookie sheets, but that seemed unrealistic. Her antsiness started to rub off on me, however, and I spent a long time tracking the apartment for the source of an irregular whistling squeak, mistaking what was by consensus a hot-water pipe for some frightened animal. Wanda left for work, and a certain Thanksgivingish torpor set in for a few hours. At some point around dusk, Maryanne pulled a reporter's tape recorder from her bag, and began to rotate it in her hands, swinging it by its little strap, waiting, it seemed, for someone to ask about it. A moment later she told me the recorder was left over from her not quite two semesters in journalism school. "I just kind of stumbled on it the other day when I was looking for spare change in drawers," she said. "I'm gonna use it to record overheard conversations, like at coffee shops and on buses and stuff. Then I'll transcribe the better ones and edit them, tighten 'em up, and leave the edited transcriptions at coffee shops and on buses."

"Fantastic," Wade said.

"Yeah, and eventually I could splice and rearrange the tapes into some kind of whole, some cohesive—well, maybe not cohesive—some whole. And that . . ."

"Yeah?" I said.

"Would be the audio for my second movie."

"Fantastic," Wade said.

"Isn't that squeaking just driving you nuts?" I said.

The movie receded into the background while Wade further commended Maryanne's project, started talking about Beckett, Joe Gould, Tony Schwartz, went into a miniature history of audio-vérité. It was pedantic but sufferable, I guess because he was so enthusiastic, so encouraging. He wasn't saying that Maryanne's experiments would in truth be replications of experiments already conducted long before she was born, as my cobwebby artistic experiments, not to be described here, have been; he was saying that she'd be honorably carrying on unfinished, unfinishable work. Now it's true that Gould's major work, an enormous social history supposedly composed of eavesdroppings, was unfinished in a more empirical sense, and as I listened to Maryanne and watched her listen to Wade, I suspected that her projects would suffer similar but less legendary fates—but that wasn't the point. "We must judge men not so much by what they do, as by what they make us feel that they *could* do," a minor English ethicist once said, italics mine, and one sensed that Maryanne could do something great, could make a great artwork, or a great creation of some other kind, and that even if she didn't create such a work, her unrealized potential, her failed, unfinished work, her refusal to "prefer mean victory to honourable defeat," as John Ruskin put it, wouldn't be shameful or pathetic but rather a calm reproof to those who toil steadily and vainly to finish mediocrities. I was falling for Maryanne, of course, and I considered that this falling was a defense mechanism, that, seeing Wanda's eye turn toward Wade, I'd simply come up with a ready turnabout, a hopeful contingency plan, though my feelings felt too sharp and instinctual to give that consideration much credence. Occasional whiffs of Maryanne's perfume led to nascent erections, for instance.

Wanda got back from work around eleven with a box of cookies (I loved all the merry sitcom coming and going) and took a seat next to Wade on the sofa. Not long after, Maryanne and I happened to get up at the same time for drinks, Diet Rite for me, a cocktail for her, very stiff—she added just one thimble of tonic to the up-brand vodka she'd brought over, smiled at me, and put the thimble back in the coin pocket of her jeans. After she finished her drink in a cowboyish gulp, we found ourselves messing around in the dining roomlet with her recorder. To facilitate transcription, the recorder had a range of playback speeds, so we taped our voices and then pitched them down and up to ursine and rodential frequencies, I speaking in my regular voice, she employing accents: hillbilly, Canadian, cockney, black (American and Jamaican). None of the accents were accurate; some were mildly offensive. We'd been sharing a joint Wade had left half-smoked on the Formica table—I can't mix narcotics, but Maryanne seemed to have no trouble with that, and I even absurdly imagined that she could choose from one minute to the next which effect she wanted to enjoy. From the living room Wade yelled for quiet, but after a while he and Wanda deserted *One-Trick Pony* to join us at the table, where we all fiddled with the tape recorder, and Wade told stories about his days with Bolling, and everyone but me did a few lines of coke and talked and laughed or cackled well into the night.

night ride home

BOLLING GREENE FIRST PERFORMED IN THE RAIL-goaded valley city of Enswell, North Dakota, on Thursday, July 28, 1977. The country station was playing his latest single every two hours, plus sprinkling in oldies with the same frequency. The station's program director was an almost discomfortingly zealous fan, and it was largely as a result of this PD's devotion that Enswell, though a city of just thirty-three thousand, became Bolling's fourth-largest market, after Austin, Dallas-Fort Worth-Arlington, and Munich. Against managerial counsel, Bolling had brought with him a three-piece horn section comprising a trombonist who ate Dexedrine like Certs and whose other job was to drive the bus, and a pair of chubby alto saxophonists, hoisted from the University of Texas marching band, who could make their horns sound exactly like teakettles. Backstage before the show, excitement was passed around like a joint; among the crowd like a beach ball. Bolling walked onstage sans introduction and yelled, as he did at the start of every show, "Y'all hungry?" The crowd cheered, and I waved my corndog in the air, splattering ketchup on my mother's shirt.

But the forecast had called for intermittent showers and it started to rain during the opening number, "The Infractor," its chorus harmonies widemouthed and sandpapery. The rain, wary of cliché, refused to fall torrentially, but it did get harder. After the third song, the dutifully fat and unstylish stage manager trotted out from the wings and said something in Bolling's ear, but the singer shook his head sheriff-like and wiped the strings of his guitar with a red bandanna, leaving cranked his Telecaster's volume thimble so the crowd might be inspirited by the strings' defiant, whooshful zip. In fancy silver letters on the guitar's neck were the words "Don't fret." Bolling looked out at a thousand view-obstructing umbrellas, at a woman in the second row tenting her gray-blond head with a fairgrounds map, at the poor planners or simply poor, or relatively poor, or penny-wise, in the sheltered, faraway seats, enjoying their rare luck, and he called out "The Storms Are on the Ocean," as if to will the storm (no storm, really, just a good rain) back to the ocean, about fifteen hundred miles away in any direction.

By the song's end the rain had stopped, and though Bolling didn't believe in an intervening God, he doffed his trademark leather havelock to the sky and the crowd unleashed a terrifying cheer. A woman climbed atop a speaker and tried to rent her poncho. Even those of us close to the speakers couldn't have distinguished the tears from the rain on her face without tasting them. As the cheers died down, the woman on the speaker started to yell: "Do you think we've given up? Do you think we ever gave up? Do you think we've given up in Enswell, North Dakota? Do you think the people of Enswell, North Dakota, have given up? Do you think we thought it was all a big joke?" And there is no typographical trick that could do justice to her concluding "No!" Bolling smiled, and the woman jumped into the arms of two burly security guards in green T-shirts, who let her return to her seat after a short lecture. Bolling sang songs about orchids, wind, love, and madness in front of sixty-five hundred North Dakota State Fairgoers, including, as has already been indicated, Marleen Deskin, who sometimes held my hand, but not Wade Salem, on his knees in a Los Angeles motel. My mother and I had great seats in the sixth or seventh row. We'd waited all afternoon.

That night the band played to beat itself. Bolling sang and danced before Enswell with such jowl-jiggling might, he may as well have been wearing King David's ephod instead of sky-blue bell-bottoms, a tight armadillo T-shirt, and a bandolier, stretched snugly across his hogshead chest like a rope round a sleeping bag. Bolling himself thought the bandolier was ridiculous, had first allowed it to be wrapped around his chest only because an art director and photographer had more or less insisted, but the longer he wore it, the more natural it felt. And as it turned out, he went on wearing the costume long after his manager dropped him, after no one cared what he wore except a few thousand diehard fans, who probably didn't care much either.

In any case, one could feel it that night. The sometimes indifferent sidemen, one could feel, felt that Bolling was feeling it, and they sweated, seemed even to call on reserve pores, so their employer (and everyone) would feel even more. "Let's try to play the music and not the background," Ornette Coleman said somewhere, and that's what Bolling and his band did. The lead guitarist wore, in the rainy heat, a black three-piece suit with trousers that squeezed his thighs and flared over his white boots, and his solos and fills seemed to loose arrows from the tear on his amplifier's silver face; when the trombonist emptied his spit valve, the spit turned on contact with the grimy stage into pools of honey; the drummer played with a necktie wrapped around his eyes but didn't miss a cue; geothermal bass notes throbbed in our chests like love. "What *is* that?" I asked my mother during the solo on "West Texas Winds." "That's a steel guitar," she said. "That's what people can do."

During the encore, Bolling felt a raindrop on his wrist. He motioned the six-stringer to make another pass through the verse changes of "Misstepchild," and then another, and another, and called on more dilatory tactics, till the time was right for Bolling to switch to the Wurlitzer electric piano, and close, as he always closed, with a wistful version of "My Red Ideal." Rocks in his throat, rocks in his bed, rocks from the fields stacked into mysterious cairns. Did he oversing it? Yes, but no. The sometimes overloud, stick-breaking drummer tapped out the beat with his paws, and the guitarists stood with fallen crests, muting their strings—"unheard melodies are sweeter," Bolling had told them before the show—while the collegiate saxophonists, slobbering for post-performance beer, triumphed again with their teakettle trick.

Moments after the death of the last D chord, not quite a common chord due to the Wurly's aphasic F-sharp above middle C, the rain resumed with full seriousness, and the crowd cheered louder even than before, and some of them danced like Gene Kelly back to their cars and trucks, vans, motorcycles, and class-B motorhomes. A few of them walked right past their vehicle and laughed over the mistake. The rain stopped again. My mother and I left the oak tree we'd been shrinking under, started for home on foot, until a family offered us a ride in the back of their pickup, and the tire humps soaked the seats of our jeans but the wind dried our hair.

COLLABORATORS

BY MID-NOVEMBER OF '91, MARYANNE STILL HADN'T found another baking job and was nearly busted. Her overdraft account was tapped. She'd sold CDs, LPs, books, vintage dresses, a somehow collectable toaster, her motorcycle as-was. She'd borrowed money from her parents and others but hadn't touched Wanda, not directly at least, perhaps because their friendship still seemed too young for loans. And Wanda hadn't made any offers, not even of twenty or thirty bucks; her parsimony—that's unfair: she treated Maryanne to a few meals and more drinks—in the face of Maryanne's crisis seemed uncharacteristic, and on a few occasions Maryanne lamented her poverty with such anxiety that I, tough-minded about such things, almost stepped in to offer a small loan myself.

In the end, Wanda came through with fifteen hundred dollars, just about all the money she had. It wasn't a loan, it was a gift, given moreover in nearly perfect concordance with the directive of anonymous generosity outlined in the Sermon on the Mount—and not the sort of Christian anonymity that scatters hints all over the place and then denies being the munificent phantom with rosy-cheeked gulping, winking, and shoulder-rolling, but a graceful, natural anonymity that doesn't even require a stone face, as if there were no internal squirming to repress. The gift wasn't fully anonymous, since I knew about it, but that's only because Wanda felt the need to involve me in its distribution.

Wanda had come up with a plan, a goofy plan that I'm reluctant to describe on account of my distaste for farce. She explained it to me one night over yet another joint. (It's surprising that I remember anything at all from those days.) We were sitting at the Formica table, her great-soled shoes resting on the table's ridged silver edge, sometimes tapping to the Sousa CD Wade had playfully brought home a week earlier. Wade was out, so we were smoking from Wanda's stash. Already I'd been spoiled by Wade's weed, worlds better in terms of aroma and potency than the green hawked by Wanda's stereotypically mindless and feckless dealer, who also ran a hat kiosk at a nearby mall. Not once did I help Wanda pay for so much as a quarter-ounce bag, though I smoked as much as she and earned more money. This injustice was never brought up. My mooching wasn't of the lowest order, I privately held (still more privately I was unconvinced), since I never strongly desired the weed, never demanded or even asked after it, never smoked it alone or missed it much during dry spells, but just accepted the joint or pipe when it came my way. Even the idea of smoking alone depressed Wanda, so in some convenient way I was being generous. Maybe our symbiosis was mutualism more than commensalism much less parasitism. I miss marijuana. I'm sober now, though unaffiliated, and take any tenuous opportunity to announce my sobriety, in hopes that people will imagine my past as a collage of Dionysian ecstasies and genuflectory humiliations, all sorts of glamorous decadence, and that after such sensational, fact-flouting images flash through their minds, they'll consider the paucity of my accomplishments in light of the routine public vomiting and bathroom-stall demise I so teeth-skinningly escaped and continue to escape through ongoing fortitude or grace.

"It seems strange to give that kind of money to someone you've only known for a month," I said at the table. "Sometimes you know the poetry before the poem," Wanda said. I thought that sounded pretty good. But answered, "Still, why give her so much? Why not just enough to make rent?" And so Wanda reminded me of the poor price Maryanne had gotten for her dinged motorcycle, the likewise insufficient profits from that other stuff; also the bicycle she'd had stolen; an obligatory, over-priced bridesmaid's dress; a few other exigencies and tough breaks. It was Wanda's money to give, of course, but if she depleted her savings, I figured, she'd soon need to borrow from me. And I was right. I didn't bring up the obvious if morally irrelevant point that Maryanne's tough times were partly self-created: it's true that she'd recently been fired (coolly and by telephone, we were more than once reminded), but only after repeated no-shows (she admitted to three, but one suspects there were more); I've already suggested that her job search was too fatigable and I'll add here that it seemed overnarrow; also it was unwise of her to live alone in a high-rise geared toward up-and-coming or low-ranked professionals when she could easily have found a bohemian studio or at least a roommate; and, from what I'd seen, she'd not been a model of jobless frugality—not all her drinking expenses, for instance, were turned over to friends. Moreover I doubted the direness of her situation. I pic-tured supportive, middle-class parents who'd ultimately bail her out with a second and larger loan. She'd made a few remarks—a shallow, classist dismissal of country music, to cite one—that seemed typically bourgeois. But that wasn't quite true, Wanda told me: Maryanne's parents were supportive but poor, poor at least in the American sense, which is often poor enough, and they'd already given all they could afford for now.

Maryanne took walks at more or less the same time every day, in the midafternoon shortly after waking from her day's sleep. In her unemployment, she had expanded but hadn't adjusted her sleep schedule, since she was looking exclusively for another graveyard gig and didn't want to drift back into a more natural circadian rhythm. Twice a week these walks led to her erotic-art class; on other days they led nowhere in particular. But always she crossed a certain footbridge in Loring Park, or at least had crossed it (and from the same direction) on each of the walks she and Wanda had taken together that fall and premature winter. Wanda's plan—goofy, as was said, but uncomplicated—sought to exploit this regularity. It called on me to wait troll-like under the just-mentioned footbridge, or rather partly under it, keeping an eye out for Maryanne, at whose approach, provided there were no other nearby pedestrians, I would obscure myself more fully under the bridge and slip a cash-fattened envelope between two of its rotting, mouse-fur-colored planks.

"How will I do that?" I said, exhaling. "The planks will be covered with snow."

"Shit, that's right," Wanda said.

"It's a good thing you have me around to—"

"But it's important that you push the envelope between two planks. That's become a real idée fixe for me as I've worked this out."

She looked at the ceiling.

"Maybe you could shovel the bridge in advance," she said.

"I don't think you can do that"

"Why not?"

"Well, it's public property," I said.

"The sidewalks belong to the city and you can shovel those."

"But the snow's gonna be really firmly packed. And we don't have a shovel."

"You could clear a gap between two planks," Wanda said. "Just enough to slide the envelope through. Make a little cunt in the bridge." She put her feet down and reached over to rub my cock through my cavalry twills. Our sex life had more than less ended, so it was hard to say what this gesture meant. We weren't fighting, weren't estranged in a way outsiders would easily recognize, weren't acknowledging a problem, but it was starting to feel as if we were staying together mostly because it was a hassle to move in winter, and because she needed me to be around Wade and I needed her to be around Maryanne. "You'll want to make sure the envelope is stop-sign red," she said.

"Isn't that just red-red?" I said.

She shrugged.

"What if Maryanne sees and recognizes me when I'm looking out for her?"

"Just tell her you're waiting on a friend," Wanda said, and we both laughed.

"Will she be wearing that snowsuit?" I asked.

"No, no. She just wore that as a joke. Probably she'll be wearing her red leather jacket."

"Okay, I think I know the one you mean."

"It has a belt, kind of *Shaft*-y."

"Right, yeah, I've seen it."

I had the next day off and could discharge the plan straight-away. That morning Wanda furtively slipped me the cash on our way out of the bank (the furtiveness was just for fun, I guess), and ran to catch her bus. After lunch I went to a drug-store and found a greeting-card envelope in stop-sign red. The card itself was for an occasion not pertinent to my life, so I left it on a park bench for someone else, using a rock as a paper-weight. I wrote "Razor Ray" on the envelope in block letters with my less serviceable left hand, twice underlining the name:

RAZOR RAY

The epithet was Wanda's idea as well, an attempt to discourage pangs of conscience from Maryanne, something of a softy. Too farcical a touch, I argued (I've just noted my antipathy for the form), but, farcical or not, one that might scare Maryanne into simply leaving the money alone, or make her doubly inclined to turn it into the police. But I didn't protest for long. At that point I saw my function as strictly executive, understood that Wanda, in addition to helping out a friend, was trying to pro-duce and direct a piece of street theater, and that my job was to help realize her vision.

I got to the basket-handle footbridge in time to unobstruct a gap between two of its planks with a letter opener. The bridge passed over a creek or brook that branched off Loring Lake. The lake probably wasn't safe to stand on yet, but the brook, creek, or branch seemed solid under the snow. I hung a stick from the gap (the snow held it in place) so I wouldn't lose track of the spot, then waited on the brook- or branch-bank, peering through the railing, my galoshes filling with snow. I only had to wait about twenty minutes for Maryanne to approach. Unfortunately, a man or tall boy in a baseball cap was walking maybe thirty paces behind her. No one, as far as I know, saw me scurry back under the footbridge, clutching the creased, damp envelope. Maryanne's footfalls crunched charmingly overhead.

On my next afternoon off (probably three days later), Maryanne was unfollowed on the path leading to the footbridge, but was with a friend—Wanda in her grandfather's old camel coat, it seemed from a distance, though that didn't make sense, and as they got closer I saw that it was the similarly statured Wade in a coat I'd not seen before, a shearling coat that he later said he'd been keeping in his pillowcase. I was taken aback to see Wade and Maryanne together and couldn't react in time to remove the envelope, which, as it happened, they walked right past. Perhaps they'd instead looked up to admire a flock of blackbirds or a snow-covered linden branch, or were too engrossed in conversation. I eavesdropped hungrily as they approached, crossed, and passed the bridge, but only caught a few unrevealing sentences. Maryanne, it seemed, was asking the supposedly polyglot Wade if other languages had a better word to represent the sound of a sneeze than *ahchoo*, or if the word is pretty much the same across languages, since *ahchoo* is about perfect, though only for one type of sneeze—or maybe, Wade broke in, once the word *ahchoo* and its variants were introduced, people unwittingly began to steer the sound of their sneezes to conform to the word, a tail-wags-the-dog thing, like when . . . and then their voices got too faint.

Four days later—Maryanne's desperation all the more pronounced, overdue notices sliding daily under her door in increasingly perturbed script, her phone soon to be muzzled—

I, holding my breath, heard her stop, heard the crinkle of her thigh-length red leather jacket when she leaned over to pick up the bulging stop-sign-red envelope, may have heard one of the belt's arrowheads graze the packed snow. My heart was pounding even faster than it had during my previous lurkings under the bridge. When Maryanne got the gist of the envelope's contents, she must have stood still and looked in all directions, because it took her awhile to start walking again, at what sounded like a faster pace than before. I stayed put for a half minute, then slowly emerged from under the bridge. The envelope was still there. She'd taken the money but left the envelope, I thought, but no, it was all there. I next tried with an unmarked envelope (Wanda had yielded to my point re Razor Ray). This time, as far as I could hear, Maryanne didn't even slow down, nor did she ever mention the strangely enduring/recurring envelope to Wanda, though they certainly talked often enough about less interesting things.

On the afternoon of that fourth unsuccessful attempt to solve Maryanne's financial trouble, I was in an unpleasant mood, a kind of tired agitation mixed with horniness. That night I told Wanda that after Maryanne had again passed over the money, I'd emerged from the bridge to see a man leaning over to pick up the envelope, an apparently homeless man whom I hadn't noticed before. There was nothing I could do, I told Wanda; I couldn't reasonably explain to the man that the money had been entrusted to me, couldn't tussle for it in good conscience. Wanda of course was dejected by this, regretted having turned a simple kindness into an entertainment. "I'm so fucking selfish," she said, and cried. When she finished, we sat in defeated, roiling silence for five minutes or so. Finally she blew her nose again (I'd brought her a roll of toilet paper). "At least the money went to someone in need," she said.

That night I lay in bed thinking about how to give the money back to Wanda, but couldn't come up with a way to confess that wouldn't end our relationship, an especially pusillanimous concern seeing as how our relationship was already in a clear lame-duck period. I spent just as much time imagining how I'd spend the money, and didn't shake these latter thoughts or even feel the need to eat till nearly a full day later, about five minutes after I'd come pathetically on the heavier prostitute's back, on which there was a disturbing welt.

Now I'm thinking of part of a poem by Gary Snyder, whom both Wade and my mother Marleen read in the seventies:

I don't mind   living this way
Green hills   the long blue beach
But sometimes   sleeping in the open
I think back   when I had you.

The brook or branch that runs under that footbridge in Loring Park seems to run down the above passage, which describes how I feel today, though there's no long beach here and the *you* I miss is plural, the *y'all* form. *Here*, in fact, is Loring Park itself. There's a flower garden nearby, full of bumblebees and helpful identifying signs. I'm trying to build my floral knowledge, but I can feel the names slipping away like a dream even as I mumble them to myself. I'm writing on a park bench. That makes me sound like a vandal—I mean I'm writing in a yellow notebook while sitting on a park bench. I'm also eating a package of oily sliced ham and a stringy, arid orange, eating hastily though not like the caffeinated wolf I was on the night described in short just above, when I ate two slices of heat-lamp pizza on the bus ride home from the thinner prostitute's humble but not seedy apartment. I see that the wooden footbridge has been replaced with one of concrete and steel, a less attractive bridge, though the steel railing has already taken on a handsome patina that makes it look considerably older than its no-more-than eighteen years. Under the bridge now are some clothes, the upended lid of a Weber grill, a sleeping bag, some bottles, some other things, not my things (there but for the grace . . .), though just now the idea isn't emphatically unimaginable, is even perversely attractive.

BLUE NUDE

ONE LATE AFTERNOON ABOUT A WEEK AFTER THE envelope interlude, Wade, Maryanne, and I were on the living room couch surrounded by five or six collections of erotic art ("porno art" in Wade's constant designation), having just returned from the U of M's main library, where Wanda had stayed behind in the video room to take notes on episodes of *Your Show of Shows*. Using a TV tray as a desk, I was slowly annotating a stack of Wanda's promotional postcards with the words "I go on at 8," but would frequently look up from my work to watch Wade and Maryanne discuss ideas for her erotic-art term paper, he playing the questionably solicitous blue-jeaned professor at some undistinguished college. He shared his incompletely coherent ideas about George Grosz's desolate bacchanals and Otto Dix's S&M watercolors, took *Erotische Kunst, Gestern und Heute* from her lap so he could better spot favorite features of a skimpily reproduced Egon Schiele nude or point out a detail in one of Eric Gill's woodcut romps, picked up another book and explicated Achille Devéria's fantastically explicit depictions of orgies, voyeurism, and bestiality. He kept flipping pages, switching books. As a rule he drew the "long sensual line" at adolescent nudes, he told Maryanne, and opposed academic porno art; thus Ingres's *The*

Source was his quintessential guilty pleasure (Cabanel's similarly tacky and arousing *The Birth of Venus,* with the goddess's right eye open a classically pornographic sliver, was another). Perhaps to evidence his bisexuality, of which he seemed proud, he praised the "glistening carnality" of William Etty's *The Wrestlers,* but he seemed more sincerely aroused by Philip Wilson Steer's *Seated Nude: The Black Hat.* The pornodelic fantasies of Ernst Fuchs and Mati Klarwein, he said, were "exalted kitsch." He was a big fan of Degas's rainy, snapshot bathers, and of Goya's *The Naked Maja,* Manet's *Olympia,* Bonnard's *Blue Nude,* and Frenhofer's *Study No. 3;* all were "impossibly sad." He was more attracted to the kneeling background maid in Titian's *The Venus of Urbino* than to the Venus herself. He'd once had a postcard, he said, of the Félicien Rops aquatint in which a zaftig, blindfolded brunette, naked save for stockings, gloves, ribbons, flowers, bows, and other accessories, walks a pig under cherubic oversight. He liked shunga, but only from a distance, he said, because he wasn't "into Oriental women." ("That's kind of lame," Maryanne said.)

A moment later Wade turned a page, and I could hardly believe Courbet's *The Origin of the World,* a close-up of a woman's nude torso, the subject-object lying in bed with her left leg spread, her right angled slightly out. "Jesus, when was this painted?" I said.

"Eighteen sixty-seven," Wade said. (Sixty-six, in fact.) We all stared at the reproduction awhile. The painting's vantage is from the foot of the bed. A sheet covers part of the model's left breast and all her head, most of which latter part would be above the painting's top edge anyway, though if not for the sheet her neck and chin would probably be exposed. The sheet and the painting's limiting focus keep the model's arms out of view as well. It seemed odd to me that her right arm wasn't even suggested, and the more I looked at the painting that afternoon (my memory now assisted by the several reproductions I have laid out in front of me *this* afternoon), the more the model seemed to be an amputee, partially unlimbed just as the bed is unlimned—it's really not a bed at all but a kind of magic sheet floating in a dark brown inane, a dark brown nearly matching the model's pubic hair.

"It's just like a centerfold," Maryanne said.

"Except a centerfold's almost always a full-body shot," I said.

"Well it may actually be a conflation of Courbet's model— who was probably this gorgeous red-haired Irishwoman named Hiffernan—a conflation of her and one of the porno photos floating around Paris back then," Wade said.

"It doesn't seem like she has red hair," I said, looking at the pubic hair.

"Yeah, but you have to remember that le réalisme wasn't a fussbudget documentarian's fidelity to prosaic reality but a prophet's allegiance to essential truth," Wade said.

"My dad has brown hair but a red beard," Maryanne said.

"Besides, this is a bad reproduction," Wade said, "though generational loss can of course be a source of great interest. Years ago—I never should have sold it—but years ago I owned the book that featured the first mass-repro of *L'origine du monde,* this wonderfully designed French book from the late sixties called *Le sexe de la femme.*"

I thought for a moment.

"It was by a doctor, maybe a friend of a Lacan's, since Lacan owned *L'origine* for a long time—how perfect is that?—and maybe through him this doctor managed to get a photo, or it might have been that—"

"Wait," I said. "*Le sexe de la femme.*"

Wade corrected my pronunciation.

"My mom owned that book too. She got it from a boyfriend when she was in Paris."

"Really?" Wade said blankly, turning the page.

"Yeah."

"That's weird," Maryanne said.

"Not so weird," Wade said. "It was quite a hot book back then."

"For Americans, though?" I said. "It doesn't seem like a lot of Americans would—"

"No, it was definitely part of the hippie samizdat," Wade said.

"She always told me that my other mom, you know, that my other mom stole it from her."

"You have two moms?" Maryanne said.

"I'm adopted."

"Well, I bought the book secondhand in Enswell," Wade said. "Maybe I bought your other mom's copy without knowing it."

"Yeah"—I spoke slowly—"that's probably it. She probably sold it to buy drugs."

"Maybe," Wade said quietly.

I craned my neck and leaned around Wade to look at Maryanne. "My real mom OD'd," I said. I wanted her to come over and comfort me, but it was Wade who put his hand lightly and awkwardly on my back. After a too-brief pause he started recommending additional sources for Maryanne's paper, which if I'm remembering correctly she never got around to writing.

WiLD THiNGS rUN FaST

O N A FEW HOT NIGHTS DURING THE SUMMER OF '78, Wade and my mother slept in his cool basement apartment, and I moved into her queen-sized bed. (The heat has never kept me awake; my contented slumber through "oppressive" heat and humidity has bred envy.) On those nights when Wade and my mother slept in the basement, I would stay up late in my mother's bed reading boy-detective stories, or so I once told Wanda, who I thought would like to picture me reading such stories on the same summer nights that found her under soft bedcovers aiming a flashlight at *Wuthering Heights, Madame Bovary,* or *Story of O.* (Wanda was always a more sophisticated reader than I, as well as sexually precocious, but you'll recall that she's five years my senior, this last difference most accounting for the contrast in our summer-of-'78 reading.) I did sometimes read boy-detective stories, but rarely, and I don't recall reading any on those nights when Wade and Marleen slept in the basement. Probably by the time Wanda was fully enraptured by her book, even stroking her flashlight as she read, her mouth slightly open, the light- and world-blocking covers too warm for summer (though Wanda's family had central air), probably by that time I was well into my night's first boring dream.

Wade generally kept the plywood door to his apartment unlocked, so I sometimes went down there to watch his fish or listen to his stereo. His speakers, Frankenstein creations made by his drumming friend Karl Tobreste, were the size of cigarette vending machines. They stood on the obligatory maroon shag, pointing toward his bed from opposite sides of his sleeping area (much of the sound got lost in the dust under his never-hidden-away hideaway). A nude by an Enswell photorealist named Lloyd Gibson hung across from the bed, above the speaker-flanked modular storage unit of bricks and boards, which held some of Wade's books, his favorite records, his stereo, some knickknacks, objets d'art, and mementoes: an ashy incense holder; a series of misshapen, variously eaten ceramic dough-nuts made by a clever but clumsy niece (these doughnuts espe-cially rattled at certain woofer eructations); a framed photo of his grandfather wrestling a bear; a broken Philco radio. Gibson's painting—which owing to the shelves was hung too high, so that it nearly touched the low ceiling—profiled an erotically fleshy woman with brick-red hair, wearing Ray Bans and a Milwaukee Brewers cap, getting out of a pink bathtub, water cascading from her liquory backside and dripping from two fangs of pubic hair. I also have some recollection of the paint-ing's fogged mirror and the grime on the tile grout, but I might have added those details later. A few times I lay on Wade's hide-away for a long while staring at Sharon Gibson (the model, though it was hard to tell with the cap and sunglasses, was Lloyd's wife, the night manager at Piggly Wiggly and an acquaintance of my mother's), listening mainly to Manilow and Manchester, sometimes to Seger or Sands. The mattress had a magnetic indentation in its center. I wish I could remember what speculative, protosexual thoughts I had during those whiles, though having wished this I feel I've abused myself.

My mother Marleen rented that house in Enswell for nine years. She was always a homebody but never bought a home, though after both her parents were dead, she took over their modest, paid-off ranch house, an arrangement my more affluent aunt accepted but resented. The inheritance from my grandparents wasn't large, I gather, but wasn't insignificant. My adoptive grandfather, an engineer for a company that made circuit breakers and other electric-power equipment, earned decent money but was something of a spendthrift. Anyway, the house in Enswell was a boxy two-bedroom with two front windows, pale gray asbestos siding, and a tiny wooden stoop that my mother called a deck. It was on Queal Street just off Foster Avenue, near where Queal's westernmost yellow center dash pointed across Foster to the front door of Oran's Bar. To our immediate west was the aforementioned parking lot of a large Lutheran church, whose chestnut bricks looked more red than brown in the sun, and whose spire sometimes cast a shadow on those entering Oran's in the arguably not-late-enough afternoon. During the warmer months of the school year, I'd routinely spend a few afternoon hours in the lot, popping my anemic wheelies, jumping off curb ramps, trying to avoid parked cars as narrowly as possible, drawing invisible zeroes, ampersands, eyeballs, and apples with my tires (if there were puddles on the lot, I could make these shapes visible, but then they weren't quite the shapes I had in mind). On some summer days, I biked around the lot all day, sometimes found the repetitive tricks and near-tricks transporting. Around six o'clock, my mother would open the back screen door and call out: "Hot dogs!" "Burgers!"

"Taco salad!" "D-Luxe Frenchies!" "Tuna casserole!" In the summer we ate on the railed, wooden front stoop almost every night, listening to the v-eights and eight tracks whizzing by on Foster, our plates in our laps, our metal folding chairs (hers silver, mine in the standard dun) facing the largely uneventful street but slanted slightly toward each other.

Wade moved into the basement apartment in early '77, probably in February. Strange, considering North Dakota's climate, to make a move at that time of year. He'd been living with Karl Tobreste, whose wife, I later heard, had lost patience with Wade and demanded a hasty exit. He and Karl made several trips to our place in an old yellow pickup, icicles hanging from its grille like drool from a Saint Bernard. They held a long, testy debate in the snow and cold about how to get Wade's plaid hideaway down the stairs and in the apartment's narrow door, Karl maintaining in a very Plains-speaking shout that such an operation was impracticable, Wade eventually hitting Karl on the back of the head with one of the hideaway's scratchy seat cushions. My mother and I, undetected as far as I know, watched the argument from our dining alcove. Karl wore an orange snowsuit, permanently stained with what looked to be day-old dirt of the kind one picks up in a corral tussle; Wade wore faded Erizeins, a parka the color of a root-beer Popsicle, and fur earmuffs. We cracked a window to hear them better. "Let's just take the door off its hinges," Wade said. "It still won't fit," Karl said. (But it did.) Without looking at me, my mother whispered, "Which one of these fools did you say is moving in?" I'd talked briefly with the men a few hours earlier. "The one with the longer hair," I whispered. Her head drew back subtly as if she'd been filliped on the chin. "Easy on the eyes," she said.

Some morning not long after he moved in, Wade jump-started my mother's car for what must have been one of its last rides. Another time, maybe three months later, he gave me the thumbs-up for a wobbly run of no-hands. But mostly he kept to himself. Then one night in what I guess was August of '77, I was eating alone on the front stoop and saw Wade coming home on foot, probably from Oran's. I held up my plate: "Wanna dog?" Really there were no extras. He declined, but I must have planted or watered an idea in his head, because a week later my mother and I were out in our small, mostly dirt backyard, I pogo-sticking, she lighting a rusty Coleman stove, when Wade's car crunched into the driveway, and he got out with a bag full of groceries, pointed to the stove, and said, "Have any room for another burger on there?" We did. He pulled out a six-pack of soda from the bag. "D'ya wanna drink your pop from the can or out of a glass?" he asked me.

"Um," I said.

"I'd like to offer you a frosty mug," he said, "but I don't have one, frosty or not. I'm thinking about buying one, though, doing some research. My buddy has a back-issue of *Consumer Reports* that rates 'em."

"Can's good," I said.

"Can's good, *please*," my mother said.

"Can's good please."

"It's not cold. How 'bout on the rocks?"

I nodded and he went downstairs to grab a glass of ice and two regular beers. The ice cubes, made of Bubble Up, were impaled with toothpick handles, which I pulled out and put in my pocket. I sat on the backyard's rotting picnic table while the adults talked, my mother flipping the burgers more than necessary.

Her connoisseur's spatula, a gift from her father that later fell to me, had been washed only by the rain, and Wade teased her about its filth, I remember, but I don't remember what else they talked about. When the burgers were almost done, my mother went inside to change out of her tank top into a silky, honeydew-green blouse (what a great word, *honeydew;* I only realized it now), and Wade sat down with me at the picnic table, shaded by a warty bur oak with conjoined trunks. The Lutheran church's brick, one-story office building, which marked the southern border of our backyard, had forced the decapitation of some of the oak's limbs, but that seemed to add to the tree's gothic charm. Wade and I talked about football. He said I was wrong to like the Cowboys. "Root for the underdog," he said. "Always." That night he and my mother sat on the stoop, talking till after my bedtime, playing Joni Mitchell, Keith Jarrett, and Bolling Greene records on the living-room stereo loud enough for the music to sift heartily through the front screen. A week later he settled in upstairs, though he continued to rent the basement apartment, as noted earlier, apparently continued to mail rent checks for a few months even after he left impetuously on the also previously mentioned morning of November 11, 1978, this time locking the door and not leaving a key. We had to ask the landlady to come over so we could save Wade's fish, which I kindly adopted.

Lectures amoureuses

MY COPY OF GÉRARD ZWANG'S *Le sexe de la femme* arrived a few days ago. Naturally I didn't expect the paperback reissue to match the original, enticingly described in one of Linda Nochlin's essays as a "limited edition, luxe, pseudoscientific, soft-porn production." Still, I hoped it would be something more than what I've been sent. The original, from what I gather, is heavily pictorial, whereas this is almost all text (of which I can only read fragments), here and there interrupted by Jacques Zwang's anatomical drawings. I should probably try to work through a few pages with a French-English dictionary, or if nothing else translate the reissue's introduction, by Jean-Jacques Pauvert, who in the fifties bravely published *Story of O*, the complete works of Sade, and other dirty classics, but, having recently given up coffee, I'm too tired for a laborious translation. I have at least browsed the book's clever glossary, made up mostly of literary quotes. Really I'm not interested in actually reading Zwang's book, though I'd skim it if it were translated into English. Last night, however, I happened to return to my apartment at the same time as my across-the-hall neighbor, to whom I've said hello a few times and who I thought might be from Côte d'Ivoire or Togo; there are small communities of Twin Citians from those countries, and he reminded me of a Togolese guy I worked with for a few months at a call center. We've hardly spoken before, and I'm not habitually so forward, but I was in good, almost giddy spirits (yesterday, to combat a headache, I allowed myself one cup of coffee), so as I was fiddling with my keys I asked this neighbor if by chance he spoke French. He is West African, as I'd guessed, though not from a Francophone country. But, it further turns out, not wholly unfamiliar with the French tongue. He told me his name and I immediately forgot it, along with his actual country of origin. I offered him dinner and he agreed to essay some rough translations of a few passages from Zwang.

The book's title and racy cover seemed to make my neighbor uncomfortable, but he voiced no complaints. He began with Pauvert's intro, translating slowly and, it seemed, inexpertly. We both got bored before he finished. I took the book back, opened it at random, and, after a few whimsical loops and spirals, landed my index finger on a sentence. Keeping my finger planted, I handed *Le sexe* back to my neighbor. He had trouble with these first fruits of my bibliomancy: "'Of course, clitoral masturbation'"—here I foolishly giggled, but he kept reading—"'persists more or less' . . . 'assiduously'—maybe there we have the false friend—'during adolescence, contrary to the theories of Papa Freud.'"

"'Papa Freud,' that's cute," I said, taking the book back and randomly choosing another sentence. This one was harder, and I've accordingly omitted internal quotation marks, since I didn't write down the page number and can't now sort out Zwang's translated words from my neighbor's guesswork and commentary: "Exploratory furor—the word might be *passion*—makes

something or other—wow, these are hard words—is . . . vulva?
. . . and the lazy—I don't think the word is lazy—"
"The lazy vulva?" I said. "Sounds like a band name."
"I don't think the word is *lazy*," he said.
"Papa Freud and the Lazy Vulvas—no, Vulvae."
"Shall I continue on?"

The third sentence didn't go much better, and by then we'd finished our frozen pizza. I've since discovered that the University of Wisconsin's Milwaukee campus has an original edition of *Le sexe* in the rare books room of their Golda Meir Library, which I plan to visit soon, though it will mean finally buying that new intake manifold for Wade's former hatchback.

BLUE FLOATED

IN MID-DECEMBER OF '91, ON MY TWENTY-FIRST BIRTHDAY, Wade, Wanda, Maryanne, and I assembled at the apartment for a makeshift dinner and a few tokes, after which we'd walk to the oversized, vaguely bohemian corner bar where Wade possibly did business. The phone rang as I was finishing my tuna sandwich, and soon my mother was wishing me a happy birthday in a vowely, asperous, often incomprehensible voice— "hot potato voice," it was later suggested, that being one of the symptoms of peritonsillar abscess, or quinsy as it's commonly called. I stretched the phone as far away from Wade as I could, not wanting my mother to hear his voice in the background. I thanked her for her card, a grievance woven into my gratitude since a card seemed a puny maternal gift for a son's twenty-first birthday. She had a sore throat, she said, was having trouble swallowing. "Hubble's hollow men?" I teased. She repeated herself. She hadn't seen a doctor yet. I told her to see one right away, but perhaps my concern seemed perfunctory. I thought about asking her a few questions about Martha Dickson but figured it wasn't the time. She told me she loved me. She said she was proud of me. "For what?" I said, to my later regret, but at least I mumbled that I loved her too and thanked her again for the card. Next I should have called my aunt. My aunt and mother, despite their proximity (roughly fifteen miles), weren't in close contact with each other just then, but certainly my aunt would have chauffeured Marleen to a clinic or hospital on my request. Probably I shouldn't forever berate myself for not leaping to action over what I took to be a bad sore throat.

It was a Friday night and the bar was crowded, lots of people trying to hail a waitress or squeeze up to the bar, others walking their drinks oafishly, gingerly, or in one case sexily back to their booths or tables, for instance with two pints raised above bumping level in the semaphoric *U,* an image I now suspect I've recalled not from that night but from a Michelob commercial. "Nothing bad had happened," as Michael Krüger wrote in *The End of the Novel,* published around the time of that twenty-first birthday, "except that everything was getting worse in the most cheerful manner." We found a booth near the jukebox, the air around which, Wade said, was doing some kind of violence to a song he'd always liked. There are some public spaces, he said, that in some moments can enrich and revive a record, even a record seemingly parched by overexposure, public spaces and collections of bodies and historical forces that can work miracles of restoration, returning, for instance, all the impudence and alienation, all the endless flux and eternal striving, to "(I Can't Get No) Satisfaction"; and there are some public spaces, he went on, that will invariably debase or deform a great record or song, though this debasement or deformation doesn't normally happen in drugstores or elevators (where traditional Muzak, if you'll excuse the oxymoron, was still played in the early nineties, whereas now my neighborhood druggist plays the Staple Singers and the Ramones, though I've not yet heard "I Wanna Be Sedated"), but rather in places where authenticity and individualism are respected, but stupidly. It was this latter fate, this kitsching and vitiation, that befell the songs limping from the corner bar's jukebox that night, Wade argued. I started to feel sympathy for the songs I liked, exaggerated contempt for those I didn't.

Wade invited me to the pool table. Predictably, he was an excellent, theatrical, erotically limber player. That's one of the things he was in general: a player, ein Spieler. He threw a strict dart too, slaughtered me at around the clock and football. When we rejoined Wanda and Maryanne, he leaned under the table to find his shearling coat, pulled from one of its pockets an unwrapped paperback of Goethe's *Die Leiden des Jungen Werthers*. "You'll pick it up," he said when I recalled my two inattentive years of high school German. Wanda's gift was a pair of saddle-brown cowboy boots with a tan-and-red filigree that I immediately began tracing with my index finger. Wade had helped her pick them out, she said. Maryanne gave me a deck of playing cards that I'm pretty sure she just happened to have in her purse.

Our plan had been to maintain a noncommittal buzz at the corner bar for an hour or so, then pile into Wade's car and claim my free half bottle of cheap champagne at Minneapolis's leading nightclub. This plan was losing its appeal, but I couldn't think up a better idea and figured that even a mild expression of ambivalence or discontentment would come off pathetically on my birthday, which really was proceeding nicely, only I no longer felt like being in a crowd. "Maybe we should just go back to your place and play records," Maryanne said, as if she'd sensed my change of heart. "We could have our *own* dance party," she added in the movie-voice of the kid impresario, then laughed her intoxicatingly sharp laugh.

Back at the apartment, I wiped the fog off my glasses while Wade looked for his bootjack. "Are we barefootin'?" he said. "Not me, pard, I'm wearin' ma new boots," I said, struggling to pull them on. "Bend your knees," he said. They fit just fine, were more comfortable than I'd expected. My twills weren't in perfect sync, as Wade needlessly pointed out, but I tucked them in the boots and earned compliments all around. Wade sat on the couch and rolled a couple numbers on a Judith Butler book, while Maryanne sang the chorus to "No Parking on the Dance Floor" in the standard robotic nasal and with accompanying gestures. Wade swayed slowly up from the sofa, holding a lit joint in each hand, his face to the floor, his hair like fresh blacktop descending a hill in the Coteau du Missouri. I scissored one of the joints from his fingers and took a long, swooning hit that seemed to relax my shoulders till they fused with my hips. Maryanne turned up the stereo.

I won't carry on about the songs we played. I've in fact just deleted a complete (and, I concede, largely falsified) set list from our utopian three-hour dance party. It should be clear and will become clearer that I'm no dogged opponent of inventories or nostalgia, though I'd like to think my nostalgia is defensibly more personal than historical, that my sentimentalities over the hour of my youth have to do with my youth, not its hour (though one can't separate oneself from history), but even if I could remember the full dance-party set list, and could then conquer the temptation to edit the list, deleting errors of taste or attributing them to one of the other dancer-deejays, inserting hipper or squarer selections, making the list broader, then narrower, then more worldly, then more provincial, then more multicultural, then more ethnocentric, then more masculine, then more feminine, then straighter, then queerer, then more timeless, then more period, even if I had magical recall and could overcome all obstacles of self-consciousness, I'd still be disinclined to trivialize this memorial polestar with a droning roll call of pop songs, which isn't to say I think the songs themselves were or are trivial, which is to say the opposite.

In Goethe's novel—I read it in translation years after Wade left Minneapolis—Werther says that when dancing with Lotte he was "no longer a person." That seems the best way to describe the transcendence I felt dancing that night. It was something like meditation, I think, though really I can't say, having not tried that. My mother Marleen meditated for a year or so in the figurative seventies (it was the eighties, but she wasn't always in her time, a trait she passed on to me, though not genetically). At any rate, I felt easy, unselfconscious, and transported that night. Voided. Maybe I skimmed the Christian ideal of Philippians 2:7, in which Jesus is said to have "emptied himself." The comparison is absurd and, obviously, blasphemous; I'm letting it stand only to humble myself for having thought it, and because I did feel blissfully emptied that night, some kind of just-Windexed mirror dumbly taking in everyone and everything. "Voided" was too strong, however; were that accurate, I doubt I'd remember having been voided.

Everyone danced better than they were. Wade Jaggered and Browned, spun and twisted, held out one leg, made circles with his calf, rotated an ankle, clapped and kicked, skated and snapped, punched and chopped the air, whirled his forearms around themselves like a lawnmower blade, like a Temptation (I was surprised when he told me he favored sweet-but-not-sugary Eddie Kendricks over salty-but-not-coarse David Ruffin). He pretended to dry dishes and dial rotary phones, did the Monkey and the Chicken and the Dog, all those animal dances, did none of the dances correctly, to the extent that I could judge, yet did all of them perfectly. He wasn't afraid to use his hips that night, and neither was I. Wanda did the same narrow sway all night, wore the same monotonously contented smile, never stopped dancing, even during songs I knew she disliked. She wore her moth-eaten sweater longer than seemed comfortable, but finally pulled it off midsway. Her tight, stop-sign-red tank top was sweat stained underneath her small breasts and around her lower spine, and when she turned away from me, her upper back looked beautiful, especially the shadow that sometimes formed between her pronounced shoulder blades. During one song I gently touched her back with my palms—really I was trying to just hover over her skin, but I couldn't be so exact while dancing and would often slip and make contact. Then I tried to touch only the fine hairs on her pale arms, never the skin, and the hairs seemed to reach out for my palms (manutropism, I believe this is called), until she herself reached out for me and we kissed for a long time. It felt like a goodbye kiss, and filled me with longing for routine kisses in the distant future.

Most of Maryanne's moves, like Wade's, were overtly referential, but never predominantly ironic. At one point she grabbed one of our mismatched dining-room chairs, a metal one with a blue vinyl seat-cushion marked with thin, wandering rips like rivers on a map, straddled it, and pushed it over and shook with a mock ecstatic frenzy that, as just indicated, wasn't really mock. Not long after she put her hands against the wall and walked in place, as on a treadmill, her camp shirt rising up her jeans, inviting one or more of us to imagine a police search, inviting me to kneel on the floor and run my hands up her thighs and ass and kiss the small of her back.

I refused this invitation, which hadn't really been made, and didn't dwell on my refusal. Our Saturnalia was hugely sexual, but not hugely lustful; when the four of us laid out our blankets and coats and prepared mutely for sleep on the hard living-room floor, there was some touching and neck kissing but no significant removal of clothes, unless some were removed after I nodded off, and I doubt that anyone felt stupid, ashamed, regretful, or even hungover the next morning, when the phonograph stylus was perhaps still stuck in the slick limbo between the last band and the paper label, and was thumping like a heart all night, though I doubt that as well, since my turntable back then was a nearly inerrant retractor.

THE ORIGIN OF THE WORLD (2)

O N THURSDAY, DECEMBER 19 OF 1991, I CAME HOME
from the closing shift somewhere around ten thirty,
carrying in each of my parka pockets a new CD for
myself, though I still hadn't done any Christmas shopping.
None marked my entrance. Wade was probably making deals at
the oversized corner bar. It was dark in the living room, dining
room, and kitchen, but a lot of light was coming from the bedroom. Wanda didn't answer when I called her name, but she was
home, naked and asleep in bed, lying on her back, her left knee
slightly bent, her right arm forming an L that finished above
her head. I lingered a moment in the doorway.

How to characterize her condition? She seemed in a state of
unconsciousness shallower than death but deeper than deep
sleep; I could see her breathing, but it was like the breathing of
a statue. The bedroom's overhead light was on, its lopsided
fixture basketing many dust-cushioned, capsized insects while
frost-shading two white bulbs of Wanda's preferred one hundred watts, hard glare-pears unchanged during Wade's renova-
tions. The light made her look even paler than she was, and
against that heightened paleness her acne-reddened face and a
few other faint lines of color, on which more soon, seemed particularly contrasting, something like the pink carnation pinned

to a white coat in the old Marty Robbins song, or, to exaggerate the contrast, like a crab-apple tree after a snowfall, menstrual blood on a new white sheet. I never liked how strongly Wanda's ribcage pushed at her skin, and often thought her stomach looked and felt weak and papery, but it looked beautiful that night, stretched like clay, her oval naval like a surprised mouth on a long face. Although she was naked or nude, not even partly covered by a blanket or sheet (recall how hot it was in our apartment during winter), from my doorway vantage she seemed somehow clothed. I held a blink as if to reset my vision. Once, not long ago, at a public swimming pool to which I'd escorted a friend and her toddler, my eyes were arrested by a woman's leg clad in fishnet stockings, odd poolside attire outside of pornography, and my penis rose out of my swimsuit's undernet. My doubletake, however, revealed that there was no woman at all, that a metal, mesh-top patio table had cast a retiform shadow on the bony legs of a prepubescent girl. Legs not unlike Wanda's, I suppose, though shorter. She—Wanda, not the poolside girl— stayed unstirred when I walked in the bedroom, in spite of my ka-thunking cowboy boots. Looking down on her, I saw that her skin was adorned with creases, marks, impressions, and other pinkened traces of rope. My later research suggested that these were more specifically traces of decorative knots such as a five-lead by seven-bight Turk's Head, or rather four traces of that knot, forming dimple-bracelets around each ankle and wrist. There was a fainter, complicated tortoiseshell pattern latticing her torso, vestigial I suspect of a presentational wrap derived from Japanese kinbaku or shibari bondage.

Wanda had often asked me to tie her up. But I've no feel for knots. Even a common square or reef knot can throw me off under certain conditions, and all of Wanda's instruction—"Right over left, left over right, makes a knot that's dandy and tight"—took a toll on the dom-sub histrionics and was no ally of my erection. She once suggested we seek out a volunteer "rigger," a man or woman who would come to our apartment and do the binding, then leave us alone, but this plan was never effected.

I leaned over to get a better look at the knot traces, and still Wanda didn't stir, even when I crawled gingerly on the bed and brought my eyes within inches of her vagina to see if I could spot drops or smears of semen. There was a small, not yet fully dried drop on her left thigh and, driven I think by some self-punishing impulse that at the time just seemed like unthinking curiosity, I licked it with a few kittenish brushstrokes. Wanda shifted but went on sleeping. I saw that our top sheet was heaped in a corner, and I positioned it to cover her partially and prettily, then went out for a riddled walk and to get a pint of ice cream.

I walked for quite a while. The plastic spoon I'd picked up at the convenience store snapped at its first dig, so I simply bit into the ice cream (I liked how my teeth marks looked under the lampposts). When I could no longer reach the ice cream by that method, I scooped it out with my mittened paw, and by the end of the carton was able to pound or squeeze-pour it directly into my mouth. I had fantasized before about watching Wanda in bed with another man, or with a group of men and women, but the others in these fantasies always had the nebulous faces of film extras or dream strangers. Now the image of Wade's scrunched face made me flinch and cringe. I tried to concentrate solely on the ice cream, how it was both warm and cool, smooth and sticky, but these thoughts were sexual too and brought me back to Wade walking around our bed with his hard-on and rope.

Years later I lived for a while in an attic apartment into which bats often squeezed their way. Usually they would announce their presence in the middle of the night, as I lay in bed trying to fall asleep, or sometimes the sound of one flying overhead would wake me. Always there'd be a period, maybe an instant, maybe several minutes, in which I'd tell myself that it wasn't a bat disturbing the air, that I'd heard or imagined something else, that I wouldn't have to get up to open a screen and wait for the bat to find its way out, or squeamishly trap it under a salad bowl, then slowly slide a cookie sheet under its resisting little rubbery feet. But of course it always was a bat.

When I got back home, Wade was asleep on the sofa, and all the marks and traces had faded from Wanda's body. She sighed when I got into bed. I brought none of this up the next morning, Friday, December 20, and neither Wade nor Wanda acted unusually.

Also that Friday, I came home from work at about six thirty to find Wade's records gone, or largely gone—a moment later I saw that twenty to thirty of his LPs and about half as many forty-fives were leaning against my tippy stereo stand. Wanda was out that evening and I was glad to be alone, hoped my solitude would last a few hours. Armies of dust mites floated into my nostrils as I flipped through the records. I put on a warped Gary Stewart forty-five and was singing along with the fade-out ("Born to lose, dying to win!") when Wade came in. "Y'all"—he startled me—"have a beautiful art deco post office." He was leaving the stack of duplicate or otherwise unneeded records for me to cherish, sell, or throw away, he said. "So you're leaving?" I said. "Tomorrow morning," he said. "Berlin via Amsterdam. I thought maybe I could take you out to dinner." I didn't feel like eating. I felt as if he were gripping my insides.

As our slices were being warmed up at the pizza-and-gyro place near our apartment, Wade reminisced about Bey's Food Host, where he'd cooked for a few years in the late sixties and early seventies. From my preschool days till we left Enswell in '83, Bey's was my favorite restaurant. Almost always I'd order a D-Luxe Frenchy, a cheese sandwich dipped in eggy batter, deep fried, and coated with crumby Corn Flakes. My mother and I didn't go out to eat often, but when we did, we went to Bey's, and later, when Wade, my mother, and I were a short-term family, we went there most Thursday nights. Bey's was one of those restaurants at which patrons, booth patrons at least, got to order by telephone. Next to the booth phones were dwarf jukeboxes. Most of the restaurant's customers preferred the booths to the half-dozen or so tables, cleared of novelties, though certain imaginative and unspoiled children, when the booths were full, entertained themselves at the tables by staging football games between sugar packets, white versus pink, pink versus pale blue. Bey's had glass walls, a white PVC floor, and orange vinyl booths. It was just explained that the booths at Bey's were more popular than the tables, but some men, especially groups of older workingmen, would request a table so they could spend more time with the waitress. This, Wade told me as we carried our red cafeteria trays back to our table in Minneapolis, was especially true when my biological mother Martha Dickson was a Bey's cashier-waitress. Her short stint at Bey's probably began in July 1969, he said, and ended there as well, or in early August, but either way partly coincided with Wade's longish stint.

Previously I'd been told that Wade had once met Martha at a party but hadn't really known her. I'd never been told they were brief colleagues. "Does my mother know this?" I said.

"Marleen?" Wade asked.

"Well, yeah. The other one would know 'cause you say she was there," I said.

"Okay, yeah."

"Yeah what?"

"Yeah Marleen came to know that Martha and I worked together."

Wade told me that Martha was a beautiful woman, as I'd heard before and as I could see from the faded instant photograph he took out of his shearling jacket and laid next to my tray. I'd never seen a picture of Martha. I'd asked my mother Marleen to see one, but she'd never taken or asked for one, which from my perspective always seemed selfish and short-sighted. I picked up and stared at the picture. Martha had lively eyes; a dimply, candid smile; two moles on her right cheek marking a shaky diagonal line like pips on a preindustrial domino; dark brown, uncommonly horizontal and uniform eyebrows, almost like Dickinsonian dashes; and long, brown hair, lighter than her eyebrows, parted slightly to the right and tied up in back, though there was a maverick, S-shaped tuft falling over her right cheek. Wade said the photo was taken in the fall of '69, though he couldn't say where it was taken. "Outside somewhere," he said, as if that weren't clear. Martha usually wore her hair up, he told me, and sometimes the maverick tuft would graze her unlipsticked lips and she'd banish it with a puff.

"What color were her eyes?" I said.

"Green."

"Green?"

"Yup."

"They don't look green," I said, bringing the photo closer to my own brown eyes.

"Well, it's an old Polaroid."

There was definitely something wrong with her blouse, I noticed.

"But they were brown. I remember now they were brown."

"You two went out?" I said.

"Well, eventually," Wade said. "We didn't talk much at the restaurant, just said hello a few times. She walked out in the middle of what I'd guess was her ninth shift, still untying her apron as she opened the door to leave. I remember she draped the apron over a newspaper box before she got into her car. I can't remember the headline her apron covered up. That'd be a nice touch, don't you think?"

"What would?"

"For me to remember the hidden headline."

"I guess."

"It was an elegant gesture, her draping the apron over the box. She draped it delicately, made sure it was balanced. She could have dropped it on the ground, you know, something contemptuous like that. But that wasn't her way. We all watched her through the glass. It was quiet when she left, midafternoon, just a few customers around. I'd been doing some cleanup, the prep cook was reading *Road & Track*, the manager was at one of the tables filling out the ledger, plaintively whistling 'It Was a Very Good Year.' He had a soft, warbling whistle. Martha's exit was apparently unprovoked is what I'm saying, seemed wholly spontaneous. This pizza is truly subpar. Then a few weeks later I found her playing the gimbri under an oak tree in Ruyak Park. Up till then I'd only seen her in her uniform, so I didn't know for sure if she was in the hippie sector or not; in the park, though, she was wearing bell-bottoms and one of her embroidered blouses, really loose in the right shoulder but nearly as tight in the left shoulder as an inflated sphygmomanometer cuff."

"What's that, some kind of drug thing?"

"No, no, a blood-pressure meter," Wade said, pantomiming a nurse squeezing that big black olive. "There were a few dollars and some change in a gray Samsonite suitcase Martha had in front of her, but probably she'd put the scratch there herself, since money in tip receptacles is said to be suggestive. Do you think that's true?"

"Do I think your story's true?"

"No, do you think money in tip receptacles is really suggestive? I might buy a cheap guitar and do some street performing on Unter den Linden, at least till I get my first check from the station. It'd be cheaper to buy the guitar here and take it on the plane. But I doubt I'll have time to buy one."

"Probably not."

"You wanna sell me your acoustic?"

"Not really."

"I'd give you five hundred bucks for it."

"It's not worth that much."

"It is to me."

"Yeah, I don't know."

"Well, think about it." Wade got up to refill our waters. There was only one other customer in the restaurant, a muscular collegian in sweats. The regular posters were on the wall: the photo of the workmen lunching on the RCA Building girder,

Ruth Orkin's shot of the American girl about to be gang-raped by Florentines. A decade later, the restaurant's Middle Eastern (pardon the vagueness) owners would feel obligated to hang a WTC commemorative poster as well. "But anyway," Wade said, sitting back down, "I added a dollar to Martha's suitcase, and she smiled, still plucking the gimbri's slack strings, drumming on its body with her thumb, swaying as she played, her embroidered blouse swaying too, where it could. All this swaying had something of the hypnotic effect the music was aiming at. I watched her awhile. Then I said, 'What do you call that thing?' and by dinner she was living in my apartment."

"Just like that," I said.

"Just like that. Would you consider a trade? I'd give you my car in exchange for your acoustic and maybe two hundred bucks."

"I don't really need a car."

"An adult should have a car."

"I don't even know how to drive stick."

"Well, Jesus, an hour in a parking lot will solve that. The insurance payments are nothing on this car; even for an ephebe like you it'll be no big deal."

"How much do you pay?"

"What? I don't have car insurance! Look, I'm selling you the car for a lot less than it's worth."

"I'm confused," I said. "Who gives who the two hundred bucks?"

"You give me the guitar and two hundred, and I give you the car. It's a nice ride. It's not the sport model but it's still a good handler."

"It seems to pull to the right."

"That's easy enough to neutralize. It's been very reliable."

"How long have you had it?"

"I've had it awhile."

"But how long?"

"So Martha had grown up in North Dakota," Wade continued after further negotiations, "first in Pennsburg, then in Enswell, where she—"

"Pennsburg? I thought it was . . . Wheeler."

"Wheeler? There's no Wheeler," he said.

"What do you mean, no Wheeler?"

"There's no town in North Dakota called Wheeler."

"You know every town in North Dakota?"

"Huff, Voltaire, Napoleon, Wimbledon, Dazey, Tuttle, Hoople, Milton, Cannon Ball, Zap, Gackle, Mott—"

"Okay."

"No, I don't know every town in North Dakota. But she was born in Pennsburg. She lost her virginity there at fourteen, underneath some kind of graveyard fruit tree. And then she'd been Enswell High's second prettiest cheerleader. Her parents died in the middle of her first year at Northern Illinois."

"Yeah, I know about that."

"Do you know about her brothers and sisters?"

"Not much."

"The firstborn died in Vietnam. The sister I think was crazy. Then there's another brother; I met him once."

"What was he like?"

"Fat."

"That's all? Fat?"

"Really fat." Wade held out his arms and puffed out his cheeks. "Not instantly likable." He took three quick bites of his second slice, resumed talking before he'd finished chewing. "[Incomprehensible] the park, Martha told me she had no fixed address. That was the phrase she used: 'no fixed address.' 'I haven't had a fixed address in two years,' she said. 'But I've had a few broken ones.' Our first months together were a lot of fun. She was a wild seed. I was no virgin, but up till then I'd only had meat-and-potatoes sex, sometimes hold the potatoes. But Martha was wild. She'd sit on my face and read highbrow pornography—to herself. Usually on my face she'd read poems out of a notebook, not her poems, just stuff she'd transcribed. Whenever we'd visit a friend she'd look around for books of poetry, or a magazine that had a poem or two—even the *Stone* published poems back then—and then she'd pick a poem at random and start copying it into her notebook. Once at a friend's house she opened to a long poem and sat there for an hour transcribing. Browning. That's how I turned on to him. You ever read Wanda's paper on Browning?"

"I've skimmed it."

"Better work than I did in college," Wade said. "'All my term papers, misspelled and overdue,'" he sang, "'My Smith Corona had a broken *W*.' As far as I know, Bolling was the first to use *term paper* in a c&w song."

"Probably," I said.

"Also the first to near-rhyme *tractor* with *dactyl*."

"Doesn't he rhyme *dactyl* with *infractor*? 'And I never knew the difference 'tween an anapest and a dactyl / ooh ooh ooh I'm the infractor.'"

"Oh yeah, you're right. But there's a *tractor* in there too."

"Sure, first verse."

"It's cool that you know Bolling's stuff so well."

"Thanks."

He took a swig of water and some of it dripped down his chin onto his cowboy shirt. "When transcribing, Martha never noted the poet. She even covered up the poet's name when she was transcribing, with a coaster or a stapler or anything handy. So she could rarely attribute the poems in her notebook, or even give them a general time or place. Like the Carters sang, 'You may forget the singer, but don't forget this song.' That's how Martha operated. I was a singer-not-the-song type, so that challenged me."

"I can't figure out poetry," I said.

"You will eventually. I tried to write some in college, and a bit afterwards. For a while I wrote 'em on the insides of match-boxes. That was my hook. On one of my poems, not a match-box one, a paper one, the prof wrote, 'You might do more with simile.' So my next poem started: 'The lemon languished on the table like a yellow lime.'"

I didn't want to laugh, but did.

"Martha mostly recited out of that notebook, but sometimes she'd set the notebook aside and pick up something else. A lot of times it was Bataille's *Story of the Eye,* sometimes Verlaine or Rimbaud, or one of their collaborations—she probably read *Sonnet du trou du cul* on my face two dozen times. She'd always announce the title and then start reading silently. The first time, I pushed her partway off me and said, 'Why don't you read it aloud?' 'Well, you won't be able to hear with me sitting on your face,' she said, and then got right back on her perch." Wade laughed loudly, drawing a pizza chef's glance. "Martha was an artist. She had no artistic talent as conventionally understood, but she had the spirit of art. She was the one who turned me on to nonart, to the art of living artistically as a nonartist, to the heroism of refusing to make art-art while every minute making nonart, art that has nothing to do with grasping for status or vaulting for glory. She was the one I told you about who claimed to be Jo Hiffernan's great-great-granddaughter." Wade got up to buy a couple pieces of baklava, and I stared without focusing at the soda machine. "Martha and I took a short road trip nearly every week," he suddenly resumed. "She had friends all over the state and in a few bordering ones. Those were fun for a while. She was a relisher and surpriser in bed, and on couches and floors when we stayed with her friends from all over."

"Uh-huh."

"She didn't think that guests should forgo sex just 'cause they'd been billeted in a living room, a living room that one of the hosts might easily peer into en route to the bathroom. Once in Jamestown, at one of her ex-boyfriends'—he was married at the time of the visit—I was sure I heard creaking and a voyeuristic quiet from the hallway. Over breakfast the next morning I looked at the hosts' faces, from the man's to the woman's and back again, trying to figure out who'd spied us the night before. One of them would have seen Martha illuminated by a torchy, sheet-muted lamp, naked except for her socks— they were my socks, in fact, long athletic socks with the stripes. Martha had the most gorgeous, round ass; she would've been hovering over me, alternately flopping her tits onto my face like car-wash mops onto a windshield." He paused. "A lot of those moments with Martha have lingered for over twenty years now in my arsenal of images autoérotique. They've degenerated in interesting ways from overuse. They'll be there forever, I hope, always degenerating, but regenerating too. Sex is a long-term investment in memory, you know; all the smart rich people have mixed portfolios."

I didn't say anything.

"Every bed is clothed in securities blankets. It'd be better, after sex, to talk of being saved rather than spent."

"Are you giving me advice?"

"So Martha made a modest income selling embroidered blouses at shops that took consignment items, and, because she was so persuasive, at shops that didn't normally take consignment items. She had a bunch of shirts hanging near the dartboard at the Sportsman's Taproom in Wahpeton, for example. She'd sell them in parking lots before concerts, or out of her car. She was charismatic, modeled the blouses auspiciously—well, on one hand her wearing them made their lapses in craftsmanship more apparent, but on the other it was easy to overlook those flaws with her wearing them, since she was beautiful and looked good in white. They didn't sell well off the rack, though, sewn as they were with such an unsteady hand and absent mind. She must have had some other source of income, is what I thought. She seemed to have money—I never figured out where she stashed it—but she had it for lamps and books and a beaded seat-cover for her car, driver's side only. For toilet paper and milk she had less money. She drank inconsiderately large glasses of milk as a soporific, often finishing or all but finishing the carton late at night, then not apologizing the next morning. I remember once how she watched me pour this teasing tablespoon of milk over my Grief-Nuggets, and watched as I grudgingly ate with my fingers before pouring the soggy rest back in the box, spilling lots of them in the process. And as I was sweeping the cereal onto a newspaper, she said—with that sort of hostile sham innocence children use, not sarcasm, something else—she said"—and here Wade assumed a cruel, coquettish voice—"'Are we out of melk?'"

"Couldn't you tell there was hardly any milk left when you picked up the carton?"

"Well, I was still waking up."

"It's not like you've been so great about picking up milk and stuff while you've been crashing with Wanda and me."

"Let's not derail my narrative with hypocrisy charges, okay? I'm just trying to tell you how I felt. So early on I complained to my friends about these sort of domestic irritants, hamming it up really, 'cause I was proud to have such adult grievances. But after a while I couldn't keep myself from being sincerely pissed off over her quirks and venial sins. Vis-à-vis the milk, for example, there was her freeloading, her selfishness, but also the fact that she pronounced the word to rhyme with *elk* or *Welk,* as in Lawrence—you may have noticed my unorthodox pronunciation a minute ago. I guess it also rhymed with one of the lower-case *w[h]elks,* like the *welk* that means 'to droop or wither.' That shouldn't have bothered me, the way she pronounced *milk,* but it did. She had this self-belittling yet cunning schoolgirlish voice, cutesy but sharp. It wasn't a grown woman's voice. Sometimes it was hard to take her seriously. 'That's right, Honey, cry those melky cock-tears right on into me': something she actually said. I almost lost my hard-on—it nearly welked. Also, she still called lunch 'dinner' and dinner 'supper'—and that's fine, I'm not snobby about that, maybe even charmed by it, but it was suspicious, because when she wanted to she could subdue her dialect, you know, hammer in prairie shibboleths like they were loose, sock-ripping nails in floorboards, and I thought she sometimes trotted out and accentuated a few rusticisms self-consciously, I mean in a self-conscious way I didn't like. These were trivialities, obviously; I had bigger complaints. I thought she was getting too selfish and aggressive and masturbatory in bed. One night I told her I didn't like it when she bit my nipples. She said, 'I'm not doing it for you.' She told me there were things I did in bed that she didn't like, but wouldn't tell me what those things were. And there was other stuff. When we met, she seemed to share my atheism and my broader skepticism about hocus-pocus of all kinds. But after a while she revealed a sort of syncretic spiritualism, part Eastern, part psychological, the typical stuff for the time. She was intelligent, very intelligent, but had indiscriminate taste, especially in books and ideas."

"So was Martha the same one who liked Mingus and the Cryan' Shames?" I said.

"Yeah, you caught me. Earlier that stuff just sort of came up, and I didn't think you were ready to hear everything right then."

"So there was no Rae Morgan."

"Morgenson, Rae Morgenson. No, there was no such person, but wasn't that good? It took me a sec to come up with a name, but then, wham: Rae Morgenson."

I looked down at the table.

"When I was with Martha, she was into this stupid book of marshmallow psychology by some quickly forgotten member of the blackguard Jungle, some . . . I can't remember the name of the book or its author. I only skimmed a few chapters."

"How do you know it was so stupid, then?"

"Well yeah, yeah, I don't. When I first met Martha, I idolized her. She was so cool. She'd walked out on Bey's in that cool way, with the apron on the newspaper box. She seemed so inner-directed. Most of the girls I'd dated before Martha were simple, but Martha was complicated, maybe even a genius, I thought. So I got disillusioned when I figured out she was just like the rest of us smarties, kind of sharp here, kind of a dupe there. The worst was this poet she was into, who wrote confessional and I guess you'd say ecological-vitalist poetry—guy we saw read in St. Paul, D. Michael Tauber."

"Really?"

"Yeah. Back then he was this bandannaed picaro, poet, and odd-jobber, just barely out of his teens. He'd ridden all over North America, had lovers everywhere, Martha among them most likely. Her smudgy copy of his chapbook—*Crossbar*—was inscribed: 'To my florid nightingale.' Pretty dumb, huh? I was no great judge of poetry back then, but I could tell Tauber's poems were false. Martha loved Blake, Rimbaud, Dickinson, Yeats. It wasn't so hard to see what the Yeats fan might see in D. Michael Tauber—Adonic calves?—but what did the D. Michael Tauber fan see in Yeats?"

"I don't know," I said.

"Kooky spiritualism is one answer, but that wasn't it. She understood the Yeats poems on many levels, many of them beyond my reach, though of course things like that can't really be measured, and a lot of Yeats's poems can't be understood in any commonplace way. Mandelstam said that when poetry can be paraphrased, the sheets haven't been rumpled: poetry hasn't spent the night. Or even taken a nap, I guess. So I'm not talking about understanding in that Boy Scout, hermeneutical way, sucking the juice out of a poem like poison from a snake bite. I'm talking about something mysterious. So finally I told Martha I was surprised to see her so into Tauber's poetry, since it didn't seem to meet the standards of the masters she knew so well. It didn't even wave at those standards from a distance, I said. I was a real prick back then. 'That's just your opinion,' she said. There was nothing to do with that. One of the ways Martha punished me was to ward off debate by playing the naïf. When I confronted her further about Tauber, she swore their relationship was 'Platonic,' that its story began and ended with an all-night colloquy after a Crow concert in Grand Forks months before I met her. At the end of the argument, she swept a pop bottle off the table and called me a 'cliché.' I was willing to concede that point, though I thought sweeping the bottle off the table was kind of cliché too. And I still thought she was fucking Tauber."

"Tauber was living in Enswell?"

"No, no, he was a wanderer, but by that time Martha'd started taking road trips on her own, leaving on short notice to storm concerts and festivals in unimaginable Fargos, checking in with her far-flung consignees, whistle-dropping in on old friends, no doubt arriving right around suppertime. I didn't remember Tauber's chapbook being part of her shack-up dowry, so I figured she'd met and fucked him while we were together, on one of her solo tours."

"But maybe just one time, right?"

"Possibly."

"Well, you said 'fucking' like it was a regular thing."

"It might not have been regular."

"Where was she living before she moved in with you?"

"In her car, she said. But I don't know. So she started taking off a lot. In some ways I was relieved when she left. But I got lonely, too, couldn't concentrate. Then her trips got longer, four or five days instead of two." Wade shifted in his seat and reached down to unbutton his tight Erizeins. "Finally she took off and never came back. I kept the dozen or so blouses she left behind."

"You don't still have any, do you?" I said.

"I wish."

Some silence.

"I guess it's good to know . . . I mean"—I was faltering. "When exactly did you say you were going out?"

He didn't answer that question. "She didn't come back to me," he said, "but she did come back to Enswell, about a year later, the next summer. By then she was married."

"Married?"

"Yeah."

"She wasn't married."

"Yes she was. And she had a little boy."

"Me, you're saying?"

"Right. Once I saw her pushing you through Piggly Wiggly. She told me about her husband. He wrote hyperviolent, pornographic Westerns, had written several of them, she said, kind of rubbing it in, since I could never finish anything beyond a few lousy poems."

"What was the husband's name?"

"I can't remember."

"But he was a novelist."

"Well, he sold annuities for Prudential, but yeah, he'd supposedly written novels too. One of them had come out on a small press under a nom de plume."

"She told you all this at Piggly Wiggly?"

"We talked awhile. And I picked up some stuff via the grapevine."

"Was she a wreck?"

"Not really. Maybe a bit stressed, new mom stuff."

"But not strung out?"

"I wouldn't say so."

"This was summer of '71 then, right?"

After a pause: "That sounds right."

"Well, my mom said that Martha was a mess by then, like constantly tripping and doing laced dope and all this shit. Hair a mess, smelly."

"She wasn't like that."

"What do you mean?"

"That just wasn't where she was at," Wade said.

"Not even into drugs?"

"Well, she wasn't a teetotaler. Sure, she did drugs."

I poked my remaining baklava with a plastic fork.

"What did I look like?" I said.

"What did *you* look like? I don't know. Like a baby. You looked old enough to have been conceived when Martha and I were together, but that doesn't say much about paternity, and I'm a poor judge of the sort of ages reckoned in months."

"Well, I have a birth certificate. It's not like my birthday was just made up."

"Where were you born, anyway?"

"Butte, Montana."

"Butte, huh. What was she doing there?"

"I don't know!"

"The annuities guy was from Pocatello, but maybe he was living in Butte. You ever been to Butte?"

"Well, I guess so; I just said I was born there."

"Happenin' town if you know where to look."

"I don't want to talk about Butte."

"We don't have to talk about Butte," Wade said. He was using a calm, therapist's tone now. "A few months after I saw Martha at the Piggly Wiggly, I heard from Karl Tobreste—"

"Karl knew her?"

"Somewhat. So I heard from Karl that Martha's baby had died of Niemann-Pick disease."

"Niemann-Pick disease?"

"It might've been Werdnig-Hoffmann disease."

"What are you saying, that I'm a ghost?"

"Just listen. For a year or so, I saw her around town from time to time. She seemed to be holding it together. She was still married."

"You don't remember the guy's name?"

"I remember he had blond hair and was short, maybe five six. Dimpled chin. I only saw him once. He was wearing cutoffs."

"What's Niemann-Pick disease?"

"It might have been Werdnig-Hoffman. So sometime in '72, they moved away, to Portland, I think, maybe Eugene, Spokane. So that was that, and then I met you and Marleen."

"What do you mean, *then?* You mean later?"

"Yeah, not right then. Later. At the house on Queal."

"And I was dead."

"Just listen. There's no call for cleverness. You remember that first night, when we had a little cookout in the backyard and ate on the porch? That night Marleen told me she was a Northern Illinois alumna, just in the course of small talk she told me that, and right away I brought up Martha. Marleen said, 'It's a big school,' as in, *What of it?*"

"She denied knowing her?"

"Not in so many words. She said that NIU is a big school. And it is."

"Well, I already knew about Martha by then. My mom never kept her secret from me."

"And that was good of her," Wade said.

"Except she never told me about husbands and diseases and all this."

Wade went on: "Later—I think I was complaining about a really disgusting lunch I'd had—and she told me about a friend of hers whose dad, whenever he didn't like his wife's cooking, would after a few bites scrape the rest of his food onto the wife's plate. I gave Marleen a real squinting look when she related this second-hand anecdote, because I'd already heard it, several times, from Martha. It was how she summarized her dad, who I gather was a real ass. So I looked into Marleen's eyes and said, 'You heard that from Martha Dickson.' And she paused for a while, then said, 'It can't be unique behavior.' That's no doubt true, but she was flustered. 'You did know her!' I said. She kept on denying it, and it turned into this big thing. I started sleeping in the basement again. This was right before Bolling's first show at the EMA."

"So right before you left."

"Well, yeah. The night before the concert, Marleen knocked on my door. I'd just gotten back from Oran's. She must've been waiting for me to get back. When I opened the door, she was crying. She said she'd tell me the whole story, because she wanted to be with me, but that for varied reasons, including legal ones, I had to swear to secrecy. I agreed, and until now I've kept my promise. I've spent a lot of time thinking about this, you know, debating whether or not to tell you." Wade held his cup to his mouth and tapped the bottom to dislodge some ice. "She told me how she'd met Martha at a sit-in at the University of Chicago, how they became fast friends, how Martha moved out of some sort of commune and into Marleen's dorm room."

"I know all that."

"And then the news of Mr. and Mrs. Dickson's death reached DeKalb after an unseemly delay. And Martha left for Enswell the next morning."

"Right."

"Yeah, so Marleen didn't hear from Martha for over two years, didn't expect to hear from her ever again. Then one weekend day, Martha called your grandparents in Palatine. Sorry: What was your grandpop's name again?"

"Dick," I said. "Richard."

"Marleen's sitting in her folks' living room, reading *Life* or something, and Dick says, 'Well, I've certainly always proceeded as if I were Marleen's dad, heh, heh. And what's more, she's living at home for a spell and can come directly to the phone.'"

"He didn't talk like that," I said.

"But something along those lines," Wade said. "Marleen came to the phone and Dick went out to mow the lawn. Martha was doing well, she told Marleen. She'd started up a small clothing line. She hadn't gotten into any of the boutiques in Chicago yet, but that would come soon, she said. Kind of talking herself up, but unpersuasively. Then she told Marleen how she'd gotten married a few months before. 'To an actuary!' she said, like *who woulda thunk it.*"

"I thought you said he sold annuities or whatever."

"He did. But when Marleen told me the story, it was actuary. I didn't correct her. It's obnoxious to correct people's stories. Martha kept her update short, I guess, only asked Marleen a few general questions. There was a lull in the conversation, Marleen told me, and then Martha explained that along with an actuary and a thriving small business, she had a baby boy, a sweet, quiet, easy, handsome baby. 'Well, that's great,' Marleen said, 'he sounds wonderful.' Martha said, 'He's absolutely amazing. You look in his eyes, and, I don't know, it's just, there it is, the music of the spheres.'" Wade was again imitating what he said was Martha's wheat-bred singsong, girlish yet slightly edgy. "'Wow,' Marleen said," Wade said. "'Yeah, it changes your life,' Martha said. 'So I've heard,' Marleen said. And Martha: 'He's just had a nice melk supper, so he's sleeping now, and I—"

"Why are you like dramatizing this phone call?" I said. "You can't possibly know how it went."

"Marleen told me how it went," Wade said.

"Why would she tell it to you like that, like a play?"

"I don't know why she told it to me like that," Wade said. "That's how she wanted to tell the story. It was her story."

I dropped my head for an instant, then looked back up at Wade.

"'I wish I could see him,' Marleen told Martha over the phone," Wade went on. "'Oh, I hope you'll be able to,' Martha said. Then there was another pause, and Martha said, 'But you have to be in the right place for that change, you know. We're still young. I know I don't feel like a grownup yet. Mike's older but he's a kid at heart.'"

"That was the husband's name, Mike?" I said.

"No, I just threw that in there," Wade said. "I really don't remember his name. So Martha said, 'I could sure use more time to run my business. And Mike's incredibly busy.'"

"If his name's not really Mike, would you stop calling him Mike?"

"I'm starting to think it *was* Mike," Wade said, and then in Martha's alleged voice: "'And we'd like to do more camping—pretty rugged camping, you know, and some rafting. Mike's heavy into white-water rafting. Some of those rocks would split a baby's head right in two, like Solomon.' 'Well, Solomon didn't actually go through with that,' Marleen said. 'But you know what I mean,' Martha said. 'And we'd just like to go to a movie on impulse every so often without having to find a sitter. It's ludicrous what these sluts want you to pay them just to sit and watch the boob tube, and as you know, my folks aren't around to help, me being an orphan, all but disowned by my surviving siblings.'"

"This is how Martha talked?" I said.

"This is how she talked in Marleen's story," Wade said.

"Did my grandpa talk like you had him talking in Marleen's story? 'Cause I don't remember him talking that way—'for a spell' and all that."

"Maybe he talked like that with his daughter's friends, you know, stressing the avuncular in some innocently flirty way," Wade said.

"But when my mom started talking as Martha, did it sound like Martha to you?"

"It didn't sound quite like the Martha I knew, but it wasn't so far off from the one I talked to at Piggly Wiggly. So I guess Martha went on for a while like that about her hard luck, then said, 'We want our weekends back, Marleen.'"

"Our weekends back?" I said.

Wade laughed. "Marleen repeated that in the exact same incredulous way. Nature/nurture, huh? Except I suppose Marleen said, '*Your* weekends.' Then Marleen said, 'Hey, I can't imagine having kids now. Christ, I'm back living at home.' Martha's voice got more serious: 'Marleen, I'd like you to imagine it.' 'I'm not sure exactly what you're driving at,' Marleen said. Martha said, 'Where are you now? Are you someplace private?' Marleen said, 'I'm alone. My dad's mowing the lawn.' Martha said, 'Is it a gas mower or a push?' 'Gas.' 'Okay,' Martha said, 'that should be pretty private. Marleen, I need to just be completely open here. I know we haven't kept in close touch, but I'm not just blowing smoke when I say you're the most amazing woman I've ever met, the most intelligent, most beautiful, most deep—deepest. The instant I saw you in the back of that car, I thought, *Now here is a great soul. Here is someone who knows what matters.*'" Wade paused. "So then there's a beat," he said.

"A heartbeat?" I said.

"No, a little pause," Wade said. "'Listen,' Martha said, 'Mike and I are looking for a permanent foster mother. We're prepared to offer three thousand dollars, cash on the barrelhead, for what we understand to be an immense commitment. We'd offer more if we could. But that's our savings. Our savings is actually a few dollars less, but Mike thought we should use a round number. That's one of the things I love about Mike: he rounds up.'"

"You're making all this up," I said.

"I'm not," Wade said.

"This is so fucking cruel of you," I said. "Everything you do is selfish and cruel."

"This is the story Marleen told me," Wade said, reaching out for my hand. "I'm telling you the story she told me."

"Martha was a fucking burnout," I said. I was crying. "It's the kind of shit you think when you're fucked up, selling a baby. That's all it is, just burnout bullshit."

"Well, Marleen reacted like you are. 'Jesus, Martha,' she said, 'that's not even funny.' But after another minute or so, she knew Martha was serious. Marleen asked how many potential foster parents Martha had propositioned so far. You know, in a cool, sarcastic tone. 'You're the only,' Martha said. 'You're the only. It struck me like lightning that you were the one.'" Wade was moving into a more earnest, womanly voice for Martha. "'As a matter of fact, it struck me twice,' Martha said," he said. "'I was still in the hospital, and the little guy was nursing, and I said—I don't think I said it aloud, but I said, *I don't know who your father is, but Marleen Deskin is your mother. That's why I had this baby, for Marleen.* I set that thought aside. It's crazy, I said. But then it hit me again, just last night, a totally external voice, your voice. It didn't sound like your voice, but it was. This baby needs you, Marleen. Needs you, needs you, needs you. And you need him.'

"Marleen hung up in disgust, not quickly, not slammingly—slowly, but in disgust. Three days later, Martha called to apologize. It was a highly emotional time . . . , she told Marleen. But by then Marleen had given the proposal more thought. And a week after that she drove to Enswell in one of the smaller U-Hauls." Wade paused for a few seconds and then began to rhapsodize: "The wheat fields, the sunflower fields, barley, flax, wheat, wheat, wheat, the stretches of tree-lined train tracks und die große Grassteppe, the hay bales, the clotheslines, the junk-yards, the peeling barns, the grain elevators, the Plains sunflow-ers yellowing the roadside, the little bluestem empurpling the prairie, the lone tree in the middle of a field, rough and spindly like a Giacometti sculpture, the seductive hills as the western edge of the Drift Prairie foreshadows the Missouri Plateau—"

"Can you stop?"

"Marleen of course was no stranger to agrarian landscapes, but rural Illinois is comparatively rather dull, and as she got closer to Enswell, everything seemed beautiful, romantic, and authentic, and when she got to Enswell itself, the city looked green and hearty, antisuburban, with squat boxes and gray rec-tangles rising without ostentation above the trees, cars muscling down Foster in and out of the valley."

I noticed the pizza chefs were staring at us.

"The next day, Marleen struggled with the faulty left rear wheel of your little stroller. 'That's the boing of a distant diving board,' she told the baby you, 'and that's the squeak of a swing set, and that's the chirp of a sparrow, on which His eye is said to be on.' And three days later, she told me, she finally got you to drink the formula. And a month later she rented the two-bedroom next to the church." Wade handed me a napkin. "Over a year passed before she told her parents, who missed her, you know, 'tremendously,' who didn't understand why they were being 'shut out.' So finally she told them she'd adopted a baby, a baby a friend couldn't take care of, because the friend was a druggie who later od'd. The story she told you."

"So Martha's still alive?" I said.

"Probably," Wade said.

"What do you mean, probably?"

"Just to infer from life-expectancy stats."

"But you don't know where she is?"

"For a while I guess it was Portland, or Eugene, Spokane, Seattle, like I said. Maybe Aberdeen. Marleen never heard from her again. An unqualified severing of contact was part of the agreement. It was a handshake agreement, but nonetheless." He paused awhile. "The last time I saw Martha, though, was Pittsburgh in '85. Bolling was playing this little club, and she came to the show, stood right up front smiling at us the whole time. I played a few flashy runs for her until Bolling gave me a gubernatorial look. She hung out with us after the show."

Wade reached into the breast pocket of his coat, draped over his chair, and took out another instant photo.

"What's that bank in Owatonna have to do with any of this?" I said.

"Oh, that's the wrong photo. Here," he said, replacing the shot of the National Farmers' Bank with one of Bolling, his bearish right arm around a woman's shoulders. They were in a skuzzy dressing room, just a few spots of black wall showing under the posters and graffiti. The woman did seem to be Martha. Her hair was permed and dyed a wheaty blond. She was wearing a yellow skirted suit with a broad-shouldered jacket, a silk blouse, and a pearl necklace. I compared the older and more recent Polaroids. It was the same face. In the later picture, Martha's clothes and the Lone Justice poster over her head fixed the date at no earlier than 1985. "I took two photos like this," Wade said. "One to give to Martha, and another for me. She'd come to the club from work. She'd been working late."

"Where'd she work?" I said.

"I can't remember. Some company."

I studied the pictures a bit more and then put them in my jacket pocket before Wade could take them back. It was hard to tell when he was telling the truth, as I said before, but this time I felt strongly that the essence of his story was true, even if some of the details were fabricated.

"The main thing Marleen stressed when she told me the story was how much she loved you," Wade said, "how Martha's vision must have been true. You know how I told you about the girlfriend who believed in booksong, that you have to develop a 'mystic's ear' for which book is calling to you?"

"Yeah."

"That was Martha. I made fun of her spiritual leanings, you know, and I wondered why she was sometimes called by what I took to be inferior books. But she really did have that mystical quality."

Wade was still holding my sweating hand across the table.

"I resisted her booksong idea for a long time. But then one day—this was after Martha and I broke up—I was at the library, and I was stopped in my tracks by the spine of Augustine's *Confessions*. It was an unassuming spine, nothing eye-grabbing in itself. I borrowed it, read it over the next few days, felt the whole time that my senses were amplified, that every stubbed toe and steak sandwich held a poetic germ, that I was living both in the book's world and in the real world and that the book's world was making the real world absurdly interesting. Schopenhauer said that life and dreams are leaves of one and the same book, and I agree with that, but the way I see it, even though the words on the real-life pages are different from those on the dream pages, you can sometimes get the words to overlay, and then they can't be read but can be understood. What's important is that I knew through booksong that *Confessions* was what I'd been meant to read that week. The weird thing is that the spine that called to me from the stacks wasn't Augustine's *Confessions* at all, or even Rousseau's *Confessions*, or *Confessions of an English Opium-Eater* or *The Confessions of Nat Turner*, or *Augie March*, or a book of Confucius, or any title that on peripheral glance might have brought Augustine's *Confessions* to mind. The book that double-took me was *Thirty Plays Hath November*. By the drama critic Walter Kerr. And yet the second I touched *Thirty Plays*, I knew that Kerr was a go-between, that Augustine's book had sounded the call. Isn't that weird? So I think it was true what Martha said to Marleen on the phone, that you were born for Marleen and that Martha somehow knew that."

"Why did you tell me this?" I said. "What good can it do me?"

Wade paused for several seconds. His expression was raw and earnest, like when he sang Joni Mitchell's song that night over pizza. "People should know the truth about their origins. You have to know where you're from to know where you're at and where you're going."

"That doesn't sound at all like something you'd believe," I said.

"No, it is."

"Are you saying you're my dad?"

"Almost certainly I'm not," Wade said.

"You're not *saying* that? Or you're *not* my dad?"

"Martha and I were probably still together when you were conceived, although my dates are a little fuzzy. But even if we were, we were pretty estranged by that point."

"You weren't having sex, you mean."

"Not that I recall."

We looked at each other.

"We don't resemble each other in the slightest, you and me," Wade said.

"But you know when we were at the vegetarian restaurant a couple weeks ago and we ran into that friend of mine from high school. She started to laugh 'cause we were standing by her booth in the same pose."

"Was it an unusual pose?" Wade said.

"I don't know, but I know that's why she laughed, 'cause later I talked to her by the bathrooms and she said we were like two peas in a pod."

"She seemed like a ditz."

"She's not a ditz."

"'Two peas in a pod': it's such a dumb thing to say."

"I've always felt something, that we were connected."

"You might be Tauber's kid. You probably saw from the author bio that he's teaching at Grinnell now, if that interests you. They have a nice bank down there. You might want to do some sightseeing and just see what happens."

"But she never said anything about me being Tauber's kid, right?"

"No, no. It's just a possibility. That's why I wanted you to have a signed copy of his book. It might open a door. If nothing else it gives you a souvenir. Did you notice anything about his inscription?"

"He didn't say much."

"Well, I don't know if handwriting has a genetic component or not, but you might study it, see if you spot a family resemblance.

Another possibility is the pedal steel player from the Seed Sacks. They broke up years ago, but he's probably still around. I could get you the name if you want."

I shook my head no. I was burping pizza but had a worse taste in my mouth. I felt that Wade was contaminating my air and wished he would stay at a motel for the night, but at the same time I wanted badly to go with him to Berlin.

"Don't dwell on the three thousand dollars," he said. "It was a grassroots adoption. Marleen didn't have any money to get you two settled."

I tried to clear my head by analyzing the pain in my stomach. I felt a cold coming on.

Wade patted my hand twice, put his coat back on, and nodded for us to leave.

THE BLUES AND THE ABSTRACT TRUTH

ONE AFTERNOON IN THE SPRING OF 1987, I WALKED two or three intermittently seedy miles from my high school to a record store I sometimes visited and where that afternoon I bought a used LP, *Hope Springs Eternal,* by the jazz pianist Elmo Hope. From the store I walked another two or three miles to our apartment, the smaller unit of a duplex in a quiet middle-class neighborhood. It wasn't a hot day—probably only in the midseventies—but I'd jogged part of the way home, holding my backpack's straps to stop its textbook-heavy bounce, and when I got home I was sweaty under my jean jacket. I wiped a damp washcloth up and down my nape, grabbed a budget-brand soda from the fridge, put Hope's record on my mother's stereo, and took a seat on the sofa. On the end table to my right was a silky, often-flowering mammillary cactus that I sometimes teased or studied, but that afternoon I mostly studied my new album, whose previous owner had written his name, Grady McGill, in neat script in the upper right corner of the jacket's verso and on the A-side's prosaically designed label. I particularly liked the tail of Grady's *y* and the ligature of his *Gr* and *Gi.* I stared at the script as I listened to Hope's trio, then read the album's liner notes, endearingly bad I see now. During the second side, my mother came home through the back door. "I love how jazz sounds from another room," she said while passing through the dining room to the living room. "There's something sirenical about it. I like how it sounds in the room where it's playing too," she clarified, maybe so I wouldn't think she was insulting my record, "but I especially like it from another room." We talked about that, and she brought up Sonny Stitt's show at the Plugged Nickel, recalled how emotive Stitt's horn had sounded from the women's room. Then we went into the kitchen to make a taco salad, and that was one of the times she told me about Martha Dickson.

A few months after I bought the Hope LP, I bought a used Wayne Shorter album that had also belonged to Grady McGill, and then, maybe a year after that, another album exiled from his collection, this one by the then-popular R&B singer Gregory Abbott. I'd taken McGill for a hardcore jazz collector, a type normally dismissive of modern pop, so his ownership, however short term, of Abbott's album surprised me. On the Shorter album, *Schizophrenia,* he'd checked his two favorite cuts; on the Abbott, he'd written the words "As will I" next to the album's closer, "I'll Find a Way."

Years later, probably in 1996, I met Grady at a birthday party thrown for a locally notable tenor saxophonist. I knew it was Grady McGill even before I learned his surname. Grady isn't a common name and it was a jazz crowd, so I can't be credited with much clairvoyance there, but for a few minutes I felt the excitement of knowing more than I was assumed to know. He was a tall, large-framed, slouchy, mostly bald computer programmer, but for all that not bad looking. Taking in Grady's size—he must have been six foot seven—I recalled the two checked cuts on *Schizophrenia,* "Playground" and "Tom

Thumb," both by a man named Shorter, and wondered if some sort of wish-fulfillment psychology had been at work or in play. We chatted comfortably about jazz for ten minutes or so. He was elegant, relaxed, melancholy. When our conversation began to lose steam, I said, "You must be Grady *McGill*." By then I had six of his old records, and named each one. Grady was flattered by my secret admiration, if that's what it was, and from the party we drove in separate cars to the studio where he kept most of his records, some twenty thousand jazz, blues, R&B, and pop LPs, plus about a thousand forty-fives, a few hundred seventy-eights, and two or three stacks of CDs.

Grady had two old floor lamps in the studio space, but ignored them in favor of unpleasant fluorescent overheads, chosen, I guess, to best illuminate my browsing. It was the kind of light Wanda liked to fuck in, I thought, risking with the thought a noticeable erection that might have misled Grady. I hate to fuck in the dark, mostly because it leaves me with so few images to return to the next day, but severe light is perhaps worse even than puritan darkness; I doubt Wanda's subsequent partners have tolerated it. "There's a stack of duplicates and some other things I'm ready to sell over there," Grady said, "if you want to look them over."

"I probably won't buy anything tonight," I said.

"That's fine," he said, standing on a stepladder to see if he could stop one of the fluorescent light tubes from buzzing (he couldn't), then resting on the concave seat of a brown recliner, in reach of which was a stereo system that probably received good marks in some early sixties issue of *HiFi Review*.

"Do you keep your favorites at home?" I said, turning away from the record shelves to look at him.

"Not exactly," Grady said. For several minutes he didn't elaborate. As I was getting to the jazz *D*'s, he said, "I spend every Sunday here, listening to my buys from the previous week. Then I stack them up in order of preference and bring home the top five or six. I listen to those at home until I feel I know them well, if they do after all seem to deserve that, to be known well. I try to bring home only deserving records, but sometimes I misjudge. My ears get tired by the end of the day."

"Sure," I said.

"Isn't that the challenge," he said, "to spend time only with things that deserve to be known well?"

"That might be."

"I mean people too, even though they're not things. That's why people move to new places."

He had some highly valuable records.

"Or for a job," Grady said. "For a lot of reasons, I guess."

"Yeah."

"But in my experience people are the same everywhere, so moving doesn't help."

I said, "That reminds me of something Werther said."

"A friend of yours?"

"No, from a book."

"A man in a book?"

"Yeah, a young man in a book," I said.

"Is that what interests you, young men in books?"

"No."

"So what did he say?"

"What you said: *What are people like here? Like everywhere!*"

"Yes, that's right," Grady said.

"Or it's something like that. I can't quote it verbatim," I said.

"Verbatim. Do you speak Latin?"

"No."

"I had to study it as a boy, but I've forgotten everything. It's horrible how much one forgets. You'll see. Even the albums I say I love: I pull them out sometimes to look at them, and I stare at the titles, try to remember the tunes, and there's nothing, often there's nothing. So every February I bring home fifty or sixty of my favorite albums, and just savor those. I really do, I savor them, and I don't bother at all with my recent acquisitions. So I should change the answer to your earlier question and say that yes, I do keep my favorites at home, but only in February."

"Maybe you should pick one of the longer months for that," I said.

"No, I need it to be February. I'm in rough straits by then."

"Yeah," I said, looking over at him. He blew his nose and put the hanky back in his khakis. I asked if he collected any country records.

"Not really. I have a Hank Garland, a few by Willie Nelson, one by Bill Wills."

"*Bob* Wills?"

"Bob, right. And you, you like country?"

"No," I said.

"Oh."

"I love it."

"Ha, that's good," he said. "*I love it*. Did you make that up?"

"No."

"Maybe I'll use that."

"Do you like jazz?" I said.

"Beg pardon?"

"Do you like jazz?"

"Oh, right. No . . . that's good. I love it."

A few weeks ago, I pulled out *Hope Springs Eternal* and listened to it on vintage, long-corded headphones, stolen from Wade, I may as well now confess, over three decades ago. Inside the jacket I found a pencil drawing of a bald man with a thick mustache, prominent cheekbones, lonely eyes, and, on his flat forehead, two differently sized avian furrows. He was wearing a plaid shirt with a narrow, button-down collar. Underneath the drawing were the words, "Grady McGill, jazz man." I knew it was Wade's drawing, both because I recognized his hand and because I knew Wade would distinguish a *jazz man*, a man who loves jazz, from a *jazzman*, a man who plays jazz, although on the other hand Wade loved ambiguity more than fine distinctions. "I'm a red man," he once said at a restaurant, meaning not that he was an American Indian but that he preferred red wines to whites, though the waiter ("My grandma was Mandan") reached the former conclusion.

I also knew it was Wade's drawing because he left a number of other scraps in my records, how many I'm not sure, since I'm trying to discover them naturally, in the course of regular listening. So far, despite periods of financial duress, I haven't had to sell any of my several thousand records. I've even kept the thousand or so that I never play and have no desire to play. Sometimes I pull out one of those undesired records, partly to challenge my ear, partly in random search of Wade's leavings (and in so doing I suppose I'm disrupting the course of what I just called regular listening). The Hope record, though not his best, isn't one I'd consider undesired, though I guess I haven't played it in nearly two decades, or I've played it but overlooked Wade's drawing. Had there not been a legend underneath the drawing, I might not have recognized Grady—I see now that the cheekbones are especially off, the whole face short on flesh. Still, there's a resemblance. Probably a coincidence, but maybe Wade knew Grady too. Maybe they're still in touch. I didn't meet Grady till long after Wade left Minneapolis, so I couldn't have described him to Wade. I'm not sure how meaningful or eerie this really is, this possibility that Wade knew Grady and left a clue pointing to their acquaintance in that Elmo Hope LP, but it seemed that way, eerie and meaningful, when I discovered the drawing a few weeks ago.

Also not so long ago—it might have been a year ago now—I found a strand of long black hair sticking like a bookmark out of a 1990 world almanac. Right away I was sure it was Wade's. I held it up to the light. It was sable. It's possible that the almanac hadn't been opened since Wade's stay with Wanda and me, and that the hair was never displaced during my several moves or at the yard sale at which the almanac was predictably passed over. In other LPs I've found Wade's pornographic drawings, an annotated take-out menu, a few defaced dollar bills, and one poem, slipped inside the Carpenters' *Close to You:*

Alison, the carpenter's wife, flaxen
maculate Mary, her laugh bawdy yet
soft,
reaches across centuries (her alchemic
chemise!) to make a middling American
hard.

I've read worse. That's the only poem I've found in my LPs, but I found another one written in minuscule script on the interior bottom of the matchbox Wade left, circled with a green rubber band, in the glove compartment of his hatchback. All the other items had been removed. This poem read:

Baby, I need your loving
Got (!)
To have all your loving.

A ready-made. If I find another of Wade's poems in my records, I'll submit the trio to literary journals. They'll be rejected without encouragement, I'm sure, but I might take some comfort in that.

CHICAGOLAND

IN LATE SEPTEMBER OR EARLY OCTOBER OF 1998, I WAS gently summoned to Chicago's northwestern suburbs to get the last of my mother's things. "There's some stuff I think you'd like to have," my aunt had said over the phone, "some keepsakes, and her favorite easy chair." I'd been to Chicagoland twice since the funeral of late '91: once in early '92, to fill Wade's former hatchback with some of Marleen's belongings; another time in '96, to finally apologize to my aunt and uncle for my callow and callous behavior at and around the time of my mother's funeral (my uninspired eulogy; my crude beseech-ments of near and distant relatives for plane fare to Berlin; my actorly tactlessness and calculated, ostentatious frazzle: the loosened knit tie; the tousled hair; the pant leg trapped inside the sock; the incoherent, vaporously metaphysical responses to simple condolences).

The hatchback wouldn't hold the chair, and I couldn't afford to rent a truck, so I borrowed the failed singer-songwriter Maggie Tollefsrud's van, which had been driven nearly three hundred thousand miles and nicknamed. Maggie and I first met as fellow temps at a print shop, assembling ad supplements for the Sunday paper. Somehow, though I dislike being onstage, she later talked me into playing bass guitar, rhythm six-string, rhythm synthesizer, ornamental electric piano, and occasional vibraslap in several of her bands, including Terrycloth, the Sullen Nieces, Hash Slingers, and Mag and Her Wheels. A few of these bands made vanity records of not entirely merited obscurity.

My other motivation for going to Chicago in '98 was to see Maryanne, who'd moved there sometime in '92. I'd thought about contacting her earlier but always came up with a reason not to. Now the idea seemed more pressing, and I managed to get her mobile number from a shared acquaintance. She seemed unsurprised to hear from me, even said she'd been meaning to call *me*, though it had been a long time since we'd seen each other, the early spring of '92 it must have been, and we'd never socialized without Wanda or Wade and Wanda. On the phone, she said she had a six-year-old son named Rowan and was working at a shop that engraved plaques and trophies for schools, businesses, chess clubs, curling leagues, and the like. She said she'd love to see me, said so with a mellow yet frank enthusiasm that made my penis creep tinglingly away from my slightly tacky testicular skin. I decided to drive directly into the city and pick up my mother's last unclaimed things on the way home.

A few mornings later, I got to see the skyscraper sunrise from the Kennedy Expressway. In the city itself I spotted what looked like a funky breakfast joint, but I couldn't find a parking space big enough for the Rhino, so I kept driving, eventually wound up at a regional franchise where I spent an hour reading the paper and eating not truly scrambled eggs and ultimately disagreeable hash browns. It still felt too early to call Maryanne—we'd discussed a midmorning meeting—so I left the van in the restaurant's lot and took a walk, sticking to a single street so I wouldn't get lost. The sky was the color of grimy snow, the trees mostly leafless, and the air felt cooler than the forty-eight degrees claimed by a bank's digital thermometer, but the walk did me some good, and by the time I returned to the van my dour achiness had given way to achy punchiness.

Maryanne lived in a warehouse in Wicker Park. I'm pretty sure it was in Wicker Park, but maybe it just seemed like Wicker Park. I don't know Chicago well. More and more I think it was probably not Wicker Park. She came down to meet me, and we took a freight elevator, the kind that requires a key to operate, up to the third floor where she lived. Like a janitrix, she had her keys on a leather ring hanging from one of her belt loops. She was wearing red jeans and a cleavage-revealing Gypsy blouse that mostly covered her full hips. "Is this a legal residence?" I asked. "I don't know," she said. "It has a bathroom." As we walked down a long hallway, she explained that she subleased a corner of a recording studio from a guy named Luke. The words "Smash Palace" were stenciled in red spray paint on the studio/apartment's heavy door. Maryanne moved closer to me and stood on the toes of her white nurses' loafers. I leaned down and her lips brushed my ear when she whispered, "I've never actually seen a band come through, and I've been living here a year and a half."

It was an enormous space, once a tea factory, Maryanne told me. The windows were covered by soundproofing material, but there was enough light from three banks of overheads and a Tiffany-style lamp that stood near Luke, who was arched over a workbench. There were faded Oriental rugs all around, overlapping each other like sleeping kittens. Luke said "hey" in a low voice when he heard us come in, raised his hand to say "just a sec." From what I could make out, he was burning a cigarette mark into a drum-machine pad. He had frizzy brown hair and was wearing pajamas, expensive but unfashionable tennis shoes, and a velour bathrobe with a torn belt loop. He officially lived in an apartment a few miles away, I later learned, but spent most of his time at the warehouse and often slept on a soft leather couch in the control room. When he finished his work with the drum machine he greeted us less passively, answered some of my questions about the studio, and handed me an unwanted rate sheet. Maryanne went to check on Rowan while Luke showed me around. The space was shaped like a fat L, with the control room at the top of the vertical line and much of the horizontal line unused except for storage. I spotted something like thirty electric and acoustic guitars on stands or in dusty cases; also a mandolin, a banjo, a cittern, and a gimbri ("What do you call that thing?" I asked, and Luke misidentified it); plus old brown synthesizers and shiny new red ones; digital samplers; garagey European organs, Hammond organs, and a Leslie speaker cabinet; a half-dozen electric pianos; four upright pianos and a disgraced grand; a Mellotron; two clavinets; a theremin; two marimbas; a vibraphone; drum machines and nonmechanical drums; several turntables; a precarious mound of boom boxes resembling installation art; a few dozen microphones and mike stands; a large, rectangular spring-reverb box; probably a hundred stomp boxes and other electronic umlauts; a yellow racetrack for toy cars; and, reportedly, in the control room, which I never entered, a British mixing board once owned by Todd Rundgren, and a German tape machine that had taken in some of the basic tracks for Don Henley's *Building the Perfect Beast*, or so Luke said, in a tone that attempted to both deprecate the album and call for its imprimatur.

Maryanne returned to the tracking room and smoked a cigarette as Luke finished giving his overlong tour. She seemed more subdued than she'd been when I knew her before (or maybe *relaxed* is better—I don't mean to say she seemed repressed or conquered). She asked Luke if Rowan could watch TV in the control room awhile; Luke seemed cheered by the idea. Then she took me to the end of the L opposite the control room, to a byroom something like a large serif off the L's horizontal line, where she and Rowan had their beds and dressers, a TV, a portable refrigerator, an enormous sculpture of some sort, and not much else. Luke's tour hadn't driven deep into the L's horizontal line, so I'd caught only a glimpse of this byroom, had heard the TV but hadn't seen Maryanne's son, who was now sitting on his single bed watching a kids' sitcom. There were toys, watercolor trays, books, loose sheets of paper, videos, and Pokémon cards heaped on, around, and underneath the bottom shelf of the old TV stand, but aside from that the byroom was fairly neat. Both beds were made. Rowan had black, home-cut hair and sounded like he needed to clear his throat. He looked a bit like Wade. "You can watch till the next commercial break," Maryanne told Rowan, "and then you're going to hang out with Luke." The three of us watched the program for a minute. I laughed politely at a punch line. When Maryanne smiled at me, I pointed to the sculpture and said, "Did you make this?" My tone might have been too incredulous. "Well, I'm *making* it," she said, and then the commercials started and she turned off the TV and took Rowan's hand.

The sculpture was about nine feet tall, an Amazonian or Lachaisian woman with a stump for a head and skin made of plastic tiles—Shrinky Dink plastic, I realized as I got closer. On each of the die-face-sized tiles Maryanne had drawn some portion of the figure's oddly shaped body in colored pencil: part of a toenail or ankle, part of a navel or areola, or just a square of peach-flesh skin. When I kneeled down, I saw that the figure's dark pubic hair was suggested by tile-sized drawings or tracings of Freud's head ("the Shrinky Shrink," Maryanne later explained). The imbricated tiles tinkled from the breeze of my waving hand, since they weren't stuck like skin to a hidden skeleton as I'd imagined on first glance, but were finely punctured and hung by fishing line from a framework of white cardboard and silver wire, resulting in an impressive if not unquestionably beautiful mosaic sculpture. I was still studying the thing when Maryanne returned to the room. "This is fantastic," I said. She thanked me and described in unintelligible detail her ingenious method for making the sculpture. I complimented her again. "It's too lumpy, though," she said, "and I can't figure out how to make her head."

She walked over to her dresser, on top of which there were maybe a dozen tapes and CDs, a boom box, and a school portrait of Rowan, manifesting the genre's ironies, I hoped, in that the most contortedly counterfeit school-photo smiles are forced by the purest of heart. She put on a Tricky CD and sat down on the edge of her queen-sized bed, dressed with a quilt made of brick-sized patches of small-town suits. I sat down next to her. "So did you go to art school?" I said.

She laughed. "I can't afford art school. I just wing it. I'm almost a folk artist. When they interview me, I'm gonna act super bumpkiny."

"You think they'll buy that? I mean, you're in Chicago and all."

"I don't really think there'll be interviews."

"There might be."

"I still need to make the head."

"I like how swirly this music sounds," I said, and lay down with my legs still hanging over the bed, my boots grazing the floor. I turned my head to look at the trophies on Rowan's dresser. The quilt smelled like the corner of a storage closet that was itself in the corner of a thrift store's back room. The trophies were topped with chess knights and kings, bowling balls and bowlers, tennis rackets and players, curling stones and brooms. "Rowan must be really smart and athletic," I said.

"Kind of," Maryanne said. "But those trophies are rejects and extras from the shop. My boss lets me take them home for him. But he is smart, and kind of athletic."

"What grade is he in, then, third?"

"First."

"He's tall."

"Yeah, so far," she said.

"What sort of stuff is he into?"

"Well, you know, regular stuff. Uno, Legos, trains, bowling. He probably could win a bowling trophy fair and square."

"That must be hard for a kid, bowling," I said.

"Except they have bumpers now, so the ball never goes in the gutter. Well, sometimes it sneaks into the gutter at the very end."

"Does he push it or roll it?"

"He drops it."

"Oh."

"WHAMP!" Maryanne yelled, startling me. "That's how it sounds." I laughed and she yelled the sound again.

"Is most of what they say about parenthood true?" I said.

"What do they say again?"

"That it's the greatest and hardest thing you'll ever do. That sort of thing."

"Yeah, I guess that's true." Pause. "There are harder things."

"Sure."

"Not things I've done, but they're out there."

"Hunger and war . . ." I said.

"I love Rowan. Beyond words, you know. But it's dull sometimes, lonely. We're having more interesting conversations now, but he's still just a kid, so they aren't real conversations. I mean, they are, they are. Now I feel bad for saying that. But sometimes they aren't, so it can be isolating."

"Yeah."

"I'm supposed to make friends with the other parents, the other moms and stuff."

"Who says?"

"It's just something I hear," she said.

"But you're not really interested in making friends with the other moms?"

"Not like I'm a misanthrope. But it's not much to have in common."

"Do some of them want to talk about home improvements? A friend of mine's married and he says that's what they talk about, kitchen remodels and stuff like that."

"No, I haven't heard much about kitchens—it's not an affluent school, the one Rowan's in. Although once at the park this Mexican lady in a Mickey Mouse sweatshirt tried to talk to me about stainless-steel appliances, how they're really fancy but show fingerprints."

"Why does it matter that she was Mexican?" I said.

"Why does it matter that she was wearing a Mickey Mouse sweatshirt?" she said.

"I guess you're right."

"My grandma was Mexican."

"Oh."

"But then the woman at the park turned out to be the nanny, or the nanny-maid or whatever. So it wasn't even her stove. Doesn't that seem worse to you, talking about a fucking stove and it's not even your stove?"

"I don't know. Maybe there was, you know, a critical subtext, like: *These norteamericanos are so dumb, they'll buy a stainless-steel stove and not even consider in advance the fingerprints.*"

"Maybe. I think she was just an idiot."

"Well, you'd have a better sense."

"Of idiocy?"

"What? No, no. Not at all! I mean, you were there at the park, you talked to the woman, so you'd have a better sense."

"Oh. 'Cause I was thinking, *Fuck you.*"

"Sure. That would've been a reasonable response."

"But now I know what you meant. I'm not mad."

"Are you still in touch with Wanda?" I asked.

"Yeah, we talk on the phone, email sometimes. You still see her?"

"No. Well, once in a while. I work with this theater troupe, so I'll see her if she comes to review one of our shows. Or just around."

"What are you doing with a theater troupe?"

"Like, *why* am I doing it?" I said.

"No, I mean, are you doing lights? Are you acting?"

"Acting? I can't act. I do publicity mostly, send out post-cards, hang fliers. I make tapes to play before the show."

"Does Wanda give you guys good reviews?"

"Sometimes, not always. She panned one of the shows, too forcefully if you ask me."

"Yeah, I just did."

"What?"

"I just did ask you."

"Oh right. The show she panned wasn't one of our better ones," I said. "She's usually pretty discerning."

"She's so smart. She should be performing again," Maryanne said.

"Do you still have that red leather jacket?"

"Huh?"

"That red leather jacket you used to have. It had a belt."

"Oh. Yeah, I still have that. I don't really wear it anymore. Why?"

"I just liked it."

"Do you want me to put it on?"

"No, that's all right."

"I will."

"Okay."

"Do you ever hear from Wade?" she said. She was on her hands and knees, fetching a big plastic bin from under her bed.

"No. We're not . . ."—I was distracted—"Before he left, he told me some strange things. I haven't sorted it all out."

"Yeah, I heard about some of that."

"You did?"

"Here it is. There's only one button left."

"I remember how the third one from the top was missing."

"Oh." She put it on.

"It looks really good."

"It's kind of tight on me."

"It's great."

"You want me to take off my shirt and then put the jacket back on?"

"Yeah."

She did that, but with her back turned, not like a striptease. I prefer to wear jockey shorts with jeans, but that day I improvidently wore blue, shark-themed boxers with several tiny rips and an exhausted elastic band. Our lovemaking wasn't depressingly hasty but it wasn't slow either. I suppose we didn't want to take advantage of Luke's generosity. After we'd fucked in a few positions on the bed, I asked Maryanne to stand up and put her loafers back on, led her out of the byroom and over to the nearest upright piano, which was in the middle of the L's horizontal line, still quite a ways from the control room but exposed enough to give me an exhibitionistic thrill. She bent over, gripped the moving handles on the back of the piano, handles like those of a very large rolling pin. We started fucking again, slowly at first. When I spanked her the piano inched forward a bit, and just then I let slip a pornographic phrase, met, to the extent that I could judge from behind, with neither hostility nor indulgence. She ignored it, would be a simple way to put it. The phrase immediately embarrassed me, but also spurred me to come too soon, not with—all these qualifiers are tiring even me—humiliating or ridiculously inconsiderate prematurity, but too soon all the same. I tried to pull out and stanch myself but with only partial success, resulting in a staggered, tentative orgasm, inferior in itself to the tremulous one I accomplished later in front of a guest sink belonging to my aunt and uncle, who were out, shopping or golfing I guessed, when I got to their unlocked house.

I wanted to watch their giant TV, but somehow that seemed too invasive, so I just sat on the floral sofa in their fussy but comfortable living room. On the coffee table there were three books on how to simplify one's life and a copy of *Time*. I reached for the magazine, but decided to rest instead. The sofa's fabric felt cool and silky on my impoverished cheek; a day later I'd need to hit up my uncle for gas money.

When my mother Marleen died, she was cash poor but debt free: no credit cards, no car loan, no mortgage on her parents' ranch house. I would have inherited the ranch house to live in or sell had I not refused it, after an English eccentric I'd read about who'd renounced a much vaster fortune. I tried to explain my refusal in meandering, philosophical terms a few times, to Wanda for instance during one of our pathetic breakup dialogues. To my aunt I simply said, "I have my reasons." I did ask for three thousand dollars, which she and my uncle sent me after they sold the house without a realtor's help. My aunt had written something on the memo line, but then crossed it out; this still bothers me.

After a pleasant if dull afternoon and a similar dinner, my aunt took me to the garage, the stopover for the last of my mother's unclaimed things: the easy chair and the contents of two white cardboard boxes. "Why don't you bring the boxes in the house where it's nicer?" she said, but I was already rummaging them so she left me alone. The keepsakes weren't much. I'd hoped for diaries, letters, maybe a letter from Wade, or another photo of Martha Dickson to accompany the two Wade had given me. There was none of that. There were a few undated, unrevealing, distantly Blakean watercolors, possibly done in the dorm room Marleen and Martha briefly shared; a not thoroughly cleaned ashtray; a couple of Christmas photos of me as a toddler; and thirty-eight notebooks filled (half-filled in one case) with Marleen's sentence diagrams. From her midtwenties till her death at age forty-four, Marleen spent a half hour or so of most evenings parsing and diagramming sentences copied from books, newspapers, magazines, flour bags, circulars. The white boxes apparently held her corpus in that field. I sat on a twenty-four-pack of soda, opened one of the notebooks at random, and planted my index finger on a sentence: "In this, it is unlike such other popular sports as golf, track and field, swimming, diving, ice skating, archery, and marksmanship." The sentence was transcribed (conventionally and without analysis) at the top of the page in blue pen, then diagrammed below in pencil, correctly and with no erasure marks. Its unstated subject ("What's this *it*?" Wade would have said) was almost certainly tennis. Marleen was a good player with a powerful left-handed serve. I remembered us resting on a courtside bench after two midday sets during the summer of '87's heat wave. It had been a close match, but she'd won all her service games and had broken me twice. She was heavy by then and her slowness around the court was my main advantage. My drop shot wasn't so masterly, but it sufficed, and by the end of the first set she didn't bother coming in for it. "Now that I'm so fat," she said on the bench, "I hate sweating and eating in public." "You're not fat," I said. "What does *fat* mean if I'm not fat?" she said. Some sweat dripped off my forehead and stung my eye. Our water bottles were pretty much empty, so she poured and shook out the last drops on our heads, first on mine, then on hers, and I enjoyed the drops' slow descent from my crown to my neck and down the back of my T-shirt. The court was badly cracked—a few points had been decided by odd bounces—and littered with tree droppings, but it was well shaded and attractively situated next to a creek, wherein two kids had been wading and fighting during much of our match, a few of their screams engendering unforced errors.

I picked up another notebook but decided it would be cheating to open randomly to a different page, so I kept browsing but in a more linear fashion. The notebooks weren't dated, except indirectly with the odd topical sentence, but eventually I found an incomplete notebook, presumably her last, the one found on her deathbedside table between a *Chicago Tribune* and a shaky-handed note that read, "I'm having my period." It took everyone awhile to recognize the amateur grammarian's parting joke.

As far as I know, my mother didn't have a favorite easy chair, as my aunt put it, but the chair in the garage was the one I'd anticipated, a round-backed chair with broken springs, upholstered in a shiny fabric of wide pink-and-sky-blue stripes, with a fringed, sky-blue skirt. At one time it must have been a comfortable chair, but that time preceded mine, and I have no clear memories of my mother sitting in it. I have clearer memories of setting laundry baskets on it when I went down to use the washer and dryer in our Minneapolis basement. Nevertheless I've become sentimental about the chair, and have moved it to four different houses and apartments. When I got home to Minneapolis in that fall of '98, I found under its cushion two cassettes—a blank Realistic and Bolling Greene's *Renegade Ticker*—along with a quarter, a green lighter, and a knife-sharpened pencil, all of which items I now keep on a thin metal shelf above my boyishly narrow bed.

CLOUDS

GROWING UP, I TOLD FRIENDS, A FEW FRIENDS, THE story of my late, drug-ruined mother Martha, and perhaps as a result some cachet and sympathy fell my way. I told Wanda the story on what must have been our fourth or fifth date. We were sitting in an uninviting nook of a large nightclub on a slow, eighteen-plus dance night. The nook was furnished with a carpeted, built-in bench splotched with blackened chewing gum, and a round, industrial table, whose bottom, my fingers discovered, was a whole textured ceiling of chewing gum. It wasn't so loud in the club that I had to shout, but I did have to speak up and was soon hoarse. Wanda listened attentively and sympathetically, but didn't go through the stock nurturing motions I may have been seeking. I came to admire her for that. Matter-of-factly she said, "If you ever want to meet your relatives, or try to, I'll help you, drive to North Dakota with you, whatever."

After hearing Wade's clouding, enriching version of my origins and adoption, I started to exploit the story, telling it with untoward frequency, first to all my friends in an increasingly exhausting, decreasingly helpful flurry of narration, then over time to new friends, who, in keeping with the normal pattern, emerged more often during my nascent adulthood than they do now, when they are wished for only abstractly. I told the story to various bandmates, in basements while waiting for the headliner to finish, in vans when the rest of the group was asleep; I told it to coworkers over drinks. I was especially eager to tell the story to girlfriends or potential girlfriends (I trust I needn't elucidate the psychology probably at work there), but nevertheless didn't rush to tell them the story. On the first mention of family, I'd usually reveal my orphanhood and hint at something beyond the death of a single mother, but surrender no specifics. If the friendship or romance proceeded, I'd tell the whole story a few weeks later, or several months later, depending on the level of intimacy attained or desired. I always tried to unwrap the story with a suggestion of inadvertence.

Well, sometimes genuine inadvertence factored into the unwrapping; it was a story I wanted to tell, and more than once I launched into it at the wrong time. I've been giving the impression that this was all very cynical and calculated, but I don't think I fully recognized the cynicism and calculation till later. Unrecognized calculation may still be calculation, but not of the shrewdest type. Perhaps that's not true, though, and anyway I'm giving myself too much/little credit: certainly I knew I was trying to use the story, and the steely candor with which I told it, seductively, spilling it over long dinners, over coffees, once on a last-legs swan boat. Sometimes the telling was postcoital, a kind of reinforcement, my narrative pace slower than usual, my voice raspy and mellow, resonating in my chest as I lay in the dark. Once, while describing Marleen's drive from Palatine to Enswell, I was interrupted by a gentle snore.

For some audiences, I'd emphasize mystery and ambiguity, comparing Marleen's and Wade's conflicting accounts and speculating on the tellers' motivations. For others, I'd tell the story more confidently, conflating Marleen's and Wade's versions but largely accepting his and not really citing my sources, or at least not letting the sources encroach on the telling. I didn't always narrate with the dry calm I was after—I wanted to hover impartially over the story as I'd hovered over the players and the little pantyhose-colored foam ball on my boyhood's vibrating football field—but I didn't force emotion either. Sometimes I'd tell the story in group settings. Not at loud parties or on open-mike nights, but at small gatherings, for example on a friend's lyrically lit porch postcookout, lounging with four or five people, most of them near-strangers to me. In these settings, my recitals aimed for stoical yet subtly vulnerable comedy. The story usually went over well, most notably with an actor and professional storyteller named Corey Gustafson. Gustafson was a guest on that dim porch, listening, I later recalled, with almost disconcerting concentration. He phoned me a few seasons later, in the spring of '96. He was working up a one-man show made up of four dramatic monologues about mothers, he said, and wondered if he could turn a mutatis mutandis version of my story into the second act. I laughed nervously. His silence proved his seriousness, and I gave him the go-ahead. Possessiveness about the story would be unbecoming, I figured, and I was flattered, though my pride and excitement quickly gave way to embarrassment and regret. The story, I knew by then, was already overexposed in my circle and possibly in some overlapping ones.

Probably I couldn't have stopped Gustafson anyway. He didn't really need my permission; he was just being courteous, and his show, *Medea Culpa*, was surely beyond its beginning stages (it opened less than two months later). In Gustafson's treatment, as I came to understand it from secondhand reports, my story included a comic yet contemplative picaresque section and concluded with a dramatic ("wrenching," said one of the dailies) reunion between my unnamed surrogate and Martha Dickson, rechristened Lacy Rugh and then living in Moon Township, Pennsylvania, where she worked as a brand manager for a pharmaceutical company and was still happily married to "Mike," "name" retained and flourishing at Prudential. The show got strong reviews, made a few of the local reviewers' Top Ten lists that December, and enjoyed three revivals. Wanda, by then on the theater beat for the Twin Cities' LGBT glossy, as has been noted in less detail, was the only critic not taken with the play, which I never saw despite Gustafson's kind invitations.

When Gustafson called about using my story, he asked me if I had ever tried to find my mother. "I'm not the questing type," I told him. In truth, I'm not wholly unquesting. I've discovered, for instance, that Martha isn't listed in any of the online phone directories, and that the leading search engines turn up no other leads. Probably she took "Mike"'s name. Keeping one's name was still leading edge in the early seventies, and my sense is that Martha's time on or near that edge was short. Wade, we know, was unsure even of "Mike"'s first name, and said nothing of his last, though I guess it wouldn't require much sleuthing on my part to find it out. I've considered taking more forceful measures to find Martha, just as I've considered paying a surprise visit to Wade, but such reunions, I'm sure, would only bring pain. It was easier when I could sympathize with Martha, when I saw her not as some flighty, selfish black marketeer but as a wasted, desperate young woman who gave me away out of love. I've often resented Wade for upending Marleen's well-meaning lies, and yet for a long time I couldn't help but think that he had some beautiful design in mind, that he was trying in his way to do right by me.

A few summers ago, I did at least take a road trip back to Enswell, where Martha's reportedly obese older brother still lives. I thought about calling him, but didn't, nor did I look up any of my grade-school playpals, a few of whom may have passed me on the street or in the mall. The paradox about my loneliness is that while I do feel the weight of the word's meaning—I do feel painfully alone—the pull to actually be with other people grows easier and easier to ignore. At the library I found Enswell High's 1967 and '68 yearbooks. In both, Martha was listed under "Students Not Pictured." She wasn't on the cheerleading squad after all, apparently, nor was she listed in any of the Enswell phone books I looked through. I did find her parents in the '67 book: "Dickson William B & Mildred D pipefitter Great Northern Railway . . ." I stopped for a few minutes in front of what was once their modest home. Also on the trip I had my cowboy boots resoled at the saddle shop on Enswell's beleaguered Main Street, where Motown and other R&B oldies piped lonesomely and I suppose incongruously from municipal loudspeakers. In Ruyak Park, the sounds of playing children sometimes drowned out by impudent exhaust tones and desperate hemispherical combustion chambers filled me with intensely sad nostalgia. There were muscle cars everywhere. At a traffic light later that same night, I pulled up behind one, an early nineties Pontiac. "If you're gonna ride my ass, at least pull my hair," read its bumper sticker, bespeaking, I thought, Enswell's enduring strain of petulance and impurity. I followed the car for a few miles, failing to get a look at the driver's face, though I felt I could make it out later that night when I masturbated twice into one of the motel's balding lemon hand towels.

THe Basement (1)

A FEW DAYS AFTER I GOT BACK FROM CHICAGOLAND in the fall of '98—Maggie Tollefsrud's van returned not noticeably the worse for wear, a cover of clutter on my pink-and-blue easy chair—I got an email from Maryanne. The body of the text: "It was great to see you." Economical to a fault, as well as redundant, those being her parting words to me at the curtain of her freight elevator. Then the playful postscript: "Do you come to Chicago often?" My sincere and quietly witty response went unanswered. My emails are often failures: too formal or too self-consciously chatty, too aloof, too earnest, too grave, too jokey, too self-assured, too pathetic, too open to misreadings, too closed to nuance. Or there's nothing wrong with the tone of my emails. Perhaps they're so frequently unanswered for other reasons. I've often loitered in my "sent" box, rereading a dangling email three or four times, and consistently I spot nothing repellent in its neutral, sometimes modestly clever subject lines, nothing estranging in the notes themselves. I've forwarded some of these to other friends, few of whom have contradicted my sense that little if anything in the forwarded email would offend or for other reasons silence a normal recipient, one friend at least finally agreeing that a laconic yet soothing response would have taken the recipient less than a minute to compose, making busyness no real excuse.

So Maryanne didn't reply to my reply to her overshort email. For a week or more I checked not infrequently for her response. (Now, though I have little reason to expect an email more uplifting than a badly punctuated concert invitation from some stranger I'm friends with on Facebook, I will generally check my email thirty times a day.) Then in April '99 I got a call from Maryanne. She'd moved back to Minneapolis, she told me, or rather to one of its southern suburbs, and was working at a RadioShack. "The district manager says I'm RadioShack's first female employee."

"What? That can't be," I said.

"There's some women at corporate, but I'm the first to work in the field."

"I still don't think that's accurate."

She didn't say anything.

"I responded to your email but you never responded to me," I said.

"I never got a response. I thought you blew me off."

"I responded. I probably still have my response in my sent folder. I could send it again."

"It might've gotten mixed up with my spam."

After letting a few skeptical seconds pass, I asked after Rowan.

"He's good. He got a new bike. So listen, I'm living with Wanda now. The house we're living in is her place; I'm helping her pay the mortgage. The main reason I'm calling, besides just to say hi, is that there's a basement apartment here, a pretty nice one, and the guy who's been living down there gave his notice.

So I told Wanda I'd make a few calls, see if anyone's looking for a place."

"Oh."

"It'd be cool to get someone in there we know."

"Well, I've already got an apartment, and, I don't know, I like being in the city."

"It's really close to the border, and the rent's cheap." She told me the figure, and it was cheap, less than I'd ever paid, except when I'd split fifty-fifty or in some other way divided household expenses with roommates. At the time I was renting a Victorian attic from a couple of gentrifiers who weren't as smart as they looked. The rent wasn't exorbitant, but it was higher than my income or the bat-ridden attic justified. (I was making small, irregular money as a musician, but mainly earned my keep as part of a street team of guerilla marketers.) The attic's temperature was always uncomfortable by ten degrees in one direction or the other, and its small windows seemed to have some cheer-filtering effect on the view. "Are you thinking about it?" Maryanne said on the phone.

I was, and was the next day thinking about the GI Bill, and an unprecedented demand for single-family homes, and—the reader, I'm guessing, roughly understands what prodded American postwar domestic architecture toward homogeneity, and won't be surprised that Wanda's taupe, postwar two-bedroom was similar in many respects to the gray, postwar two-bedroom I lived in as a kid in Enswell. It was strange, however, to see that Wanda's house, like my mother Marleen's place on Queal, was next to a church, more precisely next to its parking lot. The church next to Wanda's place was UCC rather than Lutheran, the building of yellow rather than chestnut brick, modernist, I suppose, rather than Romanesque Revival. Nevertheless. I sat in the Leveret looking at the house and then the church, the parking lot and then the house, the church, the house, the lot, the lot still more, the church again, the lot, the house.

As I approached Wanda's door, I realized I was a block south of her house, at 2304 instead of 2404.

At the correct house (slate and also very similar to Marleen's onetime two-bedroom), Wanda opened the door before I rang the bell. In the living room, Maryanne and Rowan were watching *The Andy Griffith Show*. Maryanne laughed at one of Floyd's lines, and Rowan followed suit, overdoing it. The adults talked small awhile, then Wanda took me down to the basement.

After the newish washer and drier, the second thing I noticed was Maryanne's huge, still-headless sculpture, now sleeping like Ozymandias on the basement's crumbly concrete floor. The apartment itself was not unlike Wade's old place, but as with the churches there were dozens of differences: for instance in this unit there was a silver strip separating the kitchen's white linoleum from the main room's coffee-stained baby-blue cut pile, whereas in Wade's unit a gold strip had separated beige linoleum from crimson shag. "Is that oak wainscoting?" I said, about the cheap paneling. "Rosewood," Wanda said. It felt good to easily fall back into joking. "Well," Wanda said, "it's a basement apartment, so there's the risk of depression. But it's cheap, cool in the summer. Laundry's free. Folding's extra."

"What's that?" I said.

"Just kidding—like we were gonna fold your clothes."

"Oh, folding," I said. "I just didn't hear you."

"Do you think your hearing's suffered from playing music?"

"Come again?"

"Has your hearing—"

"Gotcha. No, I think my hearing's okay." Pause. "I like your theater criticism."

"It's reviewing more than criticism," she said. "And *previewing*, even worse."

"Seems like a good gig."

"I kind of stumbled into it. I have to do temp work too."

"Oh. At first I drove up to the wrong house, a block down. I thought you lived next to that church."

"Nope, we live right here."

"That would have felt especially odd, since Wade lived in a basement place kind of like this when I was a kid, and there was a church on the corner next to that place too."

"Well, you can't really put a big church in the middle of a block," she said.

"Even without the church, it might feel repetitious to live here."

"We won't be living together, we'll just be living in the same house. You'd have your own mailbox."

"I don't mean repeating our thing." I began to stammer a further explanation but stopped before saying anything coherent.

"What if I knocked twenty-five bucks off the rent?" she said.

"Like to compensate for whatever weirdness I might feel?" I said.

"Interpret it how you will." A minute later she trotted upstairs to get the lease. I didn't know whether to wait downstairs or follow her, so I waited. After a while she called down for me to come up, and I was even invited to stay for taco night. The invitation seemed reluctant but I accepted it.

THE BASEMENT (2)

"I STARTED TO THINK OF WHAT JOHN LENNON SAID about the chair. The blues is a chair, he said. It's not a chair for admiring. You sit on it, he said. A music critic wrote about this chair in a big red book your Phoenician father was lugging though Vagabondia."

"Wade's probably not my—"

Bolling went on: "The book was falling apart; pages would float around the van when we opened the windows. One time... What was the name of that building where they wrote songs?"

Upstairs the sound of bottles being dumped on bottles.

"In New York City," he said. In May of '99, shortly after the release of his quiet comeback effort, *& Goliath*, Bolling played one of Minneapolis's smaller stages. This was after the show.

"Brill?" I said.

"That's it. One time most of the Brill chapter from Wade's book flew right out the window. Wade wondered if parts of the Beatles section would get erased as a result. I liked Wade. You ever hear my Beatles record?"

"I've heard about it," I said. A copy of Bolling's rare Beatles album, Wade said, wept gently in one of the boxes that once cornered my apartment, but I looked through those boxes with some thoroughness and never came across it.

"It's hard to find. Folks treated that record like a joke, but I wanted to *sing* those songs. I'd been singing a few of them in Austin, and one night these two dudes came up to me after the show, a young, squirrely one and an older fat one. The fat one wore a knit necktie that didn't even come close to his belly button. You think I'm fat?"

"You're kind of fat."

"Not compared to this dude. The squirrely one bought me a drink and said, 'We want you to make a record of Beatle songs.' He and his partner had a little record company. The next morning I had it all mapped out, side A to side B, who'd take the solos, everything. So they rented me a studio in Nashville for a weekend. My opinion was that we should just do it local, but they said, 'Naw, we're doing this for real.' I hadn't planned on doing it for pretend." Bolling smiled. His eyes were small for his big potato face and their whites, to borrow a line from a Porter Wagoner tune, looked like a road map of Georgia. "They wouldn't let me bring my own guys. The squirrely one said, 'Don't take this wrong, hoss, but your guys can't play their instruments.' Then the fat one jumps in: 'If they could play their instruments, they'd be welcome to play on the record.' They were a couple of a-holes, these dudes. My guys were by no stretch incapable. The drummer couldn't exactly keep time, but he lost it in one direction, by which I mean he sped up. And people like that."

"It's an accelerating culture, they say."

Bolling pointed at me: "There you go. Most of the guys they hired for the session weren't first-string guys, but they were good. Good and in one case great, since they brought in the Goat, may he rest in peace, and he could make anything sound better. You know the Goat?"

"Sure."

"No one played the steel guitar better than the Goat. Except Ralph Mooney and Speedy West. Once in the studio—this was years later—the Goat played me a solo that I'll never remember." He paused. "This solo was beyond memory, is what I'm saying."

"Like the unconscious?" I said.

"I don't know. Isn't that beneath memory? This was *beyond* memory. That's how incredible it was. It was only sixteen bars long, but every note was perfect, every space too. Lester Young would have loved that solo. That's how I grew up, breathing Lester Young out of my mouth, Jimmie Rodgers out of my nose. You ever hear Lester's speaking voice?"

"No."

"It had that lilt, just like you'd expect. Fine and mellow, right? If Lester'd heard the Goat's solo, he would've said, 'Yeah, y'know, that's about it.' The Goat played that solo, and for good measure we did a couple few more takes, and then the Goat went home to his pot roast or what all. And that night the producer insisted on using one of the other takes. I said, 'Ain't you listening to that solo?' He said, 'It's a good solo on a bad take.' I thought we were turning our backs on humanity."

Bolling emptied his glass, reached into the neck of his armadillo T-shirt to rub his liver-spotted shoulders. We were in what the Dog's Bite Boozery called its green room. It was just a corner of the basement, but it had a loveseat, a chair, a low coffee table, a few ashtrays, an out-of-place copy of *Details*. Also in the vicinity were boxes of booze, boxes of toilet paper, bowling trophies, curling trophies, trophies that curled. I was stoned.

"You were talking about the chair," I said.

"I'm leading up to that." He paused again, this time for quite a while. "They made me put on overalls and stand on a pile of manure with a shovel, so they could call my Beatles record *Dung Beatle*. They brought me out to this farm, these record-company dudes did, along with a photographer, who looked to be the fat one's cousin. They handed me a red jacket with epaulets and some cheap brassy stuff, made me wear that over the overalls. So I guess they weren't even overalls!" We both laughed. He waited for the laughter to die and said, "If you look at my face on that record, you can tell I'm hurting. Have you ever seen a girl in a dirty magazine where you can tell she's hurting?"

"Yeah," I said.

"And sometimes that hurting face is what makes you hard?"

"I'm not sure I've exactly—"

"So I was thinking about this chair, on one of those tours with your old man."

"Wade's probably not my father. I mean, he might be, but . . ."

"Well in any case I was thinking about this chair," Bolling said. His havelock was on the coffee table; he had hair on the sides of his head but only a few long, doglegged strands on top. "John Lennon said the Beatles couldn't play the chair in the same way as maybe Son House could, 'cause they was from different houses"—Bolling laughed at his own pun. "So they had to build their own chairs. I was thinking about this chair. To me it was an armless wood chair, painted yellow but maybe a bit chipped."

"Yeah, I can picture it," I said.

"Now they have chairs that come chipped. I saw one in a catalog. So I put that chipped chair into a room, and also in the room is a little tape deck on a clear plastic table. One of those desktop tape recorders with a microphone built in. And a big *Play* button, and a smaller *Record* button next to *Play*."

"Sure," I said. I was excited to be in the basement with Bolling. I thought it was a kind of achievement to be talking to him, or listening to him, in what seemed to be so natural a fashion. He'd made some beautiful things; I'll never forget how good "West Texas Winds" sounded when Wade and my mother Marleen listened to it through the screen on the stoop while I sat on the sofa watching their twilit heads, drums and guitars loping and floating all around me. But also I was getting tired. It was nearly two a.m. Soon the bar's owner would ask us to leave.

"And if you press both buttons at the same time," Bolling said, "it records whatever's happening in the air."

"Omnidirectionally," I said.

"So someone comes into the room with a guitar. That's how I picture it, but it wouldn't have to be a guitar. My daughter plays the turntable." Bolling smiled. "She's a turntab*list*. I tease her. I say, 'You sure did toast that toast in that toaster. Are you a toasterist?' I do that with all the appliances. So you walk in the room with a guitar and you sit down on the chair. You push *Play-Record* and you play-record your song. You didn't really write the song, the song wrote you, or it was already kicking around, but you put your name on it. When you finish, you lean over, and maybe the mike catches you knocking the guitar with a belt buckle or a wedding ring or something, and you push *Pause*. And then after a while someone else comes in and plays his version of the same song over the next stretch of tape. And this keeps happening. It's a ninety-minute tape, forty-five minutes per side, and eventually someone's song gets cut off in the middle, when the A-side ends. Someone else comes in, sits down on the chair, flips the tape over, and plays his version of the song. Some people, before they play their song, they listen to all the songs up to that point, and then they play their version. But other people, they just push *Play-Record* straight off. Either way, lots of 'em will walk out the room with stars in their eyes saying, 'I just played a whole new song, or played an old song so brilliantly it may as well be new. I don't know *where* it came from. Maybe from God. A gift: I have one or am one. But it's the same shit, of course, the same song. By this time folks are crowding the halls waiting to shove into the room, while inside the room the tape keeps getting flipped over, songs layered on top of songs, and it starts to wear out. Maybe at first it was a tape like the one that swept back that dude's hair in the Memorex commercial. But now it sounds like one of those no-case, normal-bias tapes that hang in long packs at drugstores, on those hooks they stick in those gaps in the wall—"

"Slatwall."

"Slatwall. And then it starts to sound like a really old version of one of those shit tapes. The little tape player, its little microphone, the little tape—all o' that's been distorting the songs from the first, but now it's distorting them nearly beyond all recognition. So some people finish their song, they give it a listen and get all excited 'cause they think they've distorted the song into a whole new song, while other folks try to play in the pure old way, just how it was supposedly meant to be played. But that comes out distorted beyond all recognition too. And some folks forget to hit record, so their song isn't quite there, though at the same time it is, you see. I thought about all this while we were driving, and I told Wade about it. We talked a lot on those tours. This band you saw tonight, they don't talk much. Sheila just looks out the window and smokes; Danny smokes and looks out the window. Sometimes we'll drive for nine hours and say as many words: 'Gotta pee,' 'Wanna stop?' 'You fading?' 'Here it is.' Maybe that's more words than nine. I don't know how you count words like *gotta* and *wanna*."

"I think it's fair to call them—"

"I didn't really mean for us to discuss that. Someday," he went on, "the tape's gonna snap. That's what I realized. Or it'll get caught in one of the spools. And no one will want to splice or untangle it." Bolling looked up through the basement ceiling to the stage. "So I wait in the hall, I go in the room, I sit down, I play-record my song, I leave, and I wait my turn to go back in. What I figured out is that I'm hoping that someday I'll be the one the tape snaps for. Have you ever been to a chiropractor?"

"No."

"It doesn't work all that well, but you always want one crunch to drive all the pain away in a flash. Now part of me knows that if I'm around to see the tape snap, it won't really be me who snapped it; it'll just have snapped with me in the room. But some nights, I start to think I *will* be able to snap it. I'm not talking about Uri Geller and what all."

"No, I think I follow you," I said.

"I'm saying that I'll play the song so well, or it'll play me so well, that I'll become the tape; I'll become the tape and destroy myself for the sake of the song."

"Right, that's it. I want something like that too."

For a moment he honored me with stretched, vulnerable eyes. "You say Wade's working as a deejay these days?" he said.

"As far as I know. In Berlin."

"No kidding? I miss Germany."

"Sometimes I think about visiting him," I said, "but it's too expensive. I haven't seen him now in almost eight years. I told you how he visited me back in '91?"

"You mentioned it," he said.

"Well, I think he got this friend of mine pregnant back then. I think he meant to, I think he meant to father a child when he was here, so that maybe I could be the kid's stepdad and have the family Wade could never have with me and my mom."

Bolling squinted. "Well, it's hard to say. Most of the time these things aren't really mapped out like that."

"I know. But it's just this feeling I've had."

By then the bar owner was indeed hovering around us. When Bolling rotated his neck in response, the owner nodded and said, "Yep." We walked upstairs, Bolling holding the railing with one hand, resting the other above his left knee. We walked through the bar, now shiny and disinfected, the mustard vinyl booths sparkling like my first bike's banana seat.

Bolling's rhythm section was waiting in the van. He took out a sheet of paper, a list of songs labeled "Second Set." It was strange that he had a set list, since that night he'd called out the songs on the fly, and when I studied the list later, I couldn't remember having heard any of the scheduled material in either the first or the second set. "Y'all hungry?" he'd yelled at the start of the show, and then he and his taciturn rhythm section barreled forth, no frills, no solos, few concessions to pacing, no fear of playing five consecutive train-beat songs in G. The set list was a photocopy; some of the longer song titles disappeared into the sheet's right side. Maybe Bolling just carried a bunch of these set lists around to distribute as souvenirs. He held the list to one of the van's windows and signed his name under the words "Encore (if demanded)." Two pieces of wrinkly duct tape were attached like teddy-bear ears to the sheet's top corners— earlier the list must have been stuck to a monitor or something, or the tape was there to lend the souvenir more authenticity. The tape left faint marks on the window after Bolling handed me the list. I hadn't asked for an autograph and don't like to have or keep them, though Bolling couldn't have known that.

THE POOR ORPHAN CHILD

BY DUMPING OR ABANDONING THINGS I DIDN'T NEED or couldn't carry unassisted, I was able to cram all my stuff, including my mother's unwieldy pink-and-blue easy chair, into Maggie Tollefsrud's van, whose remaining benches I'd removed the night before. The van was Ford's second-largest model and I'd used all but a few square inches of its cargo space, but I felt proudly Franciscan all the same. It was just after four o'clock on a bright Monday afternoon in '99, the last day of May. Wanda or Maryanne would meet me at my new basement apartment in the late afternoon, or so we'd agreed about a month earlier. I would have called to confirm the plan, but had lost Wanda's unlisted number.

I should have tried harder to track it down, because when I got to her place no one was home and the doors and windows were boarded over (naturally I thought of "Boarded Windows" from Bolling's songster-for-hire days). The boards had been nailed unevenly, I noticed, and there were several nails on the ground, their shanks curled and bent, pointing to a particularly inept carpenter. Taped to the door was a thin sheet of printer paper labeled "Notice"; under this heading were the sort of sentences once used to test typists and typewriters: "Now is the time for all good men to come to the aid of their country," and so forth.

I pounded on one of the windows, pointlessly, then grabbed a warm bottle of diet soda from the van's cockpit and started walking to the ucc church I'd mistakenly parked near on that afternoon a month or so earlier. Church secretaries, I've found, are as a rule more generous with their phones than shopkeepers.

Before I made it to the church's office, however, I saw a boy standing alone in the middle of its parking lot. As I got closer, I recognized Rowan, and when I got closer still I saw that he was crying. It was a whimpery, soft-pedal cry. I said hello, kneeled, moved within hugging distance of him, smelled his troubled breath. There was dirt on both his fat cheeks. I wanted to suck up his tears with a medicine dropper and drink them.

"They stole my bike and they kicked me," he said.

"Who did?"

"These guys." He sobbed.

"Where'd they kick you?"

"Here." He spread his arms to indicate the parking lot.

"No, I mean which parts of your body did they kick?"

"Leg," he said and pointed.

I lifted his pant leg; there was no visible injury.

"Who are you?" Rowan said.

"You know me, I'm a good friend of your mom's. Where is she?"

"Who?"

"Your mom. Where's your mom?"

"I'm an orphan."

"No, you're not, Rowan. Your mother is alive and she loves you more than anything."

"It was a new bike."

"Do you know the serial number?" He didn't.

He snuffled, and I told him that I'd once recovered a stolen bike, which was not exactly true, though a roommate of mine had. After a while he started to calm down. I told a dumb joke and just as he lightly laughed I heard a sound similar to the ring of a telephone, and he reached into a slanted zipper-pocket on the side of his pants and took out a mobile phone. "Why do you have a phone?" I said.

"For safety," he said before answering the call, soon into which he resumed crying.

"Is that your mom?" I said. He shook his head yes. "See, I told you you weren't an orphan." I held out my hand.

"This guy wants to talk to you," Rowan said, and handed me the phone.

"What's going on?" I said.

"Why don't you"—it was Wanda; Maryanne had passed off the phone—"have an answering machine?" she said.

"I hate answering machines."

"We've been trying to get in touch with you for three weeks. You didn't get my note?"

"What note?"

"I left a note with the super at your apartment."

"The super's a drug dealer," I said.

"Well, he told me he'd get it to you."

"Why is your house all boarded up?"

"For a film," Wanda said. "Maryanne and her boyfriend are making a film."

"The city allows that?"

"Filmmaking?" she said.

"No, not fucking filmmaking; boarding up a house like that just for kicks."

"It's not for kicks, it's for a film. The back door isn't boarded."

"Rowan's really distraught here. All alone, without a bike."

"We're on our way. Look, we've been trying to get in touch with you. Because it's not gonna work."

"What isn't?"

"Renting the basement."

"What do you mean?"

"Just what I said."

"I'm all moved out," I said. "I'm on the street if you renege."

"We've been trying to get in touch. All your emails bounced back."

"I got a new address. I was getting all this porn spam at my old one."

"Well, I don't know, you can stay with us a few days, but it's not gonna work long-term. Maryanne and Jeff are gonna live upstairs and I'm taking over the basement unit."

"You're gonna live in the basement of your own home?"

"That way they cover more of the mortgage. I'm overextended."

"Is that why the place is boarded up?"

"No, that's for the film. I just explained that."

"Did Maryanne write the script?"

"I don't think there's a script."

"Is this a stag film?"

"No—what? No!"

"I have a lease, Wanda."

"If you want to live in the basement for two months, fine. But in that case I'm giving you your two months' notice now."

"It's not right."

"I'm really sorry about this. We've been trying to reach you for weeks."

"You might have gone to greater lengths."

She invited me again, this time with some tenderness, to crash at their place awhile. I didn't know how to hang up the phone. I don't mean I was apoplectic, though there might have been some of that; I mean I didn't know which button to push, in part because I have little intuition for such things and in part because I cultivate a luddite or elderly helplessness that some find charming. I handed the phone back to Rowan. Seconds later the bullies returned, most on bikes, a few on foot. One of them hopped off Rowan's bike and let it fall on one of the parking lot's corners, then started running, leaving behind a few incomprehensible shouts. "Joy ride," I said to Rowan, and explained the concept while we went to inspect the bike, a discount-store BMX painted a mean black and silver like the Oakland Raiders' uniforms. Part of the joy, I told Rowan, is simply in riding on or in a strange vehicle, and part of it comes from knowing that the vehicle's owner is, for instance, crying in a parking lot. He got on the bike. "There's nothing quite like the happiness you feel when something bad didn't happen after all," I said, and he started to pedal, built up a good head of steam on the sidewalk, then sailed off the curb and back onto the lot.

I could have left then. Maryanne and Wanda were due back soon and seemingly laid-back about leaving Rowan alone with bullies. But I thought I'd better stay, so I pulled my twelve-speed out of Maggie's van, and Rowan and I pedaled around the puddly lot. He did loops of no-hands and several jumps off the sidewalk ramps, sometimes whooping with the jump, while I rode off the saddle, coasting slowly, leaning over the handlebars, my legs locked straight, sometimes turning my face to the sun. I felt a strange mixture of calm and despair. Anything and nothing were possible. Then a young man whom I took for the youth minister, who earlier must not have heard the taunts and cries during and after the bike theft, came outside and commended Rowan's balance, stayed at Rowan's request to watch a few more tricks. I stopped coasting, straddled my bike, and the sweatshirted possible youth minister and I watched Rowan together for a minute or two. As he opened his car door, the minister gave me a complimentary smile and wave, stinging in its kindness and misdirection, though I relished it for a moment.

Maryanne, Wanda, and a man unknown to me, the filmmaker-boyfriend presumably, pulled into the lot a few minutes later. I rode up to Rowan. "You're a good boy," I said, almost sternly, and booked over to Maggie's van. Rowan yelled goodbye and Maryanne yelled "Hey!" but I didn't turn around. I had some trouble wedging the bike back into the van—the boyfriend called out to offer a hand—but I managed. I climbed into the driver's seat without looking over at the group, pulled carefully away from the curb to avoid any embarrassing tire squeals, then drove abstractedly for half an hour, briefly thought about driving to some clean-slate city or town, Fostoria or Wapakoneta, say. But I had almost no money, and before long Maggie Tollefsrud and I were unloading the van and replacing some of its benches. My homelessness made me more receptive to her deathless advances, and it was in her bed, six months later, that I watched Sting and others usher in the briefly anticlimactic new millennium.

numerology

O N MY TRIP BACK TO ENSWELL, I FOUND A MICRO-
filmed review of Bolling's concert at the Enswell
Municipal Auditorium (HED: "The Greene-ing of
Enswell"; SUBHED: "Country Star Heats Up EMA"), which is
how I'm able to say that Wade, my mother, and I went to Bey's
Food Host for the last time together on November 10, 1978, just
before the show. I keep mentioning these dates, as if the dates
themselves were important. By citing them I must hope that a
few indisputable facts will offset the mysteries I'm forced or
impelled to let stand. There is something pleasing about the
certainty, about being able to mark the origins of a distant
memory on a calendar, as diarists' can, or as most of us can for
our lifetime's historically notable dates. There must be dates
from which I have two or more discrete and relatively insignificant memories whose proximity I've forgotten (this fascinates
me), as well as dates (hundreds? thousands?) that fall well
within my postmemorial life but from which I nonetheless have
no memories (these vanished days fascinate me too—today, I
suspect, will become one).

At Bey's I got a plain hamburger, black and crispy on the
outside, instead of my habitual D-Luxe Frenchy. All the booths
were full so we had to sit at one of the tables. I conducted a

football game between differently colored sugar packets. The owner-manager stood by the cash register whistling "Wichita Lineman." Wade and Marleen were reconciled uneasily, like the somewhat accusable harmonies Bolling and his band sang later that night.

From Bey's we drove Wade's dolphin-like coupe down hilly Foster Avenue to the auditorium. I sat as usual between the adults on the front bench, my mother's hand on my knee. In the parking lot, Wade kept the car running, reached over the seat, lifted a baby blanket, and picked up a compartmental black leather case, a jewelry case or, I thought at the time, a tackle box (but tackle boxes are rarely if ever made of leather). "Oh Lord, put that away," my mother said. I looked intently at the case. Bolling's "West Texas Winds" was on the radio: "The west Texas winds / Blow angles in the rain / Tinfoil down the lane / It's still a-crinklin' in my brain." Wade must have turned the dome light on, or perhaps by radio- and lot-light I got a good look at the contents of the case, the bottles of pills, the assorted plastic baggies: grams of coke, quarters of weed. Also needles— I thought I saw needles, but when I asked my mother about this much later she said that Wade never dealt heroin, that there was no real market for it in Enswell; most likely, she said, I'd seen Wade's darts, since back then he carried around his own set.

Spirits were high in the auditorium as we walked underground to the main floor or basketball court and found our seats. It was open seating, but a friend of Wade's from KECF had set aside some folding chairs for us near the front. Our names— even mine—were Sharpied on typing paper and taped to the backs of the chairs. The seats in the stands were various colors, and I tried to count if there were more empty reds or more empty greens, but soon there were hardly any empties at all. Over a tenth of the city was there (well, many attendees must have come from smaller towns nearby). I doubt Bolling's performance was cynical, impartial, or perfunctory, but I know it wasn't magical like the State Fair show. I could feel my mother's enthusiasm quickly wane. The crowd seemed satisfied, though. They stood up for some of the fast songs, so that all I could see were backs, asses, and legs, though Wade lifted me up for part of "In Spades," one of Bolling's clunkers ("But now I know I dig you in the sunshine and the shade / So darling, please come back to me in spades"). After Wade put me down he left his seat to talk with one of the security guys. During the encore, my mother told me years later, Wade leaned into her ear, said he was going backstage. She could come too if she wanted, he said. "What am I supposed to do with him?" she said, pointing at me. He gave her the car keys. "I hate driving your car," she might have said. "Well, you guys can wait for me if you want," he might have answered. They argued a bit more, and in the end he said he'd see her at home, that he'd walk or get a lift. I watched the security guard step aside to let Wade backstage. Wade was wearing a long-sleeved henley shirt, navy blue with one wide horizontal red stripe across the middle, and I could still see the red stripe through the glamorous smoke after I'd lost sight of the rest of him. My mother and I didn't stay for the whole encore. Backstage, I later learned, there was more than the average partying, and then the band, crew, and tagalongs moved to Oran's, where there was an after-hours guitar pull and dart tournament, Wade victorious.

I was awake that next morning when Wade left in the silver bus, behind schedule, the driver-trombonist hopped up for a long day of lead-footing. My mother always said I slept through his exit, as was noted earlier, implying that I'd made up my memory, but the reliability of her narration has been questioned. I clearly remember hearing the commotion, remember sneaking out to the living room, peering through the mail slot. Wade and Bolling were on the front lawn, Marleen was on the stoop, closest to me, and accordingly seemed much taller than the others (she would have been an inch or two taller than Bolling even if they'd all been standing on the same level). By the time my eyes made it to the mailbox, the three of them, it seemed, had been talking and fighting awhile. The first thing I made out was Bolling saying, "Marleen, we gots to ramble." And then my mother let loose: "Be quiet, you fucking clown. You Bozo, you charlatan, you fucking sellout. Take off that vest, that fucking hat, take off that fucking hat. You." She pointed. "You sold us out, you and all the rest. Take off that stupid hat."

Wade looked at the ground. I'm not sure why my mother took out her rage and disappointment on Bolling, who, clearly hurt, started playing the jester on cue, looking fixedly at the ground, circling one of our rented spruce trees, patting his pockets. "So where's my money, Marleen?" he said. "From the sellout. Where is it?"

"Who gave you permission to call me by my first name?" my mother said.

"Ours is an informal nation, Marleen," Bolling said.

"Get back on your bus."

"Marleen, I'm coming back," Wade said.

"No, you're not," she said. "Get on your bus. Get on your bus."

So they did, and I scampered back into my room. I listened for the front door and screen, both squeaky; they didn't open for half an hour. Maybe my mother was smoking and crying on the stoop, or maybe she cried later. I know I waited a half hour for the doors to open because I watched my little white bedside alarm clock. Its hour and minute hands were black, which is standard, but its second hand was blue, which is not; most clocks in that all-business style have red second hands. See, I remember. And then when my mother came in the room to check on me (not to wake me up, it being a Saturday), I quickly closed my eyes and expertly played asleep.

Hejira

ECONDS AFTER THE DISPIRITED YOUNG WOMAN FOR some reason walked away from preparing my toasted sub sandwich, a fly landed on a frayed, floppy edge of roast beef and started working its way to the congealing white cheese. The sandwich went unattended for at least a minute. My useless attempts to shoo the fly through the sneezeguard seemed to amuse the UPS driver behind me in line. Mentally I practiced the lordly umbrage I'd use in demanding a new sandwich, but when the young woman returned, seeming more dispirited than before, I let it slide. I left my car in the sub shop's parking lot and walked in the sunny Milwaukee afternoon to the Golda Meir Library, for several blocks tasting irrational hints of the fly's filth.

The librarian at the rare-book room's front desk was wearing a roller-derby T-shirt and reminded me slightly of Maryanne. *Le sexe de la femme,* which I'd called about earlier, was waiting for me behind her desk. Affecting a scholarly stereotype, I patted my pockets as if I'd misplaced my wallet, but the librarian seemed unconcerned about my pretended loss. She asked me where I wanted to work, then used both hands to carry Zwang's heavy book over to a long, empty desk. The book was cheekily packaged like a Bible, with a fancy slipcase, two ribbon markers, and a supple leather cover bearing the title in formal gold lettering (there might have been gilt-edged pages as well, but I can't remember). The paperback I'd ordered earlier wasn't so much a shadow of this original as a faded Polaroid of the original's shadow.

On the drive from Minneapolis to Milwaukee, I'd relistened to decades-old beginner's French cassettes (perhaps my terminally tyronic accent carries a hint of wow and flutter), but having only reached unit twenty-three of French II, I couldn't read Zwang's text beyond an occasional word or phrase. I had limited reading time anyway.

Pictorially, *Le sexe* gives an eccentric history of erotic and pornographic art, with support from nonartistic documents. It's very much a product of its time: it doesn't scrimp the reader of Day-Glo pussies or bedroom surrealism (Roland Bourigeaud, André Masson, Jane Graverol, Hans Bellmer), including the surrealism that leads into or is pyschedelia or fantastic realism (Ernst Fuchs, Félix Labisse, Mati Klarwein). But the book contains images of all sorts going back to antiquity: cave drawings; Titian; a daguerreotype of a couple fucking in a haystack; Pierre-Paul Prud'hon; anatomical drawings by Leonardo; two views of *Le grand écart*, a bronze, nineteenth-century statuette of a ballerina without, the base reveals, underwear; Modigliani; anthropological photos of the type sometimes sought out by young masturbators; Rubens; photos of chastity belts; drawings of gynecological procedures; the great George Grosz; an Egyptian statuette; an American advertisement from 1960 for Vibra-Finger ($9.99), presented as a dental aid whose "novel design allows localized massage in needed areas"; Beardsley; a Babylonian cylinder; an anonymous drawing called *La revue des inspiratrices* ("The Examination of the Muses"), in which about twenty women lift their skirts and pull their dresses below their breasts for a small team of male examiners; Rowlandson; several disturbing photographs accompanying the chapter contra female genital mutilation; photographer Lucien Clergue's arty black-and-white nudes, which I once furtively examined as a teenage B. Dalton customer. There are other images I might like to name or describe, but my notes are shoddy; I find in my yellow notebook the following phrases without further explanation: "Indo-Chinese" (Indo-Chinese what?); "horse sex"; "bending over back of chair w/ [smudge]."

Stupidly, I wrote nothing at all about how *The Origin of the World* looks in Zwang's book. It was hand-tinted I know, in pastel hues I want to say, but really I'm not sure how it looked. I spent just two hours with the book. I had a shoot in Minneapolis the next morning and a gig the next night with Papa Freud and the Lazy Vulvae, so I wanted to get a decent night's sleep. But I did find, before leaving prematurely, a surprising artifact in between the book's last page and its endleaf: a pubic hair. Or what I took to be a pubic hair; it may have been a short, squiggly, dark brown hair from someone's curly head, though I didn't entertain that possibility till later. The hair looked a lot like some of my own pubic hairs, and like others I've seen. My first explanation was that the librarian, sitting at her desk after I'd called to make sure *Le sexe* was on hand, had reached into her underwear to pluck a memento for me. (I'm said to have an attractive telephone voice, if that information seems relevant.) Snapping out of that fantasy, I then considered that the book I was about to close was the very one my mother Martha had stolen from my mother Marleen, the copy Wade had undoubtedly perused and perhaps indefinitely borrowed. The pubic hair had been Martha's, I thought, was a kind of relic. Of course if Martha is still alive, the hair wouldn't be a relic in the Catholic way I had in mind, but it could function in that way for me. I stared at the hair. I thought about touching it. I thought about slipping it into my pocket. I could keep it in a tobacco box with the strand of Wade's hair I found in that world almanac.

It was better, I decided, to leave the hair where it was. Should you happen to go to the Golda Meir Library's rare-book room and ask for Zwang's book, I suspect you'll find the hair and out of courtesy won't displace it.

I was glad that it had turned overcast for my late-afternoon walk from the library back to the sub shop, where I bought a soda that I must have left on the roof of Wade's car. It's my car, but it still feels like his. My mind continued to drift for an unremembered number of minutes, during which I drove as if in a dream but apparently avoided an accident. Just seconds after I became aware again of my surroundings, I saw a sign for I-94, from which I was soon passing the baseball stadium, wondering if I'd ever been lost at all.

I can't feel at home in this world anymore.

I drove without music or French instruction till sunset, when I put on a tape I'd made in my late teens, with Steve Reich on the A-side, Porter Wagoner on the B. The juxtaposition wasn't meant in the self-satisfied way of college-radio deejays, I don't think—well, no doubt there was some self-satisfaction behind the pairing, but I also think I'd just happened to buy and tape those two albums on the same day. Reich's music is suited to the sort of contemplative driving I enjoy, but it can be dangerously lulling, and when my eyes closed for the third time, I fast-forwarded to the B-side.

After a while I came to a Porter Wagoner song that drew incipient tears, the first I'd cried in a decade. I played the song a few more times and found that it could make me cry at the same spot every time. When I've cried in the past, I've often imagined that someone was watching me, from above or on a screen of some sort, and soon I've become too focused on how my tears might affect this unseen spectator. But this time I was able simply to cry, the tears strong and desperate by the third pass, strong and relieving by the fifth, somewhat attenuated and self-conscious by the seventh.

I drove near the speed limit in the right lane, let the other vehicles pass me, let the best lines from Wagoner's songs pass through and circle my head: "Money can't buy back your youth when you're old / Or a friend when you're lonely, or a love that's grown cold"; "What is to be will be, what ain't to be just might happen"; "The light through the knot of my boarded window / Is just enough to keep me awake"; "Lord, I guess I haven't learned a thing." When an orange Yellow truck passed me, I gave the driver the thumbs-up and thought of Magritte, thought of Wade.

I imagined him at the radio station in Berlin. The studio is large but not as state-of-the-art as he may have hoped. Maybe the microphones aren't even German. The pop guard is yellow instead of the standard black. Wade's chair—it really is his chair, and sits in a corner during the other deejays' shifts—is upholstered in torn, nubby, orange cloth; its squeaks can be heard over the air during quiet moments, such as a pause in his Porter Wagoner tribute, an emotional pause or a pause when he tries to find the German words to best describe a Nudie suit. There's a lump in his throat as he finishes, then the tears start to tingle down his nasal passages, and he presses the remote button to start Turntable B.

I hit rewind and played the song one more time. I'm a careful driver, but the next car was a football field ahead of mine on a straight stretch of highway, so I closed my eyes and with perfect clarity saw Wade pull off his headphones and lean back in his loud chair, saw him rest his boots on the console and tuck some of his gray hair behind his left ear. I could see his thoughts, and he was thinking of my mothers, thinking of me, and when he looked over at the studio phone, all the oily line buttons were flashing red in free time.

NOTES AND DOWNLOAD INSTRUCTIONS

About a year into working on *Boarded Windows,* I started actually writing some of the Bolling Greene songs I'd been referencing in the manuscript. This eventually led to the novel's companion album, *Dylan Hicks Sings Bolling Greeene,* which can be purchased as a CD or LP, or downloaded without charge (it'll be Bolling's gratis non-hit). To download the album, go to soundtrax.com, and enter the following code: s3uD6kjB.

The brief notes in the LP and CD to some extent try to proceed as if Bolling were a nonfictional country singer, though not to the point of giving him songwriting credit in the fine print, which isn't really that fine. Despite the album's title, only five of the album's songs are, to my mind, covers of songs by this secondary character in my novel, and even these are somewhat free interpretations, with a few anachronisms and perhaps two or three lines that Greene wouldn't have entertained or tolerated. The remaining songs derive from the novel's narrative in other ways, or borrow some of its phrases, images, or themes.

To incite readers to seek out the handsomely packaged LP or CD, I'm going to refuse to list personnel and other credits in this setting. If you can't find the album in a record store, or can't find a record store at all, visit dylanhicks.com. Or see me at a reading, where folks who buy the book, or already and demonstrably own it, will be given a sharply reduced price on the LP or CD.

COLOPHON

Boarded Windows was designed at Coffee House Press, in the historic Grain Belt Brewery's Bottling House near downtown Minneapolis. The text is set in Caslon. Display fonts include Pussycat Sassy and Spin Cycle.

FUNDER ACKNOWLEDGMENT

Coffee House Press is an independent nonprofit literary publisher. Our books are made possible through the generous support of grants and gifts from many foundations, corporate giving programs, state and federal support, and through donations from individuals who believe in the transformational power of literature. Coffee House Press receives major operating support from the Bush Foundation, the Jerome Foundation, the McKnight Foundation, the National Endowment for the Arts, a federal agency, from Target, and in part by a grant provided by the Minnesota State Arts Board through an appropriation by the Minnesota State Legislature from the State's general fund and its arts and cultural heritage fund with money from the vote of the people of Minnesota on November 4, 2008. Coffee House also receives support from: several anonymous donors; Elmer L. and Eleanor J. Andersen Foundation; Suzanne Allen; Around Town Literary Media Guides; Patricia Beithon; Bill Berkson; the James L. and Nancy J. Bildner Foundation; the E. Thomas Binger and Rebecca Rand Fund of the Minneapolis Foundation; the Patrick and Aimee Butler Family Foundation; Ruth and Bruce Dayton; Dorsey & Whitney, LLP; Mary Ebert and Paul Stembler; Fredrikson & Byron, P.A.; Sally French; Jennifer Haugh; Anselm Hollo and Jane Dalrymple-Hollo; Jeffrey Hom; Carl and Heidi Horsch; Stephen and Isabel Keating; the Kenneth Koch Literary Estate; the Lenfestey Family Foundation; Ethan J. Litman; Carol and Aaron Mack; Mary McDermid; Sjur Midness and Briar Andresen; the Rehael Fund of the Minneapolis Foundation; Deborah Reynolds; Schwegman, Lundberg & Woessner, P.A.; John Sjoberg; David Smith; Kiki Smith; Mary Strand and Tom Fraser; Jeffrey Sugerman; Patricia Tilton; the Archie D. & Bertha H. Walker Foundation; Stu Wilson and Mel Barker; the Woessner Freeman Family Foundation; Margaret and Angus Wurtele; and many other generous individual donors.

To you and our many readers across the country, we send our thanks for your continuing support.

DYLAN HICKS is a songwriter, musician, and writer. His work has appeared in the *Village Voice, New York Times, Star Tribune, City Pages,* and *Rain Taxi,* and he has released three albums under his own name. A fourth, *Sings Bolling Greene,* is a companion album to this novel. He lives in Minneapolis with his wife, Nina Hale, and his son, Jackson. This is his first novel.

For information on Coffee House Press and our mission, please visit coffeehousepress.org